Daughter *of* Genoa

Also by Kat Devereaux

Escape to Tuscany

Daughter *of* Genoa

KAT DEVEREAUX

An Aria Book

First published in the US in 2025 by Harper Perennial,
part of HarperCollins Publishers Ltd.

This edition first published in the UK in 2025 by Head of Zeus,
part of Bloomsbury Publishing Plc

9 7 5 3 1 2 4 6 8

A catalogue record for this book is available from the British Library.

ISBN (PB): 9781804549926
ISBN (E): 9781804549902

Cover design: Leah Jacobs Gordon
Typeset by Siliconchips Services Ltd UK

Printed and bound in Great Britain by
Clays Ltd, Popson Street, Bungay NR35 1ED

Bedford Square, London, WC1B 3DP, UK
Bloomsbury Publishing Ireland Limited,
29 Earlsfort Terrace, Dublin 2, D02 AY28, Ireland

HEAD OF ZEUS LTD
5–8 Hardwick Street
London EC1R 4RG

To find out more about our authors and books
visit www.headofzeus.com
For product safety related questions contact productsafety@bloomsbury.com

Per Giobatta Triberti, con tanto affetto e tante scuse

Essential Information

In the autumn and winter of 1938, the Fascist government in Italy promulgated a series of laws – known as the Racial Laws – that deprived the country's Jewish population of its most basic rights. The effect of these laws was cataclysmic, not only for Italy's Jewish citizens but also for the many refugees who had arrived there after 1933, and who had been promised a safe haven. Among other restrictions, Jews were forbidden to study or teach at Italian schools and universities, banned from working in a vast range of sectors, prohibited from marrying non-Jews, and severely limited in their right to own property and business. Foreign Jews who had settled in Italy were now expected to leave. These harsh measures applied to those with two Jewish parents; to those with a Jewish mother; to the children of a Jewish father and a non-Jewish, foreign mother (my protagonist, Anna, belongs to this category); and to the children of Jewish-Christian marriages who professed Judaism as their religion.

The Racial Laws constituted a U-turn on the part of Mussolini, who had previously claimed to oppose the antisemitic policies enacted in Nazi Germany. They proved divisive even within the upper ranks of the party: some leading Fascists had actively pushed for the new legislation while others opposed it, most famously Italo Balbo. Despite the controversy, however, those who were unaffected by the new measures did not often challenge or resist them; many were only too ready to enforce them. With their official existence effectively cancelled, Italy's Jews also found themselves subject to social isolation, harassment, intimidation and abuse.

The German occupation of 9 September 1943 meant that all Jews on Italian soil were now at risk of arrest, deportation and murder. A number of Italians, some of whom had been prepared to go along with Fascist discrimination, now refused to comply with Nazi persecution or even actively resisted it. This happened all over occupied North Italy; but the city of Genoa, where my story is set, was a special case in many ways.

Genoa was the operative centre of DELASEM (*Delegazione per l'Assistenza degli Emigranti Ebrei*). This organisation was originally set up in 1939, with the government's approval, to facilitate the emigration of foreign Jews. With the occupation, its entirely Jewish leadership was driven underground or into exile. DELASEM became a clandestine rescue network under the aegis of the Jesuit cardinal Pietro Boetto, Archbishop of Genoa, one of the very few Catholic hierarchs to commit wholeheartedly to resisting the Final Solution. Even within that group, he was exceptional in using his full authority, the resources at his disposal and the moral standing of his position to protect those who needed his help.

DELASEM is a big story. This novel is a small story: an attempt to imagine the experience of a handful of people engaged in resistance during the tempestuous events of April to June 1944. Only two of my chief protagonists are real people: the 'Scarlet Pimpernel' Massimo Teglio, who was head of North Italian DELASEM after November 1943; and don Francesco Repetto, Cardinal Boetto's secretary and Teglio's closest collaborator in this period. I have done my best to stay true to what I know of their personalities, and to work as far as possible within the gaps of the historical record. But their individual actions and conversations in the story that follows, the granular aspects of their clandestine work – especially the detail of the lists – and their relationships with my other, invented characters are entirely imagined.

Prologue

ANNA

It's extraordinary how the most unpleasant things stay with us the longest. I last had to look at you in 1938. That's ten years ago, and yet here you are, in my head. Even though I'm safe now, I still find myself scanning the papers for your name. *Marinaio Dead*: that's what I'd like best, but I'd settle for *Marinaio Disgraced*. It's useless, because there's never any mention of you at all. It seems that you've come through it all intact. Financially ruined, I'm sure, but alive and free.

That's far more than you deserve. I hate you for what you did to me; what you did to Stefano. I hate you for it in a particular way, but that's not why I can't forget about you. That's not why I talk to you in my mind or see you in my nightmares. No, Commendatore, the thing that makes me sick is quite simply that you are alive and that Vittorio is dead. He was a far better man than you are, and if I could talk to you – really talk to you – I would never let you forget it.

1

Genoa, 1944

I was half-asleep on the couch when the doorbell rang. I sat up, and *The Murder of Roger Ackroyd* slid off my chest and landed with a papery thud on the floor. For a moment I held my breath, hoping I'd imagined the sound of the bell; that it was one of those hallucinatory noises you sometimes hear between dreams and waking. But then it rang again – once, twice – its shrill, insistent sound assaulting my ears. I stood and approached the door with silent, flat-footed steps, my heart racing.

Please, not the Germans.

I lifted the small brass cover on the spyhole and saw my landlady, signora Pittaluga, staring angrily back as if she could see me, too. She knew I must be in, of course – that I had no choice but to be in, that I went out only for the absolute necessities. Had she come for my rent? It couldn't be that, could it? Surely she was supposed to come the day after tomorrow, when I'd had time to go to the bank and see the kind bank manager who let Stefano's account stay open, although he was dead, and let me have access to it, although that was probably illegal. As I hesitated, her finger went to the bell. I opened the door, quickly, before she could ring again and set my nerves jangling even more.

Signora Pittaluga came in as she always did, brandishing her handbag before her like a shield. She looked around as if the place were strange to her, as if she were shocked by the cramped little flat she rented to me – at a price, I might add, that had only risen as my situation became more desperate.

'Good afternoon,' she said and, as she turned her expectant gaze on me, I realised in horror that I had been wrong. The days had got away from me, slipping and blurring into one another despite all my efforts, and I should have had the money ready today. I had never been late in paying signora Pittaluga. I had never, thus far, been late in paying anyone. I cleared my throat and hoped she would have mercy on me, just this once.

'Good afternoon. I'm very sorry – I haven't had a chance to go to the bank. I can go first thing tomorrow. Or now,' I added, as her mouth pursed and her fingers tightened on the strap of her shiny black crocodile bag. 'I can go now, if you wouldn't mind waiting. It isn't far. I'm sorry.'

'Well, signora Levi, I don't quite know what to do.' Since the Germans came, she'd made a point of calling me by my father's name rather than my husband's. Before that I had always been signora Pastorino, classically Genoese and plausibly Catholic. 'I can't wait around here, I'm afraid. I simply haven't the time. I suppose I could manage to come back tomorrow, if you can assure me that you will have the money ready.'

'Of course I will,' I said.

'Then it's all right this time. But only this time,' she said, and one pencilled eyebrow crept up towards her hairline. 'My family relies on this income, you understand. If you forget again, then I shall have to see what my son-in-law has to say about it. He works at the questura.'

She mentioned him often, this son-in-law. He was one reason I'd stayed in Carignano, in the heart of Genoa, while the city emptied out around me; while those with the means to do so fled to the safer suburbs and the hillside villages. Because the bombs might spare me, but I knew that the police would not. I could not afford to alienate signora Pittaluga.

'Thank you,' I said, meekly, as if she hadn't just threatened me. As if I didn't want to snatch that shiny black bag from her hands and beat her around the head with it. 'I really do appreciate your understanding. It won't happen again, I promise.'

'I should hope not, signora Levi. I shall come past at noon tomorrow. Good day.' She went out, and I sank back down onto the couch and put my face in my hands, cursing myself.

I decided that I would go out first thing in the morning. I would go to the bank, and I'd pass by the shop on the way back to see if the man there had put aside anything for me, as he sometimes did: a spare loaf end, a half-block of margarine, sometimes a piece of fish or a cut-off scrap of meat, if he could manage it. Even the idea made my stomach squirm, and I thought of the little tin of sardines he'd given me last time. I could have them for dinner tonight, a special treat to take away the nasty taste of signora Pittaluga's threat. But now it was only four o'clock, and if I didn't want to wake up hungry in the night then I would have to wait at least until seven, ideally longer. Until then, I would simply have to distract myself.

I'd mended everything that needed to be mended and rehemmed three skirts that didn't need hemming at all. I had no accounts left to balance; I'd dusted every surface in the flat, washed all my underwear, scrubbed the bath, and trimmed my hair with the scissors I'd discarded as too blunt for sewing. There was nothing else to do. I reached down, picked *Roger Ackroyd* up from the floor and settled down to read, pretending the best I could that I didn't already know how it ended.

The air-raid siren sounded just as I'd opened the sardines. I had waited until I could stand it no longer; I could not set them aside and let them spoil. I stood over the sink and forked the little fish into my mouth, desperately revelling in their rich taste and smooth, fatty texture, the soft crunch of the small bones and the oil that dripped down my chin. Then I wiped my face, gulped down a glass of water, took my coat and bag and went downstairs.

Living so close to the port, I didn't want to risk staying home when the alarm went up, though I've since heard that plenty did. Instead I chose to run out to the shelter, relying on the crowds to keep me safe and inconspicuous. But those crowds kept dwindling, and tonight there were just a handful of people hurrying along my street towards Galliera Hospital and the public shelter that lay beneath it. An older lady and three younger women, perhaps her daughters, were a little ahead of me. I pressed on so that

I almost caught up with them: not so close that I'd alert them to my presence, close enough that any observer might have taken me for part of the group. As I pursued them along the street under the plaintive wail of the siren, one of the young women looked back and briefly caught my eye; to my relief, she smiled, but I still slowed my pace a little.

The hospital itself was busy: with so many raids and so many fresh invalids, it could hardly be otherwise. I made for the underground entrance, insinuating myself into the flow of people so that I was carried along, protected from view, into the long, narrow, echoing tunnel with its harsh electric light. I forged on further and further, letting the bustle and noise envelop me until I found a little patch of space and sank down onto the wooden floor with my back to the curved wall and my coat over my knees. Even with so many bodies in the way, I could feel a faint current of air from the round window at the far end of the tunnel, which emerged high up in the stone wall above via Banderali. Before all this began, I used to love Carignano, with its high terraces and its splendid views over the city and the sea. Now I hated it, because when the bombing started I knew that I would hear everything. There was no protective barrier, no comforting layer of soil to muffle the violence outside.

Everyone around me was mercifully absorbed, huddled together in groups, consoling one another, bickering. Nobody seemed to be paying any attention to me, and I hoped that nobody would. But the hairs on the back of my neck prickled, in the way they do when you're being watched, and I looked around. Sitting a little way away, against the opposite wall, was a Jesuit priest. I knew that he was a Jesuit because my father had taught me and my brother to spot them when we were small. And they were easy enough to identify, in their black buttonless cassocks with the wide black sash at the waist, going about solemnly in pairs – one older, one younger – with their gazes downcast as if they might see something wicked. This one was middle-aged and alone. He was slender and scholarly-looking, with a worried face and a pair of round spectacles, and he had an open prayer book in his hand, but he wasn't looking at it. He was looking at me.

I felt a surge of revulsion and anger. Who was this priest to stare at me, to single me out among all these desperate people who might actually need his help – who might *want* his help? Was it really such a novelty for him to see a woman on her own? Fury made me bold, and I raised my chin and looked him straight in the eye. For the briefest of seconds my gaze held his, and then he looked away. He closed his prayer book, got up and, with the slightest motion in my direction – it might have been a nod; it might have been a shrug – made his way towards the entrance of the tunnel.

My heart was hammering now. I was suddenly very afraid that he knew who I was and what I had to hide. My father didn't loathe the Jesuits for nothing. They were the Pope's enforcers, relentless champions of Christian supremacy. They had persecuted the Jewish people for centuries. They had supported the Racial Laws, calling on Mussolini to defend Italian Christianity against its supposed Jewish 'enemy'. They were everything that he, and I, and my good Scottish Protestant mother hated about the Catholic church. And now this one had seen me, had perhaps realised that I had reason to fear him, and for all I knew he had gone to fetch someone to take me away. I hugged my knees to my chest and shut my eyes tight, waiting miserably for a hand to descend upon my shoulder.

Nobody came. Before long the guns began to rattle, and the earth all around shook, and the noise and chatter of the tunnel gave way to a terrible, mute tension. But you can't be scared all the time, no matter how bad things are; your brain simply won't let you. At some point you have to sleep, and so after a while, I curled up on my side with my coat over me and my bag under my head, and I slept like an exhausted animal. I didn't wake until the all clear sounded at dawn.

2

Vittorio

As Vittorio emerges from the shelter and into the chilly spring morning, he finds himself looking around for the young woman he saw earlier. In his line of work, you quickly learn to spot those who live in hiding. It's not just the physical signs: the pale complexion, the mended clothing, the obvious nerves. In much-bombed Genoa, all those are common enough. No, it's something else. It's an air of wanting to vanish, of trying to be as small and as unobtrusive as possible. It's a way of holding yourself so you don't draw attention. When he saw her like that, tucked up against the wall of the shelter, he was fairly sure she needed help. The hatred and fear in her expression when she looked at him – as painful as it was – that confirmed it.

He can't approach her himself, of course; not after that. Perhaps if he can lay eyes on her, get a sense for where she might live, he can have someone else look for her once the chaos has died down: a friendly nun or, better still, a laywoman. But the crowd is dense and he can't see her, can't even bring her features to mind. He has already failed to help. Carignano is covered in dust and smoke; people are surging around him, clutching at each other and at him, begging for a prayer or a blessing. He looks into each pale, terrified face that turns to his and he does what he can to soothe them, to be the reassuring presence he knows they expect. His chest hurts with every breath of thick, cold air and he's beginning to feel very bad, worse even than usual. He's shamefully unprepared. He had come to the hospital to hear a parishioner's confession, and now he is at the centre of all this horror, sick and sleep-deprived, trying desperately to be useful and hoping that his instinct will kick in, that well-trained priest's instinct that has carried him through so many horrific situations. But it doesn't, not today. Today, apparently, he's just a man.

'Father Vittorio?'

A young, mousy-haired woman – a girl, really – in a Red Cross uniform is looking up at him. He's seen her face before, he realises. Certainly around the hospital, but somewhere else, too: perhaps the Archbishop's Palace, or his home church, the Gesù.

He must look as tired and baffled as he feels, because the girl gives him a frank smile. 'I don't expect you know me,' she says, 'but I know you. I have a patient who's asking for a priest. Will you come? Now?'

'Of course.' He turns to go back towards the hospital, but she shakes her head and sets off in the other direction. She's moving so swiftly that he has to try to keep up with her. The pain in his chest becomes tight, demanding.

There's a courtyard on the left, the gate standing open; she ducks into it and waves him after her. 'I saw you earlier in the shelter,' she says quietly, 'and I'm very relieved to find you again. I told a lie, you see. My patient doesn't need a priest, but she does need help.'

'I see,' Vittorio says. He takes out his handkerchief and wipes the sweat from his face.

'I found this lady in via Gualtieri. She'd had a nasty turn. She's very underfed – well, we all are right now, but even so – and I gather she lived in one of the houses that was destroyed. She must have come home, seen it and passed out from shock, poor soul. It took me a moment to bring her round, and she's still not right.'

'And now she hasn't anywhere to go?'

'Worse than that.' The girl looks around her, lowers her voice another notch. 'I had a look in her handbag, when I couldn't rouse her – I thought I might be able to call someone for her, a husband or a mother or some such. And I saw her identity card. Says she's from Troia.'

Vittorio knows what that means. The most rudimentary false papers, the only ones available to Jews in the first weeks of the occupation, were all stamped by the questura of Troia in the free zone of southern Italy. It was the only counterfeit stamp available in those days. He thinks of the Fascist police and the German SS, patrolling the devastated streets of Carignano to hunt for those flushed out by the bombing, and he turns cold.

'Her name's Marta Ricci,' the girl goes on. 'That's what it says on her card, anyway. There's someone sitting with her now – seems a nice enough woman, but I don't know. I said I was going to fetch her parish priest. That's you, Father Vittorio, so best you remember her name. Marta Ricci. And I'm Nurse Dora.'

'Good thinking, Nurse Dora,' Vittorio says. 'Let's go and see her, shall we?'

Via Gualtieri was once one of those typical Carignano streets lined with tall, stately buildings, a little down-at-heel these days but still grand enough, or at least respectable. Now it's a sprawl of rubble and wasted walls, laid wide open by the RAF bomb that's landed directly in the middle of it. The ruins are crawling with people: rescue parties and firemen, workers with barrows and shovels, already bringing the chaos into some kind of order. Vittorio thinks of ants.

'There she is,' Nurse Dora says, and she leads Vittorio towards a heap of masonry where two women are sitting. A wiry, headscarved matriarch who holds a broom like a sceptre; and next to her, a slight figure in a shabby tweed coat, curled up with her head resting on her knees. Something about her is familiar – the coat, perhaps, the posture – and a wild, faint hope begins to rise. Maybe this is *her*: the woman from the tunnel. Maybe he won't have failed to help her after all.

The matriarch looks up as they approach; the other woman stays as she is, a tight ball of misery. 'Here I am!' Dora says. 'And here is Father Vittorio. Thank you, signora Traverso, for sitting with Marta. We'll take care of her now.'

'Good,' signora Traverso says with a nod of evident approval. 'I was just saying to the young lady – before she took a turn again, poor thing – that it's ever so strange, the two of us living in the same street and never meeting, not even once. Don't you think that's odd?'

'Life's a funny thing.' Dora's voice is even. 'Thanks so much again for keeping an eye on her. We shan't hold you up any longer.'

But signora Traverso doesn't move. Her eyes are on Vittorio now, and she's looking him up and down in a way that makes him distinctly uncomfortable. 'You don't look like any priest I've seen around here before,' she says. 'Are you new, Father?'

'It's all in hand,' Dora says, before Vittorio can react, and she takes signora Traverso's arm and all but heaves her to her feet. 'We'll look after Marta. She needs peace and quiet, and a proper check-up.'

'But—'

'Off you go,' the nurse says, not unpleasantly but with something in her tone, something inarguable. Signora Traverso makes a face; her eyes flick from Vittorio to Dora and back again, but she hefts her broom and goes, muttering. Dora crouches down and gestures to Vittorio to do the same.

'Marta, dear, I'm afraid we need to get you moving. Father Vittorio is here. He's a good man and you can trust him. He'll find you somewhere to stay, won't you, Father?'

'Yes,' Vittorio says. His mind is already working, running through every suitable place he knows in the city: convents, private homes, apartments rented by the diocese. So many of them are full, even beyond capacity. He could easily despair, but he won't. He hasn't the option. 'I'll see that you're looked after, Marta. Please don't worry.'

But there's no reaction, no sign that he's been heard. 'Marta?' Dora prompts, leaning forward and putting her hand on the young woman's shoulder. 'Marta, please. You're not safe here. I know it's been an awful shock, but you must go with Father Vittorio right away.'

Marta raises her head. She looks at Dora and then turns her eyes to him – wide, brown, startled eyes – and Vittorio thanks God and all His mysterious ways because it's *her*.

'All right,' she says in a near-whisper. 'All right, if I must.'

3

ANNA

I wanted to stand up on my own. So much about that morning is clouded, but I remember that very distinctly. I ignored Nurse Dora's outstretched hand and got to my feet with as much dignity as I could, but the blood rushed to my head; my knees almost gave way, and she had to catch hold of me.

'Don't be silly,' she said, and she took my arm and tucked it through Vittorio's. 'And you, Father, keep hold of her. Now go!'

I hadn't a choice. I let my arm rest in his, and I let him guide me away towards the little square at the end of the street. As we turned the corner, I risked a quick glance over my shoulder and caught a glimpse of a German field-grey uniform. My stomach clenched and my legs felt weak all over again. Vittorio tightened his grasp.

'This way, I rather think,' he said, and hurried me into a narrow, ruined street leading uphill, away from the sea. The damage here was long since done: the place was deserted, the houses standing open and empty like theatre sets. I was already out of breath, nervy and unfit. My chest was burning and my calves ached, but I didn't dare slow down so long as Vittorio had hold of my arm.

'All right,' he said after a while. 'I think we're safe.' He let go and steadied himself against the wall of the nearest building. He was suffering even more than I was, red-faced and winded. I couldn't imagine how a man not so much older than me, a man who could walk freely wherever he wanted, could be so badly out of condition.

Vittorio took out a handkerchief and mopped at his brow. 'I'm sorry,' he said. 'About the tunnel, about… You thought I was watching you.'

'I did,' I said, and propped myself against a piece of fallen masonry.

He grimaced. 'I was. That sounds bad, I know. But I thought…' His voice caught, and he broke into a dry, wheezing cough, which he stifled in his handkerchief. 'Thought you might need help,' he managed to say at last. 'Didn't want to scare you.'

I saw myself as others must see me – as Vittorio, with his observant eye, had seen me. Tired and small in my old, much-mended coat and skirt, clutching my bag tightly. The indoor pallor, the anxious air. The mouse flushed out of its burrow.

'You were right,' I said. 'Thank you.' It was inadequate. Now that the immediate danger had passed, now that I was beginning to feel something, I had a sudden affection for this strange priest. I might almost have hugged him, as I'd hug a friend who'd done me a good turn. But something in his bearing discouraged me. He was so very clerical, upright and contained, even while wheezing. It might have dawned on me then that this was not a man who would ever touch anyone casually, whose entire discipline revolved around keeping his distance. It might have, but it didn't.

'Least I could do.' Vittorio wiped his face again and took a few slow, cautious breaths. The crisis over, he tucked his handkerchief away in the pocket of his cassock and cleared his throat. 'Sorry. Now, what shall we do next? If you've anywhere you can go, anyone who can help you...'

'No,' I said. The magnitude of the situation was starting to bear down on me again. I had nowhere to go. I had nobody I knew well enough to ask for shelter. That flat had been my last and only refuge, and now it was gone and I was alone, quite alone and entirely defenceless. 'I haven't. I...'

'Then we'll find you somewhere – don't worry. Just let me... Oh!' His face brightened. 'I have friends, a married couple who live near via Assarotti. I know,' he added as I shook my head. 'I know it's less than ideal...'

'No,' I said. 'No, I can't go there. I won't.' The Germans had made their headquarters at the foot of via Assarotti, just a little way from the synagogue. The synagogue they had raided the previous November, arresting many Jews including brave Rabbi Pacifici, who had stayed to look after his community. I could not imagine going anywhere near via Assarotti.

'I understand,' Vittorio said. 'I really do, but I assure you that the house is quite safe. And my friends, and their friends, and their neighbours – they're all trustworthy. They all understand, too. Please let me take you there, if only for now. I can't leave you out here alone, I simply can't – it's far too dangerous. My conscience won't let me. God won't let me. Please.'

He was so earnest. And I was exhausted and frightened, and he'd saved me once already. Of course I didn't trust him. Quite apart from his being a Jesuit – and that alone was grounds for distrust – there were enough people like my landlady, people prepared to 'help' Jews only to exploit them afterwards. You could never tell who might do a thing like that. But what other choice did I have? How could I tell him to leave me, and stay here in the ruins of Carignano with the SS prowling around and nowhere to hide, nowhere to sleep, nothing to eat? It was impossible: I could see that, even as I wanted to run away from him and from via Assarotti and all that it meant. It was simply impossible.

'Yes, then,' I said, and hoped with every fibre of myself that he was as good-hearted as he seemed. 'I'll come with you.'

Vittorio smiled. He looked genuinely relieved. 'Wonderful. That's wonderful. Come on, then.'

The next hour was excruciating. Public transport was too dangerous – too many Germans, too many Fascists, too many checks – so we had to walk together, uphill all the way. First towards via XX Settembre, where we crossed beneath the monumental bridge, trying to look inconspicuous among the crowds of people and cars. Then further up, following the high stone wall that underpinned the Spianata dell'Acquasola, until we reached via Serra. I looked to my left and glimpsed the equestrian statue of King Victor Emmanuel II, brandishing his hat with a flourish, in the middle of piazza Corvetto at the very bottom of via Assarotti. My father used to grumble every time he saw that statue.

'Don't worry,' Vittorio said. His voice was hoarse. We'd had to stop several times for him to get his breath back, and I'd been equal parts relieved and terrified at every interruption. He nodded towards a small, winding street that led off directly ahead of us. 'Up there,' he said. 'Not far.'

And so we climbed on and on. The street was narrow and mercifully quiet, but that was another kind of peril. Anyone could have looked out of a window and seen us – we were nothing if not conspicuous. But eventually we emerged into a broader street with houses along the left side and, on the right, a view over the city towards Brignole station. It was a horrific sight: a wasteland of rubble and broken roofs, punctuated by the ragged shards of bombed-out buildings. Vittorio touched my wrist.

'Up ahead,' he said, pointing to a small shopfront. Over the door was a sign reading TIPOGRAFIA GUICHARD. 'My friends are Waldensians,' Vittorio explained. 'Protestants, of a sort. Good people, though.'

Though. I bit back sharp words.

The shop, once we reached it, didn't look promising. It was one of those dark little places with a display window full of faded, out-of-date calendars and old ferry schedules. I wondered what I had let myself get into, and whether I ought not after all to go back and take my chances with the Germans. Vittorio rang the bell in three short bursts, brrring-brrring-brrring, and a man's voice from somewhere inside called: 'Coming! Coming!'

There was movement now behind the glazed door. The

green blind was pulled aside just enough for a round, suspicious eye to peer past it, and then there was the click and grind of an elderly lock and the door swung open. Vittorio ushered me through and then quickly closed it behind us.

The presumed typographer, a large, silver-haired man with a drooping moustache and a green apron, looked at me and then fixed a baleful gaze on Vittorio. 'You didn't warn us.' He had a strange, melodic accent. A Piedmontese, of course, and one from the high valleys.

'No time,' Vittorio said. 'I found this lady just now. She's lost her home.'

'Is that a fact?' The typographer looked at me again. I was starting to shiver now, the next stage of shock setting in. His stern face softened just a little. 'Don't stand there,' he said, still gruff. 'Come through.'

He raised the countertop and we followed him through a heavy velvet curtain that led to a neat but shabby back room, half-office, half-stockroom. From here, a flight of stairs led up to a warm kitchen, all polished wood and neatly pressed, Alpine-looking embroidered linen. The typographer pulled out two chairs at the round table and said: 'Sit.'

We sat. He put two cups in front of us and poured out a hot, herby-smelling tisane from a pot that sat on the stove. 'My wife makes it,' he said. 'I don't know what's in it, but it's better than what passes for coffee these days.'

'Is she…' Vittorio began.

The typographer nodded. 'Gone to buy bread. Back any moment.'

'Good,' Vittorio said. 'Good. We'll talk once she's here.'

An awkward silence descended. I can almost laugh

remembering it now, but back then it wasn't funny at all. I was as much a stranger to them as they were strangers to me, and each of us had very good cause to fear strangers. Vittorio looked at the floor, I looked into my cup as if I could read my fortune in it, and the typographer bent down and picked up a sleek orange cat, which settled smugly in his lap and began to wash itself.

I remember telling myself: These men must mean well. If they didn't mean well, they wouldn't be doggedly waiting for the woman of the house to return. But my hands were trembling and my nerves screamed at me to flee.

And then there was the sound of a door opening and closing, of footsteps on the stairs. Vittorio all but leapt to his feet. The typographer got up with a grunt of satisfaction and decanted the warm cat into my lap, where it lay and blinked up at me with trusting green eyes. The softness of it was almost a shock. I stroked its ears and a low purr started up in its throat.

'I see you've met Tiberio,' a female voice said. A stout woman, with a rosy complexion and silver hair like her husband's, but without the accent.

'No names,' the typographer said.

The woman turned a look on him: half-loving, half-irritated. 'I hardly think,' she said, 'that it matters if she knows what the cat is called. So what's happening here? Has our Jesuit friend been out picking up young ladies?'

'Very funny,' Vittorio said, sitting down again. 'Signora,' he asked me, 'may I tell my friends what happened?'

I nodded and kept on stroking Tiberio's ears while Vittorio told the typographer and his wife about the English bomb, and the suspicious neighbour, and how I had nowhere to be.

'Oh, the poor soul,' the typographer's wife said. 'What a dreadful thing to happen.' She sat down across from me and leaned forward. 'Dear, I'm going to have to ask you some questions. Not to be nosy, you understand. I want to be able to help you – we all do. All right?'

'All right,' I said.

'Now, is there something we can call you? A first name? A nickname?'

'Marta.'

'Very well. Now, Marta, do you have family here in the city? Relatives, friends? Anyone?'

'No,' I said. 'I'm all alone.' And I burst into tears.

Everyone was splendid. It was as if they worked to a well-rehearsed routine. The two men vanished: Vittorio went to 'put a few things in order,' and the typographer, whom I'd come to know as Bernardo, went downstairs to open the shop. The woman, whose name I'd learn was Silvia, sat down beside me and put an arm around me while I cried. And I did cry, like I hadn't since I was a little girl. I sobbed and sobbed, running my hands compulsively over Tiberio's fur while he squirmed and purred and butted his head into the crook of my arm.

Once I finally managed to come to a stop, Silvia gave me a handkerchief, a big blue checked one. 'It's one of my husband's,' she said as I mopped my face and blew my nose. 'Ladies' handkerchiefs don't quite do the job in this kind of situation. Now, I'm going to be very honest with you, Marta, because there's no point in being otherwise.'

I nodded.

She sighed. 'I'd like to tell you that you're safe now, but I can't promise that. You know that very well yourself. I can only promise that you'll be much safer here than you were on your own. So if you would like, you can stay here, and we'll all do our best for you. And if you're thinking you'll have to pay your way, you can forget that right now. A few old clothes, an extra place at table – that's nothing to us, and I shall be very offended if you protest, so don't you try. Understood?'

'Understood,' I said. I was too exhausted, to dazed even to wonder if she meant it or not. She patted my arm.

'Poor thing, you look like you want a rest. Come on. Let's get you settled in.'

Silvia stood, and the cat Tiberio jumped down from my lap and wound his way around her legs. I followed her out and along the corridor.

'Your room is next to the bathroom. That's important for a few reasons. Ah, thank you,' she said as Vittorio came hurrying towards us, clutching an enamel jug. 'Hot water. Good idea. That man should have been a hotelier.'

Silvia led me to the end of the corridor, where two doors stood ajar. She opened the first door: a bathroom with a big white tub and brass fittings, far nicer than anything I'd seen before. 'My father had all this put in,' Silvia explained. 'The business was doing rather better back then. Anyway, you're welcome to use the bath once a week, as we do. Now, here is the most important feature.' She opened a small cupboard that stood at floor level next to the window and gestured for me to look inside. A sturdy metal ring had been fixed to the wall behind, and attached to it was a coil of knotted rope: a sort of escape ladder. It was then, I believe, that I tentatively began to trust my new hosts.

'A friend gave us the idea,' Silvia said. 'If the Germans come, or the Fascists, then you must climb out of the window and down into the courtyard.' She pulled aside the net curtain and pointed across the narrow paved area to the building opposite. 'See that house? The custodian is a member of our church. You must go straight to the back door and ring three times and he'll let you in. Understood?'

'Understood,' I said again.

'Good. And now let's get you set up in your room.' Silvia went out into the corridor and opened the other door, motioning me through. 'Just look what a job Father Vittorio has done with the bed. They train them well, the Jesuits.'

I looked. It was a small room but high-ceilinged, with plain white walls. In one corner was an iron-framed bed with a neat sprigged cover and two pillows, and it was immaculately made. On the wall above its head, where a cross might have been, there was a small oil painting of a jug of flowers. A blue-and-white woven rug covered part of the tiled floor, and there was a wooden chest of drawers and a washstand, with a white towel hanging up next to it and a pink tablet of soap on a dish. But best of all was the window. The shutters stood open, letting in light and air. It was all a world away from my chaotic, dark little flat in Carignano with my books and my clothes and my sewing things, all gone now.

Silvia had read my mind, or perhaps my face. 'You can soak up the sun all you please. Nobody overlooks you on that side. Just pull the curtains when you don't want the light – don't go leaning out the window to get to the shutters. And here he is,' she said brightly, as Vittorio came back in with the jug of hot water. 'Now, Marta, you have a good rest and when you're ready, we shall have something to eat. Sleep well, dear.' And she and Vittorio went out, closing the door behind them.

I was exhausted. I wanted to lie down more than anything, but for a moment I just sat on the bed, looked at my feet and tried to make sense of it all. I knew that anyone who helped a Jew – or even a '*Mischling* of the first degree,' as the Germans would define me: in the eyes of the Fascists I was a 'full Jew' on account of my foreign-born mother – was subject to the same treatment as the Jews themselves. Everyone knew that; you couldn't avoid knowing, for there were posters on every street corner warning you of it. The kind bank manager, the friendly shopkeeper, anyone who saw that I kept to myself and who knew that I must be afraid of something, and yet who chose to look the other way… if the smallest of their actions had come to the attention of the Gestapo, or the Fascist police, they would have been arrested and taken away. I didn't yet know what was done to those who were taken away, like Rabbi Pacifici, and my mother's friend Giuditta and her daughters Lea and Laura, who had been my playmates. But I had garnered enough information to know that they had been sent out of Italy and that they had not returned.

I could not believe that these two gruff and practical people I'd never met before had decided, not only to defy the law, but to take me into their home and all of that risk along with me. I couldn't understand. I could only wonder at it.

After a while, need overcame wonder. I drew the flower-sprigged curtains, undressed and washed with the still-hot water and the geranium-scented soap, and then I lay down in that neat white bed and let myself begin to drift off. After a few moments, the door softly opened and shut, and Tiberio jumped up on the bed with an enquiring chirp. I opened my arms and he curled against me, starting up a deep rumbling purr that blotted out all else and lulled me into sleep. My last conscious thought was that signora Pittaluga would never exploit me again.

4

Vittorio

Back when the Jesuits were powerful, before the Society was dissolved and then restored, the community house at the Gesù stood next to the church: on piazza De Ferrari, where the Italia Flotte Riunite building is now. There was even a covered bridge leading directly from the upper floor to that of the Palazzo Ducale, the seat of the Doges of Genoa. Now Vittorio and his fellow priests live on top of the church itself, in a set of rooms accessible by elevator. As he steps into the wood-and-iron cage, a wave of tiredness hits him and he has to lean against the wall until it passes.

He'd hoped there might be something for him to do, something urgent and necessary that would carry him through the rest of this long day. But when he reported to Cardinal Boetto on the way here – or rather to the cardinal's secretary, an earnest young secular priest called Francesco Repetto – there were no orders waiting. Don Francesco had listened to his account of the bombing in Carignano, the finding of Marta and how she'd come to stay with Silvia and Bernardo at the Tipografia Guichard. He'd taken off his round spectacles and polished them, and he'd said in his gentle, worried voice: 'Waldensians, I suppose, to judge by the name. And you know them, do you, this couple?'

'I know them well enough, yes. They work with Mr X.'

Don Francesco instantly relaxed. 'Oh, that's splendid. Then I shall tell him all about it when he gets here. Well done, Father Vittorio. You go and have something to eat, and get some sleep, too – you've had a rough night.'

Vittorio wanted to protest. But as soon as he opened his mouth, his breath snagged in his throat and he broke out coughing: that spasmodic, dry cough that's been bothering him more and more lately. He'd just about managed to stifle it, clamping his handkerchief to his mouth and swallowing repeatedly so that the saliva ran down the back of his throat, but it was too late.

'Yes, you had really better rest up,' don Francesco said firmly. 'It's not going away, is it, that cold of yours? Have you been to the infirmary?'

Vittorio wiped his eyes, which were streaming now; on top of everything else, he thought. 'Just dust,' he said. 'The air, you know, after…'

'Yes, I can imagine,' don Francesco said. 'Shall I fetch you some water?'

Vittorio shook his head. The back of his throat was tightening again, itchy and threatening. 'Quite all right,' he said. 'Thank you.'

'If you're sure. Then I shall see you tomorrow morning, so long as you're feeling up to it. Take care, won't you?'

Vittorio nodded, managed to splutter out some polite words. Then he left, in rather more of a hurry than he'd wanted to. As soon as he got out of the Archbishop's Palace into the fresh air, he coughed until he gagged and almost vomited.

It really is just a cold, he tells himself now as the elevator doors open and he steps out into the familiar corridor. *I've always had a weak chest, ever since… well, anyway. Damp weather and nervous strain, that's all that's causing it now. Nothing to worry about.*

For a moment he stands there and wonders what to do. Since he's been ordered to work with Cardinal Boetto, his time outside of that work is his own. Apart from the odd report to his superior, he accounts to nobody but God and don Francesco; because, while the cardinal oversees the Archdiocese of Genoa's clandestine activity, it's really his secretary who has his eye on the sparrow. And don Francesco has told him to eat and sleep and do nothing. He could do exactly that, if he wanted.

It's a tempting thought – the sleep, anyway. He doesn't want anything to eat, has to force himself even at mealtimes. The strain of it all has taken his appetite as well as stealing his breath. But he's spent a terrible night sitting on the floor of the tunnel under Galliera Hospital, dozing off only to be startled awake again. He never sleeps in the daytime, not unless he's severely unwell. Perhaps today, however… He eyes the stairs that lead up to the priests' quarters, and he thinks longingly of his bed.

Whatever he does, he must check in on the library first. He certainly won't rest unless he knows it's in good order. He heads along the corridor towards the small room with its handful of bookcases. It's a modest enough domain for one who trained at the Vatican Apostolic Library. Still, it's his

– no, not *his* as such, but he's responsible for it – and he's spent a bit of time teaching one of the junior members of the community, Brother Carlo, how to look after it when his own duties for Cardinal Boetto keep him away.

Let's see how well he's managing, Vittorio thinks, and he pushes the door open to find chaos. The little returns trolley, where the priests and brothers leave books when they're done with them, is stacked perilously high. There are more books abandoned on the librarian's desk, and those that remain on the shelves are clustered haphazardly together, out of line and out of sequence.

'No,' Vittorio says out loud. 'No, no, no.' He pushes the trolley over to the desk and starts pulling books out of it, grouping them into the sections where they belong. He'll replace them all, at least – he can't bear to do less than that – and then perhaps he'll give the whole place a once-over. Make sure the shelves are all in order and the books perfectly lined up: what he once heard an English Jesuit, the librarian at Farm Street, call *stricting*. Yes, that would be a good use of his time, much better than going to bed and languishing there.

He's done this so often, he doesn't even have to think. The work takes him over as it always does: the steady rhythm of it, the comforting heft of the books and the satisfaction of looking at each finished shelf. Before long, he's forgotten that he meant to rest at all.

When Vittorio gets into bed that night, he finds that he can't lie on his back. There's an oppressive heaviness in his chest, like a weight bearing down on him. Instinctively he rolls onto his side and feels the heaviness loosen and shift, letting him breathe again. But his heart is racing and the fear he's managed to suppress all day is surging up. What if he really is sick, and not with a cold? What if he's sick again like he was as a boy? He can't bring himself to name the disease, not even to himself. The idea of it is too terrible.

But it *can't* be that, can it? There's no fever, no sputum, no blood. All he has is a dry cough and a sore chest. He's tired, yes, but who wouldn't be tired after four years of air raids? He has no appetite, but who would be hungry when the food on offer is so scanty and poor? He's probably got some deficiency, some long-running infection that's sapping his strength. If he were to go to the infirmary tomorrow and tell them all about his symptoms, they'd doubtless just tell him to rest. Maybe that's what he should do, though. Go to the infirmary and quell his worries once and for all.

All right, then, he thinks as his eyes begin to close and his limbs to relax. *I'll go first thing in the morning. I won't let that old fear stop me. I shall list everything that's wrong with me, and whatever they tell me to do for the sake of my health, I shall do it. Even if it means stopping work for a while. Even if it means leaving the library to Brother Carlo. Yes, even that.*

And the decision feels right – of course it does. It's the correct thing to do. But even as he drifts off to sleep in the warm glow of righteousness, he knows deep down that he still won't bring himself to do it.

5

Anna

For the first while, I couldn't get out of bed. It was as if something had given way, something that had been holding me upright. I was like a sick child or an elderly invalid, waking only to use the lavatory or to eat the simple meals Silvia brought to me on a tray. The rest of the time I slept, with Tiberio rolled into a warm ball in the small of my back or the crook of my knee, indignantly rearranging himself whenever I drifted into consciousness for long enough to shift position and ease my stiff shoulders, my aching hips.

'It's quite usual,' Silvia said to me on the first day. I was finishing my soup while she filled the chest of drawers with freshly washed and ironed clothes – a neighbour, she'd told me, had a daughter who'd moved away and left them behind. 'You've been surviving on your own for so long, you haven't had a chance to rest.'

'But I haven't been doing anything,' I said. 'I haven't been able to.'

'And that's the whole problem.' She shook out a wool skirt, rolled it into a tight cylinder and tucked it in with the others. 'Forced idleness isn't restful. Quite the opposite, in fact – it saps all your strength. Have a good rest now, a proper rest, and you'll soon be back on your feet again.'

'I don't feel like I'll ever be back on my feet,' I said.

Silvia smiled. 'You will be.'

And I was. A couple of days later, I woke up ravenously hungry and with the strong desire to be upright and active. I washed and put on my 'new' wool skirt and a jumper in a pretty rose colour, and I went along the corridor to the kitchen. The door stood ajar and Silvia was sitting at the table, staring at a fat ledger that lay open before her with a stack of papers next to it. She smiled when I came in, but she looked tired.

'Good morning, Marta. How nice that pink looks on you. Would you like some breakfast?'

'Yes, please. But let me make it,' I said as she pushed back her chair.

'No,' Silvia said, so sternly that I didn't dare object. 'This is my kitchen. Sit down.'

'But I really do want to help.' My eyes were drawn to the ledger that lay open on the table – the need to do *something* was as urgent as thirst. 'I can dust my room, if you show me where everything is. I can…'

'Marta, no.' Silvia turned to face me, tying an apron around her waist. 'You mustn't worry. You've had enough worry for a lifetime already. Just rest and concentrate on feeling better. I'm not about to put you to work.'

'But I want to be put to work,' I said. 'I must be put to work, or I shall go mad. What's this?' I went on, gesturing to the ledger book, before she could object. 'I could help with this, I'm sure of it.'

Silvia's shoulders drooped. She eyed the book as if it were her worst enemy. 'Oh, that's just the sales ledger for the shop. Bernardo does his best at keeping it, and I do my best at checking it, but neither of us finds it easy. We used to have a clerk, but...'

'Let me do it,' I said. 'It's easy for me.'

Silvia looked at me for a moment. She was still wary, but I could see hope breaking through, and that made me hopeful in turn. 'Really?'

'Really. This is what I do. Well, what I did before...' I hesitated, the bleakness of the last years opening out before me.

'Before things changed,' Silvia supplied.

'Yes. I was a sort of secretary-bookkeeper. Honestly, it won't take me long at all.'

'Well, if you're quite sure you must,' she said, turning back to the stove. 'But you shall have an egg for your breakfast. This is the kind of work that merits an egg.'

I sat down in her abandoned chair, picked up the pencil and got to work. Before long I'd found two transposed numbers and a miscalculation, and I was so absorbed in the process that I didn't realise breakfast was ready until Silvia tapped my shoulder. There was a plate at my elbow with a fried egg, a beautiful one with a deep-orange yolk.

'I'll leave you to it, as you seem to be having fun. But enjoy the egg, I beg you. It came all the way from Bernardo's cousin's village – it deserves to be appreciated.' Silvia poured out a bowl of chicory 'coffee' and placed it next to the plate along with a slice of bread. 'If you need me, I'll be in the back office.'

I ate quickly, like I used to do before hurrying out to work, though I lingered a little over the rich egg yolk. Then I gulped down the chicory and went back to my ledger. My eyes were weaker than they used to be, and at first I found myself triple- and quadruple-checking every calculation, but as I went I picked up speed and confidence until I felt very nearly like my old self again. I was finishing up the very last page when the kitchen door creaked open.

'You see,' I said triumphantly, 'I told you it wouldn't take long! Haven't you any more?' I looked up with a big grin, expecting to see Silvia. But it was Vittorio.

'What's this about?' he said. 'Silvia and Bernardo making you earn your keep?'

'Oh, no, they wouldn't do that. I wanted to help.'

'Don't worry – that's quite clear.' Vittorio sat down at the table, a respectable distance away, and looked at me. His eyes were very green; I hadn't noticed that before. 'And now – may I call you Marta? Is that all right?'

'Of course,' I said.

'Thank you. Anyway, how are you feeling? I imagine you've had a bad shock.'

'I have, yes. I've been quite…' I had to swallow. 'Silvia's been very kind. And Bernardo, though I don't see him so much. I've been sleeping, mostly,' I admitted, and Vittorio nodded.

'Of course,' he said. 'Well, we know what we need at such moments. But you're up and at your work now.'

'Yes, well.' I tried to smile, and he rewarded me with a smile back. 'Silvia found me something to do. I know I oughtn't to be in the way, but I couldn't stay in bed any longer. I was just so… I was so *bored*. I know that's terrible, but it's true. I've been bored for years, bored and scared and tired. And I suppose I'm not so tired now, and I'm a bit less scared, so now I'm mostly bored.' My cheeks were hot. Something about Vittorio's steady gaze, his air of total attention, was rather unnerving. I wondered if this was what confession felt like. 'Anyway, I'm afraid I nagged her until she gave me this ledger to look at. And now I've finished it, so I shall have to nag her for something else to do.'

'Entirely reasonable. It's very hard to do nothing if you're someone who's always worked. Someone who likes working, dare I say.'

'That's exactly it,' I said. 'I do like working. I like having a purpose.'

'I understand that very well. May I see?' Vittorio gestured to the ledger.

I didn't know why he should want to, but I obligingly pushed it towards him and he flicked back through the pages. 'Now look at this,' he said. 'You've done such a neat job here. It's like darning a sock.'

I must have given him an odd look, because he went on. 'I mean that as a compliment – don't worry. It's very fine repair work.' He was studying the page in front of him. 'I'm imagining that you were some kind of high-powered secretary, before all this.'

'Secretary-bookkeeper, but nothing high-powered about it. Really, I was just an office girl.' I smiled, trying to look carefree, as if it were true. As if there were nothing at all painful or troubling in talking about my old life – nothing that made my heart speed up and my hands clammy. 'I worked for a very busy man, a shopkeeper down by the port. He had a lot to do, but he liked to keep an eye on everything himself, and so...'

'And so he needed a skilled helper, someone he could trust to do everything he wanted in exactly the way he wanted it. Trust being a relative term.' He laughed, a short, wry laugh. 'I know that type. My father is that type.'

I didn't know what to say to that. I couldn't imagine him having a father, much less one he could be wry about.

Vittorio shut the ledger and rested one hand on it, as if he were taking an oath. His eyes were fixed on the table in front of him. He was a Jesuit again, the kind you see in the street. 'Anyway, I'm glad you've found something to do. Silvia and Bernardo are good people and they'll look after you well. And if you ever need to talk about anything, you need only ask one of them and they'll find a way to send for me. It goes without saying that whatever you tell me is confidential,' he added. 'That isn't just for the confessional. It applies to anything we say to each other here. All right?'

'All right,' I said, but I couldn't imagine pouring my heart out to this rather ascetic-looking priest. I didn't know how anyone could. 'Thank you.'

Vittorio nodded and got to his feet. 'It's what I am for. Good day, Marta.'

'Wait.' I didn't really know what I was going to say next, but I knew I couldn't let him go yet. 'I do need to talk. To ask you something. If you have time, that is.'

He nodded again and sat back down, returned his gaze to the table. 'I have a few minutes.'

'Look, I... you don't have to tell me what exactly you're

doing, or who you're working with. It's enough that I know what you want to do for me. But you're helping other people, aren't you, the three of you? I know it's secret,' I said as his mouth tightened, just a little, at the corner. 'Believe me, I know all about confidentiality. But I'm in on the secret, too. I'm in on it simply because I'm here, being helped. And since I am here, and since I am in on it, and since we all have to trust each other… I want to contribute. I don't know exactly what I can do, but if there is something, then I want to do it.'

Vittorio smiled, but he still didn't look at me. 'You are a good person,' he said. 'God will bless you for it.'

'I'm serious,' I said. 'Just tell me what I can do.'

For a moment, he was silent. His gaze drifted to the ledger and I hoped desperately that he was assessing my skills, lining up some role for me – though I really didn't know what. 'Why?' he asked at last.

'What do you mean, why?'

'Why are you asking me this? Even assuming that Silvia and Bernardo and I were doing anything riskier than dispensing simple charity – and that's quite risky enough on its own – why would you want to involve yourself? Don't you think you're in enough danger as it is?'

'I'm in danger because of who I am. I don't see how I can make it any worse by what I do. If the Germans find me, they'll send me away regardless.'

Now Vittorio raised his head. His face was still, but there was something terrible in the way he looked at me. 'Then you know they'll send you away,' he said.

'Yes. I've gathered that much.'

'And do you know where?'

'No. If I were a young man, I expect they'd conscript me, send me off somewhere to fight or to die of hard work. As it is, maybe I'd end up in a factory or a labour camp.' I could say it with a certain bravura, because the idea of it had become so horribly familiar. I'd spent whole days, entire nights thinking about it.

'A labour camp. I see. I... well.' He cleared his throat. 'Marta, I admire your courage. I truly do. But you must know that if the Germans believed you had information that could help them, any information at all, then they would do everything they could to extract it from you. Any sensible person, in your position, would make the greatest effort to stay ignorant.'

'I know.'

'And that would be a perfectly reasonable choice. The only reasonable choice, in fact, for you and for anyone who might wait and hope to see you again.'

'You have to understand that I have nobody waiting or even hoping for me. I'm alone, and that changes everything.' I had not consciously chosen the words, but as I said them, I knew that they were true. 'All I have here and now, Father Vittorio, is myself. I still have my free will, so why shouldn't I use it?'

Vittorio cracked a faint smile. 'Oh, well, if we're going to start getting in about Maimonides...' He shook his head. 'Look, all this is theoretical. There's nothing going on here beyond what you've seen already, and even that is something you'd be well advised to ignore. The single most important thing you can do is look after yourself.'

'Father Vittorio—'

'I'll pass by tomorrow if I can, or someone will. Just

remember what I've said to you, please, and limit your enquiries to the state of Bernardo's accounts.' He stood, tucking the ledger under his arm. 'I'll take this to Silvia on my way out. Good day.'

6

Work has always been important to me. I think you knew that, Commendatore. I think you took it for granted, assumed that I was simply delighted to help you in your own supremely important work. But I don't think you really understood. I didn't come to work for you every day because I respected you as a man or cared about your business, although you clearly believed both to be true and, for expediency's sake, I let you continue believing. Working for you was a necessary compromise – or so I let myself believe until harsh reality taught me otherwise.

Let me tell you just how big that compromise was.

I come from a family where people do not compromise. My mother had left her comfortable schoolteacher job in her well-to-do, insular Edinburgh suburb to marry a man she had met while on holiday with her parents in Rapallo. And her parents, who had been happy enough for their daughter to talk to this man when he was merely a charming foreigner and a free tour guide – and not, emphatically, a prospective member of their family – now threatened to cut her off unless she abandoned him and came home. I don't know whether they were more upset that he was an Italian or that he was a Jew. I don't know to this day whether my mother's parents are alive or dead. My mother wasn't prepared to put up with anyone who would not love my father as warmly and unconditionally as she did. She made her choice.

My father's secular, socialist family adored his staunchly principled new bride; there was no question of a rift on their side. His turn to choose came in 1931, when I was seventeen years old and my brother Filippo was twelve. That was the year the Fascist regime required all university professors to sign a loyalty oath in order to keep their jobs. My father was a professor of literature at the University of Genoa. He loved his work – it is not too much to say that he lived for it, for Machiavelli and Dante and all his beloved souls. He loved teaching, and he loved his students. But he hadn't risked his life in the Great War to end up swearing fealty to a man like Mussolini: a brute and a demagogue, an enemy of liberty, a man whose entire claim to power was founded on violence. That was unthinkable to him. And so my father did not sign the oath, although a great number of good, principled men held their noses and did precisely that. He made his choice and resigned instead. Only twelve other professors in the whole of Italy did the same.

Our family was now cast adrift. My father had not only lost his salary, but he had also lost all chance of finding a job again – at least, so long as the Fascists were still in power. The only sensible thing was to leave. My parents decided to go to New York, where my father's brother and his wife lived. My uncle and aunt had even written to them, years before, to say that they must come if Italy became too dangerous. Of course, without my father's income, going to America was much easier said than done. We needed to raise money, but we also had to stay afloat. We sold everything we could afford to spare: clothes, books, furniture. My mother gave English lessons from morning to night, while I did my bookkeeping course and took in typing for the students at the university and the naval academy.

It was through this work that I met Stefano, who was then a first-year student in naval architecture. By the time my parents had got the money they needed and had gone through the gruelling process of getting all the necessary paperwork and securing guarantees from their New York relatives and enduring the long wait for visas, he and I were married.

Now came my turn to choose. Would I – would we – leave now along with my parents and brother, or stay in Genoa until Stefano had finished his degree? There were so many practical reasons to stay. Once he was qualified, Stefano would be able to get a far better job in America. We wouldn't have to burden my parents, but could support them as they grew older; we could start a family of our own. And I thought that I could afford to stay for a while, because Stefano was so very respectable: a well-connected Catholic, the youngest son of a Genoese seafaring dynasty. His parents weren't warm and affectionate like mine, but they were unfailingly polite to me and, in my innocence, I thought that was their version of love. When Stefano assured me that they'd support us whatever we chose to do, I believed him. After all, his father had earned his fortune working abroad. How could he object to Stefano leaving to do the same?

And so we worked out a plan, Stefano and I. He would continue his studies, and I would take a job that would support us both. We'd put aside every spare bit of money we could, and when the time came, he'd look for an employer in New York. It was so logical, so beautifully simple that I actually thought it might work. And when Stefano's first cautious enquiries threw up a job for me – a good job, even a little better than we'd hoped – it seemed like a sign from that benign, universal force I didn't really believe in.

That's how I came to you in the summer of 1934, Commendatore: not as the daughter of a known antifascist, but as the wife of a bright young shipbuilder-in-training and the daughter-in-law of a renowned sea captain. Had you looked into my family background even a little, I'm sure you wouldn't have hired me at all. But I had my husband's name and my father-in-law's recommendation, and you hoped to employ one and charm the other, so you didn't enquire any further. You made your choice based on partial information, as I had made mine.

7

I ignored Vittorio's strictures, of course. I repeated my offer to Silvia when she came in, a little after he had gone, to make a fresh pot of tisane. She shook her head.

'We haven't anything for you to do, Bernardo and I. We don't really do anything ourselves.'

'But—'

'What you see is all there is,' Silvia cut across me. 'Someone from our church asked if we would offer our spare room to people like you, people who needed somewhere safe to stay, and we said yes. It was perfectly obvious that we must. But that's it, I'm afraid.'

I think I knew even then that this wasn't the whole truth. But Silvia's manner brooked no argument, so I just nodded and let her pour me a cup of herbal tea.

'Did you ask Father Vittorio if you could help?' she asked, sitting down opposite me with her own cup.

'Yes.'

'And what did he say?'

'That I am a good person and that God will bless me for it.'

Silvia snorted. 'Yes, well. I dare say *they* prefer to do things their own way.'

I didn't ask her what she meant by that, for I knew exactly. Of course, I was grateful to Vittorio for finding me and bringing me to my safe haven. I was prepared to believe that he was a decent man who happened to belong to a wicked institution. But I was also quite ready to assume that he had acted, at best, out of high-handed Christian charity; that he didn't see me as an equal at all.

'I'm sorry,' Silvia went on. 'It must be very frustrating for you – but just hold on. Some day, hopefully soon, this will all be over and we can go back to our usual lives.'

She smiled at me and I tried to smile back. She was being kind, I knew; more than kind, given everything she and Bernardo were doing for me. But something in me rebelled. What was the good in setting aside all my justified fears, in choosing to trust these people if they couldn't bring themselves to trust me? What threat, exactly, did they think I posed to them and their operation? I went to bed that night feeling well and truly low, as angry and helpless as I had been since that horrible day when I ceased to exist in the eyes of the law.

It wasn't long before everything changed.

A couple of days later, we were just finishing our meagre lunch when the shop doorbell rang, in three short bursts. Bernardo looked at Silvia. 'Are we expecting someone?'

'No,' she said. 'Shall I…'

'I'll go.' Bernardo got to his feet, putting his napkin down on the table next to his plate. He seemed impassive, but I'd learned by then that he was a man who grew quieter and stiller the more worried he was. He went out and I heard his slow, heavy footsteps on the stairs.

I felt cold. I stood without thinking and started towards the bathroom, but Silvia caught hold of my arm.

'Wait.'

For an instant we stood there and listened. And then came the most welcome sound in the world: Bernardo saying gruffly, just as he'd said when I first arrived, 'You didn't warn us.' I could hear a cultured male voice offering excuses.

Silvia let go of me and sank into her chair, covering her face with her hands. 'It's all right,' she said. 'It's quite all right. Oh, thank God, it's only him.'

The stairs creaked, and she sprang up and began clearing the dishes away. I barely had time to help her before Bernardo cleared his throat behind us. I turned and saw him standing in the doorway next to an elegant man in his middle forties, clean-shaven and wearing large horn-rimmed spectacles. He had thick dark eyebrows and dark, swept-back hair touched with silver at the temples. And his eyes were extraordinary, even behind those ridiculous glasses: a deep liquid brown, sombre and watchful.

'This is Mr X,' Bernardo said, and the man made a small bow. 'He's a friend of ours, and he's come to see if you need any help.'

I haven't censored the man's name. Bernardo really did call him Mr X. But the ruse was useless, because I knew exactly who he was. This was Massimo Teglio, the aviator, and I knew him because my little brother Filippo was mad about aeroplanes: an unusual obsession in our literary family. He had begged each of us in turn to take him to the Genoa Aero Club on one of its open days; my mother had finally relented, and Filippo had even been granted a short ride in Teglio's seaplane. After that, the daredevil pilot with his neat moustache was firmly established as an object of worship. Filippo used to keep a scrapbook where he pasted in every clipping he could find, and in pride of place was a big newspaper photograph of Teglio alongside another flying ace: the Fascist hierarch Italo Balbo, Mussolini's rival, freshly relegated to his final posting as Governor of Libya.

When my mother found that photograph, she carefully unstuck it from my brother's scrapbook, cut it in half so that only Teglio remained, and glued it back in again. My brother was furious. I suspect he rather admired Balbo, who had made his Atlantic crossing the previous year, and he tried to argue that his feats in aviation were quite separate from his political record. My mother would not have it.

'I don't care what he does in the air,' she said. She usually spoke quietly in a clipped, measured accent, but when she was angry she became exaggeratedly Italian, like someone doing a comic impression of a Genoese. 'Nothing, nothing could excuse the things he's done on the ground. Or have you forgotten the March on Rome? The murder of don Minzoni? I will not have that man celebrated, not in this house, not for anything. And *he* should know better than to consort with Fascists,' she went on, tapping a disapproving finger against Teglio's face in the photograph.

'But Balbo doesn't hate Jews,' Filippo protested. 'He wouldn't fly with Teglio if he did.'

My mother shook her head. 'I dare say he has his pets. He might even tolerate the Jews in Tripoli, if they don't get in the way of his plans, but he wants to remake the world just the same as any other Fascist – and just as violently. No sensible man would have anything to do with him, and if you think otherwise, then I despair of your education.'

As I have said, my parents did not compromise. And now here was Massimo Teglio in front of me, trying his best not to look like Massimo Teglio. It made no sense. Teglio was Jewish, and therefore hunted. He was also a rich man, and even with Balbo gone he must still have had powerful friends. Why hadn't he left? Why would he stay in Genoa, going about with glasses on and his moustache shaved off, when he could be safe in Switzerland by now?

Teglio gave me a brief, tight smile, and I realised that I was staring. I quickly looked down, and stood there while he removed his overcoat and sat down at the table, accepting a cup of tisane from Silvia. I didn't know what to do with myself, and I missed my parents and brother terribly in that moment, as you might suddenly miss people who died years ago.

'Won't you have some tea, too?' Silvia asked me. I shook my head, and she put a hand on my shoulder and gave it a pat. 'Then I'll leave you to it,' she said, and hustled Bernardo out of the door before I could ask her to stay.

'Do sit down, please,' Teglio said, gesturing to the chair opposite him. I reluctantly sat, and he leaned back and looked at me. 'Now, signora...'

'Ricci,' I said. 'Marta Ricci.'

'Signora Ricci, I'd say it's a pleasure to meet you, but given the circumstances... well, I'm glad you're here, let's put it that way. It's a good thing you ran across Father Vittorio.'

'You know him?'

'Oh, yes. In fact, I'm substituting for him today. He was meant to come and drop this off.' Teglio reached into the inner pocket of his jacket and brought out an envelope, which he handed to me. I opened it to find a new trimestral ration card, valid for the months of April through June, and a bundle of five- and ten-lire notes.

Whatever unease I felt about Teglio's presence, in that moment, the sight of the ration card blotted it out. I had not seen one up close since the Germans came: obtaining one would have meant showing my false documents, and I tried to avoid that at all costs. The card bore an official stamp in purple ink, and some of the boxes for soap, sugar and fat had already been crossed off; which wasn't surprising, since we were now some way into April. But the paper was pristine and unhandled, the ink clear and fresh as if recently printed. I couldn't understand how Teglio had got hold of such a thing, or how he could walk around carrying it. If I had recognised him, then surely anyone might.

'Silvia will do the shopping, of course,' Teglio said. 'Leave all that to her. You've landed among good people: the Waldensians are very sound. You might have spotted their church on the way here. You shouldn't have to worry too much about the neighbours, but the usual security measures apply. Stay away from windows, keep as quiet as you can, and don't go outside unless absolutely necessary. The nearest shelter's across the road and up a few steps, which isn't so bad. I presume they've shown you the escape route from the bathroom?'

'Yes, they have.'

'Splendid. Now, you should know that if anyone comes by who means to help you – Father Vittorio, say, or me – we'll always ring the doorbell three times. Of course, we'll try to send word we're coming, but that isn't always possible. The best procedure is to assume that any unheralded visitor is a potential threat. If Bernardo happens to be downstairs...'

I tried to listen as I knew I ought, but my attention was already pulling away from him. I couldn't stop looking at the ration card, turning it over in my hands. After a year and a half of begging and bargaining for whatever scraps of food I could get, simply to have one was miracle enough. But its strange perfection set my mind racing. I felt sure that if I brought it to my nose, I'd smell fresh ink and warm paper: the same smell that drifted up from the shop downstairs.

Teglio fell silent, and I realised with a jolt that he was watching me. I quickly put the card back into the envelope and laid it to one side. 'I understand,' I said. 'And thank you for this.'

'It's nothing.' His eyes were still fixed on me, his face impassive. 'Signora Ricci, I have to ask you a few questions. I know it's hard to trust a stranger, but I assure you that I'm not asking in order to pry. I need some basic information to do my work.'

'Your work,' I echoed.

'Yes. I operate on a strictly need-to-know basis. But if there's anyone else who needs help, or who can help me help you, then it's important you tell me.'

'That's quite simple,' I said. 'There's nobody.'

Teglio raised his eyebrows. He'd trimmed them back, I realised, the stubble growing in around the edges. Another attempt at disguise. 'What, nobody at all?'

'Nobody at all.' I couldn't look at him any more. I fixed my eyes on the knot of his tie – dark-blue patterned silk – and tried to fight back the tightness that was growing in my chest. 'My parents and brother are safe. They're in America with my aunt and uncle.'

'I'm glad to hear they're all right, but I'm sorry you didn't get to go with them.'

'Yes. Well, I stayed here with my husband. That was my choice. But then he died, so now it really is just me.' The tears were threatening now, as they always did on the rare occasions I let myself think of Stefano. I blinked them away.

'I'm so sorry,' Teglio said. 'I'm a widower myself – I know how it is.' There was a terrible compassion in his voice. For a long moment we sat together in silence, and then he cleared his throat and said: 'If I may ask, where were you living before? What part of town?'

'Carignano, near Galliera Hospital.'

'Right by the port? I didn't think there was much left standing around there.'

'Well, there isn't now,' I said, and blew my nose.

'And did you have anyone to help you in Carignano? Or did you manage alone?'

'I managed. I'm healthy, thrifty and good with a needle. I rarely needed anything, and when I did, I just got it myself.' I didn't mention the shopkeeper or the bank manager. There was no need.

'Brave woman,' Teglio said. 'Living alone in Carignano,

dodging the bombs and the Germans. You might find life here almost too quiet.'

'I doubt that,' I said. 'I never want that kind of excitement again.'

He smiled properly for the first time then: a warm, eye-crinkling smile that made him look far less forbidding. 'Still, nobody likes to be bored. I hear you've already been sorting out Bernardo's accounts. Surely that can't be your idea of fun?'

'It is, actually,' I said, and he laughed.

'But that isn't all you do, is it? Don't you read, or draw, or embroider, or write poetry? I don't write it myself, but I like to be around people who do. It makes me feel intellectual by association.'

'I don't write at all any more, I'm afraid – I got out of the habit, but I do like to read.'

'Do you? Well, that's capital,' Teglio said. 'It should be easy enough to find you some books.'

'Really?' The idea seemed wonderful to me, as miraculously welcome as that pristine ration card. 'I wouldn't want to put you to any trouble.'

'You wouldn't. Books are hardly shortage material. And I know very well that survival is about more than simply staying alive and intact. This is a dreadful life, signora Ricci, and if I can lighten it for you a little, then I shall.' Teglio leaned forward. 'So tell me what you like to read, and I'll see what I can do about it.'

Perhaps it was because we were in the same situation, for all our differences. Perhaps it was his sudden kindness, or the promise of something to read, or the relief of discussing a safe topic. Whatever the case, I found myself talking to him as I might to a friend. I told him how my father loved Machiavelli and Dante and my mother loved Stevenson and Scott, but I preferred short, sleek, modern books, the kind you could fit in your pocket and take with you anywhere. I told him how I missed reading a murder mystery on the tram or a love story on a bench at the viewpoint of Spianata Castelletto, back in the days when I could take public transport and sit on any bench I liked.

I told him that I'd read Scott and Stevenson and Machiavelli and Dante, but that if I absolutely had to return to the great Scottish classics then it really ought to be Conan Doyle; and as for Machiavelli, I much preferred his comic plays to anything he'd written about statecraft or warfare. I told him that I'd read every paperback in my old flat a thousand times over, so that their familiarity became nauseating and the story meaningless; but I had loved them anyway, because each carried a memory of the first place I'd read it, and so I was sorry that they had all been destroyed. I carried on along these lines and all the time he listened intently, studying my face as if I were the only thing in the world to him.

When I finally came to a blushing, rather self-conscious stop, Teglio nodded gravely. 'Yes,' he said, 'I'm definitely glad Father Vittorio found you. I have to go now, but I shall do my best to come back and bring you some reading matter.'

'Thank you, Mr X.' My outburst over, I was beginning to feel unsettled and vulnerable, like I'd shown some secret part of myself to this famous-but-unfamiliar man. And yet I hadn't really told him anything, had I? I'd only talked about books.

'It's my great pleasure.' He shrugged on his overcoat and opened the kitchen door. 'Ah, Silvia,' he said, hailing her as she approached along the corridor. 'My apologies for the unannounced visit. I'll come past again tomorrow, if that's all right.'

'Of course it is,' Silvia said. 'We're always happy to see you, whether Bernardo shows it or not.'

'Ha! Well. Oh, now, would you look out some books for our friend here? She's a great reader and desperately needs something light and amusing. No Walter Scott, I beg you.' He nodded to me, kissed Silvia's hand and was gone.

Silvia and I looked at each other. 'He's quite something, Mr X,' I said. 'Very… gallant.' And I searched Silvia's face for any sign that she knew who he was, too – but she gave nothing away.

'Oh, he's a terrible flirt when he turns on the charm,' she said comfortably, picking up Teglio's cup and saucer and taking them to the sink. 'But it's a great weapon. It lets him do what he does.' She turned on the tap and started washing the cup, humming to herself.

I was dying to know what exactly it was that he did, but I forced myself not to ask. I didn't quite trust anyone yet; not Bernardo, not Vittorio, not even motherly, pragmatic Silvia. Teglio's sudden appearance had only unsettled me more. I couldn't forget that photograph in my brother's scrapbook: Teglio slender and upright, Balbo a broad, swaggering figure with his chest riddled with medals. I didn't understand how the Massimo Teglio I knew by reputation – the daredevil playboy who flew with Fascists – could possibly be reconciled with the serious man I'd met that day, the man who dealt in forged ration cards and secret signals. The man who knew what it was to be alone and afraid.

Until I understood, I knew that I couldn't trust him either. It didn't matter how much I wanted to help; how much his work intrigued me. I could only wait, and watch, and keep my counsel.

8

The next day, everyone was anxious and muted. Silvia didn't even argue when I offered to help with preparing lunch; I didn't linger once the plates were washed and stacked, but went straight back to my room and lay down on the bed, listening to the sounds of the street outside and the shop below. Even Tiberio seemed unsettled, and slipped away to hide under the couch in the parlour. For the first time since my arrival, I felt that my hosts were as unsure of me as I was of them; Teglio's visit seemed to have thrown everything into disorder. By the time he finally returned, just before dinner and carrying a tantalisingly book-shaped parcel, I had run through every potential disaster scenario and had all but decided that I would have to go back out on the street and take my chances with the Germans.

'I need to speak to signora Ricci in private,' Teglio said, without niceties. 'I'm sorry to throw you out of your own kitchen, Silvia, but needs must.'

'Of course,' Silvia said. 'I completely understand.'

'And I appreciate your understanding.' He waited until Silvia had gone out, and then he turned to me and said: 'I hope you'll forgive me taking up your time, signora Ricci. I'm using that name as a courtesy, of course. Your real name is Anna Pastorino, though you were born Anna Levi.'

He was looking me straight in the eye. I couldn't think, couldn't speak. 'Sit, please,' he said, and indicated the chair at right angles to his. I sank into it.

'How?' I eventually managed to ask. 'How did you…'

'Oh, I checked you out. It wasn't difficult. There are very few half-Scottish, half-Italian daughters of Machiavelli scholars in Genoa.'

I looked down, my face burning. I hadn't just talked about books. I'd stupidly given away my whole family history, and I hadn't even realised I was doing it. 'I thought you operated on a need-to-know basis,' I said.

'I do, yes. And if somebody wants to work with my organisation – which I was given to understand that you do, very much – then I need to know who they are and what might have driven them to it.'

'Father Vittorio spoke to you,' I said.

'Yes, and Silvia, too. That's part of the reason I came: I wanted to get a look at you myself, find out if you were trustworthy. It's quite all right,' he added, a little more gently. 'You knew who you were talking to. And on that, I very much appreciated your keeping up the pretence. That gave me a degree of confidence even before I discovered more about you.'

'And what did you discover?' My heart was in my throat.

'Well, let's see.' He sat back, considering me. 'You were

born here in Genoa, in March 1914, to Jacopo Levi and his wife, Miriam MacPherson—'

'MacPhail. My mother's name is MacPhail.'

'Indeed. Miriam MacPhail, who loves Stevenson and Scott. You have one younger brother, Filippo, whose great passion is aeroplanes. And yes, I do remember him,' Teglio said. 'I don't think that anyone has ever asked me so many questions. You, meanwhile, studied at the Liceo Regina Margherita and then went on to train as a bookkeeper. I wonder why you did that? An intelligent young lady with two such academic parents. Surely they would have encouraged you to pursue any career you pleased.'

'Of course. But I needed to find a practical job, something steady, something that would help. You know why,' I added.

He held up his hands as if to say: *touché*. 'Yes. I do know, of course. And it's quite in keeping with everything I've heard about your character.'

'Tell me,' I said.

'I heard about the daughter of a staunchly antifascist family. A serious, responsible soul who put her husband and parents first, at grave cost to herself – the kind of cost she could never have anticipated.'

'Then you know what happened to Stefano.' I couldn't look at Teglio now, couldn't bear his sympathy.

'Yes, I do, and I know how his family treated you when he was gone. I'm very sorry. You told me that you were alone in the world, and I'm afraid to say I doubted you. I rather had to doubt anything you told me, as a matter of protocol. I know the truth now.'

I couldn't speak. I could only nod, and hope he understood.

'I found all that out,' Teglio went on. 'And in the process, I also discovered that your capacity for discretion was far greater than it may appear. Because you hadn't been a mere assistant to some piddling local shopkeeper, as you had told Silvia and Father Vittorio and they, in turn, told me. You had, in fact, spent four years as confidential secretary to one of Genoa's more prominent businessmen. A man who did you a very poor turn indeed. I should think he was intolerable even at the best of times.'

'I hated him,' I said. 'I still do.'

Teglio grimaced. 'I can imagine. I once had to sit opposite him at a dinner. I spent all evening fighting the urge to thump him.'

'I wish you'd given in.'

'Frankly, so do I. It would have been deeply satisfying. But we can't change the past. We can only look to the present – and in the present, there is work to do. A great deal of pressing work that brings serious danger with it. It's imperative you know what's at stake. If you embark on this course of action, the Germans and their Fascist hangmen won't just want to be rid of you.'

'They'll want to get information from me first,' I said, remembering Vittorio's words.

'Correct. I have contacts inside their prisons. I know something of their methods, and I hate to broach such topics with a lady, but I must tell you that they are far more sadistic than they are efficient.' Teglio cleared his throat, and his hand went to his upper lip, feeling for the moustache that wasn't there any more. 'I am speaking of violence, bodily violence of the most depraved kind. Do you understand me, signora Ricci?'

I suppressed a shiver of fear. 'Yes, I understand.'

'That's why I must urge you to caution: for your sake, first of all, but also for mine and for all those who need my help. You must ask yourself whether you are willing to do all you can to keep silent, even as you are tortured to death. There's no cowardice in deciding that you are not. Your survival alone is a gift. It defies every foul act, every vile intention. Don't underestimate it, I beg you.'

He was looking at me so earnestly that I knew he was telling the truth. And I knew that I must be truthful with him in return. 'I'm not going to pretend I'm not afraid of the Germans or the Fascists,' I said. 'I'm terrified of them, but I'm willing to face that terror. Besides, I'm already compromised, aren't I? If the Germans have half a brain between them, they could easily decide to raid the shop downstairs simply because Silvia and Bernardo are typographers, and there must be typographers in Genoa doing clandestine work. The brand-new ration card you gave me is proof of that – I should wear those in rather better, if I were you. And if the Germans do come here, and they do find me, then I'll have to stay silent anyway for Father Vittorio's sake, and now for yours. I know who I'm talking to, Mr X. You observed it yourself.'

'Quite so,' he said. 'But it's a matter of scale. Father Vittorio and I signed up for this work – we can take our chances. If you join us, you'll pick up all kinds of sensitive details about other people, innocent people who depend on our discretion. You won't be able to avoid it.'

'And I'll do all I can to protect them, just as I'm prepared to protect the two of you. That's not in question. But if we are to work together, then you don't just need to know that I'm trustworthy. I also need to know that I can trust you.'

I thought he might be offended, or dismiss me, but he merely nodded. 'Of course. You must ask me anything you want to know.'

There were so many questions. What was this organisation of his, and how many people did he command? How did he come to have contacts within Nazi prisons? How far did his network reach, and how many people was he helping? I knew, though, that I mustn't ask. Flouting Teglio's need-to-know rule would be the quickest way to lose his confidence.

But there was one thing I could ask, one that had been nagging at me since I first saw him. 'Italo Balbo,' I said. 'You flew with him. Why?'

'Ah.' He nodded again, almost as if he were expecting the question. 'Yes. I rather had the privilege of being apolitical in those days. Though I expect your father wouldn't describe it in those terms.'

'My mother had even more to say.' I knew that I was being rude to him, but I was unable to stop. 'If I may speak frankly, she thought you stupid, frivolous, and a very bad influence on Filippo. If she didn't suspect you of active Fascism, it was only because she thought you lacked application.'

Teglio snorted. 'A strong-minded woman.'

'She was,' I said. 'She is.'

'And you, signora Ricci? What do you think? I have a feeling you're about to tell me.'

'What I think depends on the facts.' My mouth was dry, and I dreaded what I had to ask next. 'Was my mother wrong? Were you an active Fascist?'

'Never,' he said. 'I wasn't interested in joining any party. I didn't much care which party those around me were in, either, so long as they treated me well – which was a tremendous luxury, of course. I like to think I'm not stupid, but your mother wasn't wrong about my being frivolous. All I wanted to do back then was fly planes, and damn everything else. But I had a few socialist and antifascist friends even in those days. In fact, you and I have a number of people in common.'

'That's how you checked me out,' I said.

'Yes. As I say, it didn't take long.'

'And Balbo? Was he a friend of yours?'

'I wouldn't go so far as to call it a friendship.' Teglio's voice was cool and steady. 'But we certainly got on well. We flew together a number of times – he was a seaplane pilot, too. He spoke his mind around me, as did I around him. When the Racial Laws were passed, he did what he could in my favour, and I often wonder how my life would have gone if his plane hadn't been shot down. So, yes, before 1938, he was my good acquaintance. After 1938, he was something like an ally to me and my family. And now he's something far more powerful. He's an asset.'

'How can he be an asset?' I said, rather stupidly. 'He's dead.'

'Precisely. He's dead, and so we'll never know whether he'd have recanted his opposition to the Racial Laws, or to the alliance with Germany. There are men in our city's administration, influential men who have made their entire careers in the Fascist system, who cherish Balbo's memory as something like a lost hope. Now, I may be rather more cynical, and I'm certain that you are. But the fact remains that these people are sympathetic to me because they know that I was, in some small way, once valued by him. They are even willing to help me, although I am not a Fascist – although I am a Jew, and their German masters dictate that I should be rounded up and deported. But if I were a communist, or even a member of some social democratic party, then I don't think I'd find much goodwill in those particular quarters.'

'But—'

'We all compromise, signora Ricci,' he cut across me. 'We all deal with people we would rather avoid, especially when it means helping ourselves and others. You ought to understand that – you, of all people.'

The reproach landed like a blow. I lifted my chin, determined not to show him that he'd got to me. 'And how, exactly, do these powerful men help you? Can you tell me something about that?'

'Better yet, I can show you. Perhaps you'd be so good as to fetch me your identity card? I mean to say, the one you've been carrying?'

Still smarting, I went to my room and got my false identity card out of my bag. When I returned, Teglio waved me back into my seat and held out his hand for the card. I gave it to him and he opened it.

'Oh, dear, I thought so.' He shook his head. 'Yes, this is a classic case. The wrong paper, the hastily re-stuck photograph – though whoever made this did a nice job of trimming off the old stamps – and this new stamp here, the one from Troia. What a good thing we found you before anyone else could. Now, compare it to this example.'

He reached into an inner pocket and brought out another

identity card, which he handed to me. A real-looking card, nothing like my poor, shabby forged one. It belonged to a man called Giovanni Episcopo who was born in 1910 in Caltanissetta, in free Sicily. It seemed in every respect authentic, and it even had a stamp on it from Caltanissetta questura.

'I can get hold of the right paper,' Teglio said as I inspected it. 'I can get the forms printed. I can get stamps cut, I can even manage new photographs if those are needed, but what I cannot do is apply the imprimatur.' His finger traced the round, embossed police stamp that covered part of Giovanni Episcopo's photograph. 'That can only be done by somebody with access to the right equipment.'

I looked at him. 'Is it *real*?'

Teglio smiled. 'The partisans fight on their front, signora Ricci, and I fight on mine.'

'Then I want to help you,' I said.

His smile grew wider, warmer. 'Does that mean you're no longer horrified by my past choice of flying mates?'

'No, I am. I'll never understand that. But this... this is wonderful.' I reluctantly closed the card and handed it back to him; he tucked it safely away again. 'Do you make many of these?'

'As many as I can manage, and as quickly as I can. There's a great demand for them, and not only in Genoa. I get requests from all over North Italy – and each and every one is urgent, because the situation is urgent. So an extra pair of skilled hands can be of significant use; if you're prepared to take up forgery, that is.'

Take up forgery. The words thrilled me. Finally, someone

was offering me a real task to do: something new and skilful, something worthwhile. 'There's nothing I'd rather do,' I said. 'Thank you.'

'I'm the thankful one. Here.' Teglio slid the book-shaped parcel towards me. I'd quite forgotten about it, and now it tantalised me again.

'May I?' I was already undoing the string.

'Please do.'

I pulled away the brown-paper wrapping and found a battered paperback: an Italian edition of *The Adventures of Sherlock Holmes*, published in 1898 in Rome. And although I knew that everything Silvia had said was true – that Teglio was a habitual flirt, that his charm was all part of the game he had to play – I couldn't help but feel touched. He had remembered that I liked Conan Doyle, and he had brought me this.

'Thank you,' I said again. 'Thank you so much. I love these stories.'

'I do, too. I read them over and over as a boy – that was my father's copy, in fact. But we're getting away from the point,' he said. 'Turn to *The Speckled Band*, if you would.'

I did as instructed and found a folded piece of paper tucked in between the pages. It contained a list of names, each with the standard information – marital status, date of birth, distinguishing features – and an address in Caltanissetta.

'I thought you might start off by filling this batch in by hand,' Teglio explained, 'since your work on Bernardo's ledger was so beautifully done. Silvia and Bernardo will print the cards tonight, and I shall ask Father Vittorio to come around tomorrow and show you the ropes. He's rather a good forger – I've had occasion to call on him before. I haven't told any of them what I found out about you, by the way, and I shan't tell them. Need-to-know applies here, too. It works rather well in this case, because the three of them are truly decent people, but we all inhabit quite different worlds. In other circumstances, our paths would most likely never have crossed. I don't even know Father Vittorio's last name.'

'But didn't you check him out, too?'

'I didn't have to. He came to me from an absolutely unimpeachable source. If I don't have to know, then there's no sense in asking. So I go on calling him Father Vittorio, as if we've known one another for years, and he goes on calling me Mr X. It's extraordinary how the social niceties are thrown into disorder at a time like this.'

'I suppose it's more like having code names,' I said, and he nodded.

'Yes, that's exactly what it is. I end up on the most informal terms with intensely respectable people, simply because we must deal with one another and keep it all as quiet as possible.'

'Then you really ought to call me Marta, since we're going to be working together now. Father Vittorio calls me Marta,' I added.

'Oh, well. If he can, then I most certainly can, too.' He stood, and on impulse I held out my hand for him to shake. His grasp was firm, his skin warm and dry. 'Marta, thank you for helping me.'

'It's my pleasure, Mr X. I'm glad to do it.'

'Then we are of one mind, at least on this. Out of interest,' he said, 'do you happen to have your original papers, in your legal name? I mean to say, have you managed to keep them?'

'Oh.' I thought of my real identity card, which I'd kept taped into a secret place in my beloved roll-top desk. 'No. They were in the old house when… Is it a problem?'

'Not at all,' Teglio said. 'Mere curiosity. Forget I asked.' He opened the door to the hallway, knocking smartly on the doorframe, before I could ask any further questions. 'Silvia, we're ready for you now.'

'On my way!' There were hurried footsteps and then Silvia appeared. She looked expectantly from me to Teglio and then back again. 'Well?'

'Marta will be helping us from now on,' Teglio said. 'I've given her the list, and you should expect Father Vittorio in the morning, assuming he can be spared. And may I please give you this to hold?' He reached into his pocket and took out a small object bundled up in a handkerchief. 'I hadn't planned to bring it, but the place I've been keeping it isn't safe any more. If you could possibly hang on to it overnight…'

'Nonsense,' Silvia said. 'You'll leave it here with us, and for as long as you need to. It's not as if we could get into *more* trouble, is it?'

Teglio hesitated. 'If you're quite sure,' he said at last. 'It would certainly get me out of a bind. But only for a short while. I'll find it another home as soon as I can.'

'Fine, if you absolutely insist. But I mean what I say.' Silvia held out her hand and he obediently placed the object into it.

'Thank you,' Teglio said. 'Thank you both very much indeed. Good evening Silvia, Marta.'

'Good evening, Mr X,' we chorused.

When he'd gone, Silvia put the object into the pocket of her skirt. 'It's probably a stamp. He keeps pieces of kit all over the city. That way, if the Germans raid one hiding place, they won't get everything at once.'

'I see,' I said. 'Yes, that's very sensible.'

Silvia looked at me, and for a moment I thought that she, too, was going to warn me about what the Germans would do if they caught me. But she merely gave me a warm pat on the arm and said: 'I'm glad to have you on board. And now I must get on and make some tea, or Bernardo will be all out of sorts.'

Somehow, the rest of the evening proceeded as normal. We covered the windows and lit the lamps, and then took our usual seats by the still-warm stove. Silvia and Bernardo read aloud to each other from the Bible, while I allowed myself a couple more chapters of a novel from the small stash Silvia had got from her neighbour, the one who had donated her daughter's old clothes. I expect the novels had been left by the daughter, too: they were decidedly young women's books, romances and school stories and translations of Woolf and Sayers. It occurred to me briefly to wonder whether Bernardo and Silvia had any children; whether they, too, had grown up and left. But I immediately suppressed the thought. As Teglio himself would say, if I didn't need to know, then there was no sense in asking.

When the reading hour was over, we listened to Radio Londra for a while: that strange mix of bolstering speeches, news updates, and coded messages to partisan brigades. ('The chicken has hatched three eggs. The sacristan's daughter is lonely.') Then Silvia got to her feet and said: 'Goodnight, Marta.' And then, putting her hand on Bernardo's shoulder: 'Let's get started on those papers, shall we?'

Bernardo hauled himself to his feet. 'Yes, let's.'

'Isn't there anything I can do?' I asked.

He shook his head. 'No, you must leave it to us. This part is our job. But you can get a good night's sleep,' he said. 'You'll need a clear eye and a steady hand tomorrow. We can't afford any waste.'

'Have a bath if you like,' Silvia added. 'That might help.'

They went downstairs, and I went along the corridor to the bathroom to do as I was told. I sat on the lidded lavatory in the weak lamplight, the cat Tiberio in my lap – he had insisted on coming in, yowling and scratching his discontent until I yielded and opened the door – and waited as the pipes creaked and rattled and the wide-mouthed brass tap spat gouts of water into the tub. Then I undressed and lay down in the warm water, trying to still my mind. I was conscious that I had been allowed a very great luxury, but I couldn't enjoy it. Now that I was alone, all I could do was rehearse the conversation with Teglio in my mind, wondering at it over and over. And as for Vittorio... Vittorio, who had listened to me after all. He hadn't rejected my offer of help any more than Silvia had. He had absorbed it in his quiet way, and then had gone and found me something to do.

For the first time, I didn't see him just as someone who had saved me, who had acted out of duty or even charity. Even though he was a Jesuit – even though I was primed to dislike him, and distrust his motives – in that moment, strange as it was, I could almost imagine him as a friend.

I stayed there thinking until the water was cold. Then I washed and dried myself and went to try and sleep. I didn't sleep, of course. I lay in bed and listened to the sounds below me, the whirr and clank of the press and the indistinct voices of Silvia and Bernardo, while Tiberio slept curled up in the crook of my knee, as if nothing, as if nothing at all were strange.

9

Vittorio

If he sleeps on his side, it's all right. If he sleeps on his side, and doesn't walk too fast, and sits down just as often as he can, then he can manage perfectly well. The cough doesn't even bother him too much, so long as he does all those things and drinks plenty of water. So what's the point in going to the infirmary, really? Why interrupt his work, why cause trouble, why abandon all the people who depend on him when he's certainly not getting worse, and may even be getting better?

That's how he reasons, and on the whole it makes sense. He has his moments of weakness, of course. Like earlier this morning, when he rolled over in his sleep and woke up gasping for breath, as if some malign force were trying to crush the air out of him. As he lay there with his heart pounding and strange patterns shimmering before his eyes, he was horribly afraid that something was wrong after all. But once he'd washed, shaved and dressed, and settled down to his morning meditation, the fear had subsided and his breathing was beginning to slow. He could see the episode for what it was: a passing panic, a nervous fit, a shameful slackening of resolve. And he can't give in to that, he knows, or else he won't be much use to anyone.

By the time he reports to don Francesco, he's feeling quite as usual and has even managed some breakfast. He finds the young priest seated at his desk in the frescoed antechamber of Cardinal Boetto's office, deep in discussion with Mr X. They both look up as Vittorio enters.

'Am I interrupting?' he asks. 'Shall I come back?'

'No, no,' don Francesco says, and waves him into the chair next to Mr X. 'You're just the man we want to see. How do you feel about doing some forgery?'

'Forgery? You mean making cards again?'

'That's right,' Mr X says, turning to Vittorio as he takes his seat. 'I haven't forgotten how much you helped me before, and now I thought you might help Marta for a while. I'm glad you alerted me to her, I must say.'

His tone is polite, friendly but detached as it always is. Vittorio doesn't actually know very much about Mr X. He knows that he's a layman, of course, and that he's Jewish; that he's a friend of DELASEM's previous leader, a lawyer called Valobra, who had to flee to Switzerland when the Germans invaded. Beyond the extraordinary fact of Mr X having chosen to stay, the rest is a mystery. And that's as it should be. The less he knows, the less there is to give away should the worst happen.

'I thought it might be a good idea, too,' don Francesco adds. 'A nice quiet task while you get over that lingering cold of yours. Give you a break from running here and there all over the city.'

'So what do you think?' Mr X asks. 'Will you help me – or, rather, Marta?'

It's a genuine question, Vittorio can tell. Because what Mr X doesn't understand, being a layman, is that there's no point in asking. It doesn't matter that Vittorio *likes* 'running here and there', shepherding people from point to point, delivering ration cards and money and moral support. It doesn't matter that he dearly wants to keep watch over every soul that's been entrusted to him; that he resents the idea of giving them over to someone else, someone who won't know them like he does. Cardinal Boetto has endowed don Francesco with the power of decision. Don Francesco has decided, and Vittorio must obey.

'Of course I will,' he says.

Mr X breaks into a broad smile. 'Good man!' he exclaims, and gives Vittorio a clap on the shoulder, startling him so that he narrowly avoids a coughing fit. 'Thank you, Father Vittorio. I really do appreciate it. And thank you, don Francesco, for sparing him.'

'It's no trouble,' don Francesco says, and gets to his feet. 'Then I shall brief Father Vittorio, and you can get on. Good day for now.'

He shakes Mr X's hand; Mr X shakes Vittorio's, gathers up his hat and coat and goes out. Don Francesco sits back down, and Vittorio sits too, feeling gloomier and gloomier.

'Remind me,' don Francesco says. 'The Tipografia Guichard is somewhere off via Assarotti, isn't it? Via…'

'Via degli Armeni,' Vittorio supplies.

'Right.' Don Francesco rifles around in one of the desk drawers and brings out a map of Genoa, which he unfolds and spreads out between them. His finger follows the long curve of via degli Armeni. 'Yes, here, I see. Now, if I recall, you've placed one family in that empty flat in via Durazzo, haven't you? Then you have a couple just off piazza Manin, another near Corvetto… I think that if you could continue to keep an eye on those, plus any new arrivals – let's say as far as Brignole – rather hilly territory, of course, but at least it's all close by… What?' he asks as he looks up and catches Vittorio's eye. 'You didn't think I was going to take away all your duties? Send you away to make identity cards for Mr X and wash my hands of you entirely?'

Vittorio looks down. He's too embarrassed to admit that this is exactly what he thought. 'Well…'

'Father Vittorio, really,' don Francesco says, and the lack of reproach in his voice is somehow worse than any reproach could be. 'Even if I could do that, I wouldn't – and let us be honest here, I can't. I rely on you, and so does His Eminence. But you aren't well. I know you aren't well, not yet, and so I want to lighten the strain until you're back on form again. Do you understand now?'

'Yes,' Vittorio says. 'Thank you.' He feels irrationally as if he's been reprieved.

'So you'll keep on looking after your charges in this area here.' Don Francesco traces an invisible triangle: Corvetto-Manin-Brignole. 'And for the rest, I think don Giuseppe and Sister Assunta should be able to manage between them. We shall set up a proper handover, of course. But if you could just remind me for now roughly how many there are, and whereabouts they're currently living, that would be a great help.'

He turns the map around so that it faces Vittorio. And

there is Genoa, spread out before him: that thin, staggered strip of a city wedged in between the mountains and the sea. The line of the seafront is changed now, fretted and eroded by repeated bombing. Churches, palaces, theatres and monuments lie in ruins, but here on the map they survive as neat little symbols. And scattered around this now-imagined city are the people he looks after – the people he loves, with that fierce but dispassionate love that surpasses all sentimental attachment. Here's the orphaned boy who now lives with a big, chaotic family just off piazza del Carmine. Here's the mother sheltering with her two grown daughters in a flat in via di Vallechiara. In via Balbi, near the university, is the doctor's widow from Vienna who talks to him about Spinoza; not far from her, in vico della Pace, the young Czech couple with the toddler he keeps supplied with scrap paper and pencil stubs. He's taken to collecting those wherever he can find them, assembling a stash for his next visit – except that there won't be a next visit, and his throat is irrationally tight.

'May I have a pencil?' he asks don Francesco now. 'It's probably easier if I mark the locations. We can erase them afterwards.'

'Help yourself.' Don Francesco pushes a tin towards him, and he takes one: a brand-new pencil, shiny and beautiful. If Vittorio must give up visiting the Czechs, he resolves, he'll ask don Francesco to set aside a whole tin of pencils just for them.

Vittorio looks again at the city as it was: still beautiful, still intact. He says a silent prayer for everyone he loves, and then he squares his shoulders and gets to work.

10

Anna

I didn't doze off until it must have been near daybreak, and I didn't wake until Tiberio pawed at my face, demanding to be let out. I opened the door and he ran off down the corridor. Then I washed and dressed as quickly as I could and went to the kitchen. Silvia was sitting by the stove, darning a sock. She set her work aside and got to her feet.

'Oh, good, you're up at last. Did you sleep well? Quick, let's have our breakfast before Father Vittorio arrives. I expect he'll be here any moment.'

I was staring at the forms on the kitchen table. A neat stack with Giovanni Episcopo's card sitting on top. Teglio's list lay next to it, along with two pens and an inkwell. 'Is that…?'

'Yes, yes. Sit down, Marta, that's a good girl. I just don't feel right about eating in front of him.' Silvia was sawing at the loaf of greyish bread that sat on the counter. 'Not when he's fasting. And I know he is, for all he'd never say anything,' she went on darkly. 'I smelled it on him the other day. That nasty rotten-fruit smell, ugh!'

'He's fasting? But it isn't Lent any more, is it?' A memory came back to me: lying in bed in my old flat, listening to the bells peal and peal and peal for Easter Sunday. Days, weeks ago now.

'Doesn't have to be Lent. It's all part of their discipline. He's probably doing penance for some minor sin.' She put two slices of bread in front of me with an indignant flourish. 'As if a man like him could ever want punishing. Honestly!'

We ate and drank in haste, and had the kitchen cleaned up by the time Vittorio arrived, carrying a black bag rather like the sort doctors use. I imagined him going from house to house with it, doing whatever priests do at the bedsides of the dying. As he took off his cloak and folded it over the back of a chair, I found myself watching him. He looked a little paler, it was true, but all I could smell on him was a faint odour of carbolic soap.

'Ready to get started?' His voice was constricted. He took out his handkerchief, turned away and coughed into it – that same dry, wheezing cough I'd heard before. It seemed to go on and on.

Silvia sprang into action. 'For heaven's sake, Father, sit down. Do you want tea? Water? Brandy? Tea would be best,' she said firmly. 'Heat loosens the chest. And you know my tea – it's practically medicine.'

Vittorio nodded, his hand pressed to his chest. 'Tea, then,' he managed to say. 'Thank you.'

'Quite right.' Silvia poured out a cup of tisane and then somehow, without touching him, managed to hustle Vittorio into her own abandoned chair by the stove. 'There are cigarettes in the drawer nearest you. I have a couple of things to sort out with Bernardo before you start on the papers, anyway. Marta, will you help?'

'Of course,' I said.

Silvia ushered me out into the corridor, closing the door firmly behind us. 'In here,' she mouthed, and headed for the door next to the bathroom. She opened it to reveal a neat parlour, very like the one my mother kept for best. The furniture was old but immaculate, and there were doilies on every surface.

'Sorry,' she said, sitting down in one of the upright brown armchairs while I perched on the matching couch. 'There's nothing to sort out. I just needed a reason to leave him alone. He needs to have a good cough and a spit, maybe close his eyes for a moment, and he won't do any of that while we're around.'

'Is he…' I was having difficulty finding the words. 'Has he always been so sick?'

'Not always. Well, he can't have been, can he? The Jesuits don't accept invalids. They want strong soldiers of the Church Militant, and so forth. He must have been quite healthy when they got hold of him, or at least healthy enough for their purposes. But since we've known him…' Silvia sighed. 'Sometimes he's better and sometimes he's worse, but recently he's mostly worse. I don't know if it's the weather or the time of day, or all of this.' She waved her hand as if to take it all in: Genoa, and the bombs, and the Germans, and the Fascists. 'But he isn't helping himself by refusing to eat – that much I do know.'

We sat in silence for a moment, in grim acknowledgement of this truth. And then coughing sounded out from along the corridor, but now it sounded painful, wrenching. Silvia grimaced and shook her head.

'I don't like that, not one bit. Whatever there is that's clogging up his lungs – it needs to get out. It needs to be moving or else it will fester, and if it festers then you're in trouble. That's why a cigarette helps. Believe me,' she added, 'I know all this too well. My father died of pneumonia.'

'I'm sorry,' I said.

'He was a lot older than our Father Vittorio. Let's leave him for just a little longer, and then you two can start work.'

We waited until the coughing peaked and subsided, then gave way to silence. 'Come on,' Silvia said.

The window in the kitchen was open, letting in cold damp air, and there was a lingering smell of cigarette smoke. Vittorio sat at the table in the same seat Teglio had occupied the evening before. I was relieved to see that he looked somewhat better.

'Ready?' he asked, and I nodded. 'Then sit down, Marta, please.'

I sat down next to him with the stack of forms before me. He'd anchored Teglio's list between us, using the inkwell and a small metal ashtray.

'How shall we do this?' I asked.

'I thought you could fill out the details in your best secretarial hand and pass each one to me. I'll check it against the list, and then I'll do the signature.'

'And I shall sit here by the stove and finish my darning,' Silvia said. 'But I'll make us some more tea first. Father, you'll have a spoonful of honey in yours.'

'No, thank you,' Vittorio said. His abrupt tone startled me into looking at him. His eyes were fixed on the table and his brows were drawn together. At first I thought he was angry, but no – this was longing. This was a man who wanted a spoonful of honey in his tea.

'Don't you argue with me,' Silvia retorted. 'You'll have one. It's medicine. Marta, how about you?'

'I'm fine, thank you so much. I don't need anything to drink.' In fact, I'd have liked a cup of hot tea more than anything – my mouth was dry and the draught from the open window was caressing my right ear in a very unpleasant way. But I could just imagine knocking it over and ruining this whole precious batch of forms.

'Come to think of it, I shall take my tea by the window,' Vittorio said. 'Hot drinks and important paperwork don't mix. If you don't mind getting started, Marta?'

I didn't mind. I took a form, pulled the list towards me and started filling in the details. I was aware of Silvia by the stove, trying to keep Tiberio from stealing her wool; Vittorio by the window, sipping his tea and taking in fresh air. I concentrated on my work, tracing each letter of each word with steady deliberation, Bernardo's words echoing in my mind. *We can't afford any waste.*

By the time I finished the tenth form, my hand was cramping and my wrist was beginning to complain. It had been years since I had been employed, since I had written by hand for any length of time. I put the pen down and sat back, trying to shake out the tension. Vittorio closed the window and took his seat.

'Have a break now. My turn to concentrate. Well,' he said, looking at the forms in front of him. 'This is beautiful work. I'm not at all surprised, but I am very pleased. Thank you, Marta.'

And he picked up his pen and drew one of the cards towards him. I forgot all about the pot of tea waiting on the stove; I forgot to stand or stretch or go over to warm myself, as I'd been planning to do the whole time I was copying out the first batch. I simply watched Vittorio. First, he compared the details on the card with those on Teglio's list, nodding in approval. Then he perfectly copied the mayor's signature from Giovanni Episcopo's card, working in swift, confident pen-strokes. He picked up the card and held it between finger and thumb, whether to admire it or help it to dry I'm not sure.

'How do you do that?' I asked. 'I mean, so easily?'

'I suppose it's a gift. My training helps,' he added.

'What did you train as, a master criminal?'

A brief, dry laugh. 'No, a librarian. Librarian-conservator, really.' He set down the card and picked up a fresh one, his eyes already scanning the text I'd copied out. I had been dismissed. I accepted a cup of tea from Silvia and went to sit by the stove.

We worked like that, in shifts, until every name on the list was crossed off. But one blank form remained. Vittorio filled in the mayor's signature and then passed it over to me.

'Fill this in with the details you have on your current card, and sign it. You'll need an address in Caltanissetta, so pick one from the list and change the house number. Unless you'd prefer to wait for another batch and come from a different town instead?'

'No, thanks,' I said. 'Caltanissetta will do very well.'

Vittorio nodded. 'When you're done, fetch me your old card and we'll transfer over the photograph. Then you'll be all set up.'

'Except for the stamps and the imprimatur,' I said.

'Quite so. But Mr X will take care of that once we've done our part.'

When I'd filled in my details, I hurried to my room and dug out my false identity card once again. When I returned, Vittorio had set out a scalpel and a tiny pot of clear, thin glue, and my new Caltanissetta papers lay before him. I handed him my card – it now looked very shabby indeed, to my eyes – and he carefully prised off the photograph, sliding the scalpel underneath it with a surgeon's precision and shaving off the remnants of the glue. Then he opened the new card, added a small drop of fresh glue to the back of the photograph and positioned it in the right spot, pressing it firmly down and holding it there with the tips of his fingers.

'Shouldn't you use gloves for that?' Silvia asked.

Vittorio shook his head. 'Makes you clumsy. And you only glue your fingers together once before you learn to be careful.' He considered for a moment. 'Maybe twice.'

We sat in silence while he waited for the adhesive to dry. Then, once he judged it was time, he picked up the card and passed it over.

'Here you are. But keep it flat for a little while, with a book to weigh it down.'

'Marta has plenty of those,' Silvia said.

'I'm glad to hear it.' Vittorio stood and packed away the glue and scalpel in his black bag. Silvia got up, too, tipping Tiberio gently out of her lap.

'I'll burn this in the stove,' she said, picking up the list. 'Shall I parcel the cards up for you, Father? We have some old orders of service – from our church, not yours, but they should do as cover.'

'Not this time, thank you. Mr X will come past for them later today.'

'Any idea when?' she asked. 'Just so we can be prepared.'

'I don't know, I'm afraid. Most likely around dinnertime.'

'All right, then,' Silvia said. 'Won't you have something else before you go? More tea, a cigarette? Or stay for lunch?'

'That's very kind, but I can't stay.' Vittorio put on his round hat and his cloak and turned to me. 'Thank you for your hard work today, Marta. I think we make a very good team.'

'I think so, too,' I said, and he smiled, just a little.

'Good day, then. I shall see you again soon.'

Once he'd left, my broken night started to creep up on me. I had my lunchtime soup with Silvia and Bernardo, and then they went back to work and I went to my room. I lay on my bed with Tiberio curled up on my legs and tried to read *A Study in Scarlet*, comparing the Italian translation with my memory of the English original, which I'd read so many times before. It was the kind of mental exercise I liked very much, as mental exercises go. But my eyes were heavy and I was dizzyingly tired. I only managed a few lines before sleep claimed me.

11

I woke up what felt like hours later, my eyes dry and my mouth foul with sleep. Tiberio had moved up the bed to stretch out on my pillow – his fur tickled my ear and made my nose itch – and *The Adventures of Sherlock Holmes* lay open on the floor where I'd let it fall. Somehow, I felt worse than I had when I lay down. I pushed myself up and went to the window: pulling the curtain aside, I saw bright sunshine over the roofs of Genoa. I couldn't have been asleep for all that long, but I felt as groggy and bewildered as if I'd been shaken awake in the small hours. I understood now, better than ever, why my mother had been so strongly against afternoon naps.

It should be a crime to waste daylight, her voice rang in my ear. *Go to sleep now and you'll only lie awake all night!*

Well, I would listen to her, even if she wasn't here to nag me. I would wash my face and brush my teeth, and I'd take *Sherlock Holmes* and read it sitting upright, in the parlour, like a respectable citizen.

But when I opened the door, I found Teglio sitting on the sofa. Stacks of identity cards were set out on the table before him, and he was absorbed in applying a small rubber stamp to each one.

'Oh, sorry,' I said, and he looked up at me. He'd taken off his jacket, rolled up his cuffs and loosened his tie – his horn-rimmed spectacles were discarded on the arm of the sofa. It was strange to see him so informal, and I had to suppress the urge to turn and bolt back to my bedroom.

'Marta! Am I clogging up your reading room? I do apologise.'

'No, no, it's fine.' I was clutching *Sherlock Holmes* to my chest like a shameful secret. 'Unless I can help, of course. Is there anything I can do?'

'No, no, this is all very boring. But this is your home. If you want to sit in here and read, then that is what you must do.'

I still wanted to bolt. But the idea of getting to see him work, of understanding a little more of the whole forgery business, was tremendously compelling. 'If you're sure…'

'I wouldn't say so otherwise. What's that you're reading?' he asked as I settled into the nearest armchair. He leaned over to look at the book in my hand, and I caught the scent of his cedarwood cologne. 'Good, good. I'm glad my little offering was some use. Are you enjoying it?'

'I am, thank you. It's lovely to revisit these stories. I hadn't read the Italian version before.'

'Haven't you? Oh, of course,' Teglio said. 'You wouldn't need to, would you?'

'No, but that's what's so interesting about reading them now. It's like seeing them from a new angle.'

'Excellent stuff. Well, you sit and read, and I'll get on with these.' He leaned forward and pressed the stamp against the ink pad, lining up a fresh card. I opened my book and held it in my lap, keeping my head bowed. But from the corner of my eye, I was watching him.

I tried to observe, to leave him to it while I pretended to read. I really had no intention of muscling in. But he was clearly tired, or simply unused to this kind of work, and the irregular, slow thud of the stamp began to wear at my nerves. Worst of all, it kept drawing my attention to his hands, and I hadn't really looked at them before; hadn't noticed his capable fingers, the heavy silver watch on his left wrist, the dark hair exposed by his rolled-back cuffs. Now they were the only thing I wanted to look at, and I found myself taking refuge in my book.

He's just a man, I told myself sternly. *There's no need to gawp at him just because he happens to be close at hand. Just because he's including you in his work. Just because it's been five years since you went to bed with anyone.*

My nerves frayed and snapped. 'Why don't you let me take over?' I asked – as politely as I could, but not nearly as politely as I ought.

'It's quite all right. There's no need.'

'But there is,' I said. 'You're being terribly inefficient.'

'Now, steady on—'

'I'm sorry, but you are. You're paying the whole process far too much attention, and that wastes time and energy. I can get through these much faster. And you can have a rest,' I added. 'I don't suppose you get to rest very often.'

'That's true,' he admitted.

'Then leave it to me. Just show me where to put the

stamp. Come on,' I said. 'I wore Silvia down and I shall wear you down, too.'

'I suppose it's more efficient to admit defeat, then. Very well.' He picked up one of the already-stamped cards to show me. The details had been filled in and the mayor's signature applied – only the photograph was missing. 'The stamp goes here,' he said, pointing to the bottom right corner. 'It should partially cover the signature, like this.'

'All right. It's probably best if I sit where you are.' I gestured at the couch and he obligingly got up and moved to the armchair on the other side, leaving me to settle into his abandoned spot, which was warm and smelled of cedarwood. I hadn't anticipated that, and it was very distracting. But I focused on the task at hand – take a card from one pile, open it, apply the stamp, close it, place it in the next pile – and within moments I was genuinely absorbed. I worked steadily and didn't let myself look away until the final card was stamped.

Teglio was stretched out in the armchair with a hand over his eyes. He was clearly exhausted, and my heart gave a sharp tug of sympathy. 'All finished,' I said.

'Thank you, Marta. You were quite right – I did need a rest. And you've finished this in record time,' he added, sitting up and looking at the four neat piles of cards lined up on the table. 'It all seemed to be over in two minutes.'

'Not quite,' I said diplomatically. His eyes were bleary, and I suspected he'd dropped off at some point. 'But it didn't take long. Hopefully I've saved you some time.'

He looked at his watch. 'Oh. Yes, as a matter of fact, you have. It's quite a bit earlier than I thought.'

He said it lightly, but there was a note in his voice,

something that might have been surprise or even alarm. I thought of the walk I'd endured with Vittorio: that brief, stressful immersion in the world outside my lost street. The dangers everywhere. 'Do you have to go on somewhere?' I asked. 'Another meeting?'

'Well, yes, but—'

'Then you must stay,' I said. 'Until you have to leave, I mean. If you want to.'

'Oh, I shouldn't impose on you any further,' Teglio said. 'Not when you've helped me so much already. I ought to go and leave you to your own devices.'

'I get left to my own devices all day long. You wouldn't be imposing at all, really. If you want to wait here for a while first – if it's safer than leaving now – then I shall be glad of the company.' It sounded terribly bold when I said it out loud. But if I wanted to keep him safe, then I had to be bold about it.

'I really wouldn't be disturbing you?'

'You really wouldn't.'

Teglio smiled. He looked relieved, and I was relieved, too. 'Then I shan't argue. Thank you.' He settled back into his chair and let out a long, slow breath. 'Do go on with your reading,' he said. 'Pretend I'm not here, if you like.'

That was impossible, of course. Because all of a sudden we were alone together, not working, and with nothing we had to discuss. I had practically begged him to stay. It was all I could think about.

'Could I fetch you something?' I asked. 'Coffee? Well, not coffee, but you know what I mean. Or tea? There's bound to be a pot on the stove.'

'No, thank you, I'm all right.'

'Are you sure?' I felt suddenly desperate, as if I might say something stupid unless I had some innocent distraction. 'It's no trouble at all.'

'I'm quite sure. If I'm honest,' he said, passing a hand over his face, 'I could do with something a bit stronger than tea.'

'I think Silvia keeps a bottle of brandy somewhere,' I said.

He turned his head and looked at me. 'Really? Do Waldensians approve of brandy?'

'I don't know. It's probably medicinal.'

'Of course.' Teglio thought for a moment. 'No, I don't think it's even the drink I want, not as such. I suppose what I want is… no, it's far too silly.'

'I'm sure it isn't silly at all,' I said.

He sighed. 'Well, I think it's really the idea of going out somewhere and having a drink. If I could – if everything were different – I should walk out of here and just wander along to the Galleria Mazzini. Not as it is now, but as it used to be. Before it was such a dangerous place.'

'You could walk straight down via Assarotti,' I said, imagining it. 'Around piazza Corvetto and to the left by the prefecture.' The sun on my face, the fresh air, the leisurely sense of freedom. The great glass-topped arcade ahead, full of people drinking and chatting and enjoying themselves. I was suddenly full of painful longing for the Galleria Mazzini, even though I'd scarcely spent any time there myself. It had always been my father's haunt more than mine. And now I knew it had been Teglio's haunt, too.

'That's exactly it,' Teglio said. 'A nice, gentle stroll, none of this nipping around back streets to avoid the Germans. And then I'd sit down at a bar and drink a glass of something and smoke a cigarette, and I'd do nothing at all for the rest of the day. Does that sound frivolous?'

'Yes,' I said, and he laughed.

'I should have known. I expect you'd rather be devouring a novel on a bench somewhere.'

'But that's frivolous, too,' I protested. 'I didn't say being frivolous was wrong.'

'I know,' he said. 'I know you understand.' Of course, he'd been teasing me. I didn't quite know what to do about it.

'Come to think of it,' Teglio went on, 'maybe it is the drink I want after all. Did you say there's brandy?'

'Yes. I expect they keep it in here somewhere.' I got up, relieved to have something to do, and went over to the big, polished-wood cabinet that stood against the wall. I hadn't looked at it properly the last time I'd been in here, and now I saw that it had a large panel at the front that locked at the top with a brass key. I turned the key and the panel fell forward to reveal an almost-full bottle on a salver, with a set of small, plain glasses.

'You're not going to tell me you found that by accident,' Teglio said.

I poured out a modest glass of brandy and handed it to him, keeping a careful eye on the level in the bottle. 'I wonder if they'll notice,' I said. 'Do you think they will?'

'I shouldn't think so,' he said. 'It's probably been sitting there untouched since the old king died. And Silvia and Bernardo are hospitable souls. I'm sure they wouldn't begrudge either of us a bit of refreshment.'

'I know. They really are very kind. And they've never told

me that anything's off-limits, not even the best parlour. It's just...'

'What is it?' Teglio prompted.

'Well, they don't have to tell me, do they? This is their home, not mine. I'm an interloper here – I'm not even allowed to pitch in like a friend would, or a proper guest. I'm sure they don't see it that way, but I can't see it otherwise.'

'I think you're very hard on yourself,' he said. 'And you're being hard on Bernardo and Silvia, too, but I do understand. If you like, I'll come clean to them and offer to replace the bottle. I said I wanted a drink, after all. You were just being a sort of substitute hostess.'

'Would you? I'd feel a lot better if you did.'

'Of course I will. They'll probably turn me down, but I shall offer and mean it. I'm bound to have a spare bottle tucked away somewhere I can give them. Now, with that off your conscience, will you have a glass, too?'

I knew it would be unwise. I hadn't slept properly, and I hadn't drunk any alcohol in years, but I found that wanted to sit and keep talking with Teglio. I liked this new friendliness between us. I liked seeing him relaxed; I liked his jokes and his banter, though I knew I'd have to have a stern word with myself about that later on. So I poured myself a half-glass and sat down, daringly, at the end of the sofa nearest to him. He raised his glass to me.

'Just imagine we're in the Galleria Mazzini. *Cin cin.*' He took a draught of brandy and winced. 'This stuff really is medicinal.'

I took a cautious sip from my own drink. The alcohol

burned my lips and caught at my throat – I burst into a spluttering cough.

'Rough, isn't it?' Teglio said. I could only nod, eyes streaming. I felt in my pocket for my handkerchief and realised I'd left it in my room.

'Here you go.' He put his own into my hand. A silk handkerchief, altogether too nice to use, but I didn't have a choice. I pressed it to my mouth, desperately trying to suppress the tickle in my gullet, but it was hopeless. I gave way to a fresh paroxysm of coughing. 'Oh dear,' Teglio said.

When the worst had finally died down and I could breathe, I wiped the tears from my face and cautiously lowered the handkerchief. It was a crumpled, damp mess, and I suspect I was, too. 'Thank you,' I managed to say.

'I'm just glad you survived the experience. Keep the handkerchief – I have hundreds. And I shall be replacing this bottle whether Silvia wants me to or not. Medicinal, indeed.' He picked up his glass and drained it in one.

'Maybe it's more like anaesthetic,' I said.

'What for, horses? I suppose it's crudely effective, though,' he said thoughtfully. 'Not an unpleasant warmth, if you can get it down in the first place.'

I pushed my glass along the table towards him. 'Please,' I said as he raised an enquiring eyebrow. 'Silvia might forgive us for drinking her brandy, but she can't abide waste.'

'Yes, fair point.' He tipped it back, set the glass down and got to his feet. 'I'll go and explain myself to Silvia and get her to wrap these cards up. Fetch me your new card, would you?'

By the time I returned – having checked my reflection, dabbed my face with cold water and run a comb through my hair, which was a fright – Teglio had put his jacket and glasses back on and adjusted his tie. He stood with the cards tucked under one arm, every inch the respectable, debonair Mr X. I felt oddly bereft.

'Thank you, Marta,' he said as I handed him my identity card. 'I'll have the imprimatur applied and get this back to you as soon as possible. Tomorrow morning, if I can. I know it's worrying to be without it, but a card without the imprimatur… well, you may as well have your old card back, or none at all. Not very comforting, I'm sure,' he added. 'But it's true.'

'I know,' I said. 'I know it is. I trust you.'

I said it casually enough, but Teglio smiled: a warm, open smile that lit up his whole face. 'I'm glad.'

I held out my hand, and he shook it. 'Thank you,' he said again. And he was off down the corridor, calling for Silvia, before I could respond.

What I felt in that moment is hard to describe. Teglio – he, of all people – was the first person in years who had treated me not as a problem to solve, not as a victim to rescue, not as a resource to exploit but quite simply as a human being, a woman, an equal. And now he had gone outside into that danger-ridden world where I wasn't brave or foolish enough to go. I didn't know whether I wanted to run after him and beg him to stay inside, to keep himself safe, or insist that he take me along.

I sat down and tried to read, but I couldn't focus. I went to my room and threw myself on the bed and tried to sleep, for all my mother's strictures, but it was impossible. I was agitated, desperate, restless in body and mind. I wanted to leap up and pace, do something to work off my energy, but for all I knew there were customers downstairs; I couldn't afford to draw their attention. I wanted to scream.

In the end, I did what I so often did during those long, tense, silent days. I took a chair from the kitchen and placed it at my bedroom window, and I put my elbows on the windowsill and my chin in my hands and stared up at the sky outside. I couldn't bear to stand and look down, to see the wreck of the city I loved. I could only rest my eyes on the never-ending blue and force myself to breathe, in and out, until my heart gradually began to slow and a familiar feeling crept over me: that comforting numbness I'd learned to cultivate when Stefano died and left me alone, quite alone in a world that had already turned against me.

12

The front doorbell rang early the next morning, three times, when the shop was still closed and Silvia and Bernardo and I hadn't even started breakfast. Bernardo started downstairs to answer it while Silvia and I crept out into the hallway, craning our necks, listening.

'It's got to be *him*,' Silvia whispered. 'Hasn't it?'

I nodded, but I felt thoroughly sick. All I could think about was the remains of my old identity card, that battered scrap of thick paper – the wrong paper – without even a photograph, with nothing about it that might fool anyone. If it wasn't Teglio at the door…

I acted before I could finish the thought. I ran along the corridor to the bathroom – that quiet, flat-footed run I'd long since learned to perfect – slid the bolt across and went to the window. My hands were slick with sweat, but I managed to unlock it and slide the old wooden frame upwards in a jerky but, thankfully, silent motion. I knelt down, opened the cupboard and pulled out the rope, resting it across my knees. I fixed my eyes on the back door of the house across the courtyard, the one I was to run to, and I waited.

After a far too long a moment, the stairs creaked and I heard footsteps coming up. Heavy, slow, familiar footsteps, just one set of them. It had to be Bernardo, surely; but I didn't trust my senses and so I kept kneeling there, the rope clutched in my hands, until there was a soft knock at the door and Silvia's voice said: 'Marta, dear? You can come out now. You're quite safe.'

Now I got to my feet, letting the rope fall. I tottered the few shaky steps to the door, pulled back the bolt and walked out into Silvia's waiting arms. 'It's all right,' she said, patting me on the back. 'But it doesn't get any easier, does it? It's just a whole new fright, every single time.'

'That's it,' I said, and did my best to smile.

'Come on,' she said. 'Come back through. There's been a delivery for you.'

Bernardo was hovering by the kitchen table, clutching a small parcel and looking quite pale himself. 'Something from Mr X,' he said. 'It was a girl who brought it. A wee girl in a Red Cross uniform, with a bicycle. She looked about twelve.'

He held the parcel out to me and I took it, untying the string with trembling fingers. I had lain awake all night, disaster scenarios playing out in my head: a night-time air raid, a visit from the Gestapo or the Fascist police. I tore the paper off and found a small hardback copy of Conan Doyle's *The Lost World*, again in Italian translation. Tucked inside was my new identity card, with the Caltanissetta police stamp and the imprimatur in place. I ran my thumb over the embossed surface, scarcely able to believe it was real.

'Yes, yes, all right,' Bernardo was saying in response to some protest of Silvia's. 'Maybe she was a bit older than that. But she was a funny little lass, anyway. Ever so serious. You wouldn't want to be on the wrong side of her.'

'Well, Marta?' Silvia asked. 'Is that your card?'

'Yes.' I stared at it for a moment, and then something in Bernardo's words rang a belated bell. 'Did you say she was Red Cross, the woman who brought this? Not very tall, medium-brownish hair? Quite a determined manner?'

'That's right.'

'I think that's Nurse Dora,' I said. 'She's the one who found me, when... you know. I don't think I'd have survived if not for her.'

'And you called her a wee girl,' Silvia said reproachfully.

Bernardo protested, and the two of them fell into amicable bickering while I went back to looking at my card. I'd never seen a finished one before, and now I had one in my hand, and it was mine. *This is what I'm working for*, I thought, and the thought made me happier than I had been in a long time. *This is my purpose.*

Vittorio came the next morning with his black bag. He put the bag on the table, opened it and took out a slender purple-and-gold stole, which he kissed and laid reverently to one side. Then he reached in again and brought out a little brown-paper parcel. He held it out to me.

'The list's inside,' he said. 'But this is also for you. Mr X asked if I had anything for you to read, and this is the best I could manage.'

I opened the parcel and found a paperback novel: an

Italian edition of Graham Greene's *Brighton Rock*. The cover was a lurid affair with cars and guns and men in sharp suits, and the whole thing looked delightful.

'Oh,' I said. 'Thank you! Thank you, Father Vittorio.'

'It washed up in our library, somehow – people bring us all kinds of things. I suppose Greene is a Catholic, at least. Thank you,' Vittorio said as Silvia put a cup of tea on the table in front of him. He sat down and wiped his brow with a handkerchief. He seemed better than the last time I'd seen him, at least. But there was something about the set of his mouth I didn't like, and his chest was rising and falling in a rapid, shallow rhythm.

'Drink,' Silvia ordered him, and he brought the cup to his lips and made a wry face.

'There's honey in this.' It wasn't quite a reproach.

'Of course there is,' she said. 'And now get on with your work, the two of you, and I shall get on with mine.'

'Very well. Let's get started, shall we?' Vittorio rubbed his hands together. 'Now, Marta, I thought about trying a sophisticated system where you would tackle the first ten names on the list while I take the second, and then we would swap over and start again. But on reflection, perhaps we ought to carry on working in shifts, as we did before. We'll tire quickly without breaks, and tiredness leads to sloppiness. What do you think?'

'I agree,' I said; and Silvia, who was knitting by the stove, nodded approvingly.

'Good,' Vittorio said. 'Then I'll let you take the first shift and perhaps drink another cup of tea.'

And so we embarked on our routine. It's a strange thing, but I think of those mornings with Vittorio as one of the great constants of my life. It seems as if we spent months, years together in that way, working comfortably at right angles to one another. But it wasn't like that at all; we had only a little time.

During the final stretch of that particular morning, while Vittorio was applying signatures to the last ten cards, I glanced over at Silvia and realised she'd fallen asleep with Tiberio curled upside down in her lap. I found myself wondering if she had stayed as a sort of chaperone: a way for Vittorio to be alone with a woman without infringing his Jesuit discipline. But is a chaperone still a chaperone if she's unconscious? What would Ignatius of Loyola say about that? I smiled to imagine it, and then realised I was smiling and stopped.

Vittorio set down the last of the cards. 'There,' he said. 'Another batch done. We are getting very efficient.'

The vivid cover of the paperback caught my eye. It was so very un-Jesuit. And yet Vittorio, who barely knew me, had lit on just my sort of book. Had Teglio told him something, even though he'd promised he wouldn't? Was that even a real promise he'd made, or was it all part of his charming-Mr-X routine? I thought back to our first conversation and how I'd let my guard down with him, how I'd chatted on merrily about Conan Doyle and Machiavelli while he took notes in his head, and I felt suddenly exposed.

'Have you read it?' I asked before I even knew I was asking. '*Brighton Rock*, I mean.'

'Oh. No. No, I haven't read any Greene at all. But I have read his great preceptor, G.K. Chesterton. I enjoyed the *Father Brown* stories very much.'

'Did you read them in Italian, or...'

'In English.' He was looking at the table, but he was smiling. A soft, involuntary smile. 'I like to read in English.'

I have rehearsed that conversation so many times since then, playing it over in my mind. I should never have said what I said next. But I wanted to know exactly what he knew about me – what Teglio, whom I was already coming to like and to trust like I hadn't dared to trust anyone in years, might have given away without my knowing.

'Then we can speak English with one another.'

For one startling moment, his green eyes were fixed on mine. I knew then that Teglio hadn't said anything about who I was. He had kept it all to himself, and I felt thoroughly disloyal.

Vittorio looked at the kitchen door and said: '*Well, I… my English isn't very good. Sorry. I try to speak when I can, but I have few chances.*'

'*You speak it very nicely,*' I said. '*How did you learn?*'

'*I spent time in London many years ago. At Farm Street, for my regency. After I was a novice,*' he explained – simplifying it, I suspect, so that I could understand. '*But before I was a priest. And then also I have been to St Beuno's in Wales, where was Gerard Manley Hopkins. I do not much like his poetry. But you speak better than I,*' he said, still talking to the door. '*Like an Englishwoman, or perhaps not quite an Englishwoman.*'

I hesitated for a moment, weighing up what to tell him. '*My mother's from Edinburgh,*' I said at last.

'I see. And she… she is…'

'*She's with my father and brother in America. They're all safe, so far as I know. She's a Protestant,*' I couldn't resist adding. '*My mother. She's a good person, though.*'

Vittorio laughed, a sharp, sudden laugh that turned to coughing. Silvia awoke with a snort and sat upright, her hands going to her hair. Indignant, Tiberio fled her lap and retreated to a corner of the kitchen, where he sat primly on his haunches and began to wash himself.

'Sorry,' Silvia said. 'This weather… Have you finished?'

'Yes, we have.' Vittorio rose to his feet, gathering cloak and stole and bag. 'Mr X will come past later. Good day, Silvia; good day, Marta.' He nodded to each of us and went out.

Silvia leaned towards me. 'I'm so sorry,' she said in a low voice. 'I just closed my eyes for a moment and then I was gone. Was it horribly awkward? Or didn't he notice?'

'I'm quite sure he didn't,' I said, although in fact I had no idea. 'Don't worry at all. We were busy working.'

'Oh, good. That is a relief. And now you shall see Mr X again, and so soon. I won't have to play at being a duenna then.' She bent down to pick up her knitting from where it had fallen on the floor, and settled back in her chair. 'By the way, I don't mind you two drinking my brandy, but if you are going to be alone together then I must insist you leave the door open.'

'Of course,' I said. The suggestion of impropriety made me blush, a fierce hot-cold blush, and I hoped Silvia wouldn't look at me. She didn't, thankfully. She seemed to be busy counting her stitches.

'Thank you,' she said. 'I know you're a grown woman, but…' She trailed off, and I wondered what she was about to say next. *But those are the rules. But this is a respectable house. But I would tell my daughter the same.* Except that she didn't have a daughter, did she? Or was there one who'd grown up and married, or gone away to work, or simply… gone away? I thought of my own mother, who hadn't seen me in ten years – who didn't know whether I was alive or dead – and the thought was almost unbearable.

'Silvia?'

'Yes, Marta dear?' Her attention was still on her knitting.

'I wanted to ask…' Now she looked at me, and I realised that I was being foolish. I couldn't actually ask her if she had a child, or children. It wasn't any of my business; and besides, who knew what painful feelings I might stir up. 'Can I help with anything?' I offered.

'You can cut up some bread, if you absolutely must.' Silvia nodded towards the loaf-end sitting on the counter. 'Nice and small. I'll fry it up and we can have it in our soup.'

'All right. Is there anything else?' I said it far more earnestly than I meant to, because the thought of my mother had shaken me up. 'Anything at all.'

Silvia reached across and patted my arm. 'You're a kind girl,' she said. 'But no, the bread will do.'

13

Teglio arrived just after dinner, and asked Bernardo and Silvia if we could take over the kitchen table. 'Of course,' Silvia said – answering, as ever, for both of them. 'We'll sit and read in the parlour. Won't we, Bernardo?'

'Yes, love,' Bernardo said, but he was pulling at his moustache. He didn't look too happy to give up the warmth of the stove.

'Come on, then.' Silvia scooped up Tiberio in one arm and almost propelled Bernardo out of the door, leaving it pointedly open. She gave me a meaningful look over her shoulder as she departed.

'Right,' Teglio said, and cleared his throat. He seemed uncharacteristically flustered, and I wondered if he'd had to hear the same talk that Silvia had given me. 'Now, these are the cards you and Father Vittorio filled out today?' He nodded to the pile that stood on the table by his elbow.

'That's right,' I said.

'Good.' He reached into his jacket and brought out another

parcel, which he handed to me. 'Here are some I did myself last night, along with the list. Perhaps you could double-check them, make sure all the details are present and correct?'

'Like Father Vittorio does for me.'

'Exactly. Hang on, just let me fetch the stamp.'

By the time he returned, I'd unpacked the folded cards and set them in front of me along with the list and a pencil. Teglio pulled up his chair alongside mine and flourished the stamp with a smile.

'I'll stamp yours and Father Vittorio's while you start going through mine. I won't be nearly as efficient as you, of course, but I can give it my best try. Ready?'

'Ready,' I said. I opened the first card in the stack and saw, to my surprise, that it had a photograph already attached. I'd only worked on blank cards before, and now here was the face of a young woman, much younger than I was. Her hair was loosely pulled back and she watched the camera with wary, tired eyes.

'All right there?' Teglio asked.

'Yes. Yes, of course.' I moved the list closer and began to check the details, forcing myself to ignore the woman's gaze. Next came a middle-aged man with a moustache and a striped tie; then a woman with a round face and a billowy, old-fashioned hairstyle; then another, an angular, elderly lady with a look of fierce determination. And each of them was looking at the camera – looking at me. My nerve began to fail: I checked names, birth dates, distinguishing features and then went back to check them again, fearing that I'd overlook some detail that would alert the Germans. My work became slower and slower, more and more agonised. And then I opened the next card, and I stopped.

This was an older man. A man around my father's age, with my father's intelligent eyes and his greying hair and his frank, open expression. He wasn't my father, of course, but he was so like him. He was so like him.

'Marta,' Teglio said quietly. 'Listen.'

I tore my eyes away from the man's face. Teglio was looking at me, his gaze calm and steady. 'This is a normal procedure,' he said. 'A standard safety check. I'm new at this forgery business, too, but I've spent a couple of decades flying aeroplanes, and that means I'm damn good at safety checks. I'd be long since dead if I weren't. You know that, don't you?'

'Yes.'

'Very well. Now, I've already reviewed all these cards, so your job is to act as a second pair of eyes. The best way to do that – the only way – is to work methodically. Look at each detail in order, just once, with your complete attention. Then cross it off and move on. If you keep on going back over your own tracks, you'll lose sight of what you're doing and you're far, far more likely to miss an error if one does crop up. Do you understand?'

'Yes,' I said. 'Yes, I understand.'

'Good.' He hesitated. 'It's a shock, isn't it, when you first see the pictures. All those faces. Makes it suddenly very real.'

'It does.' It came out as a choked whisper. I looked away and bit my lip, fighting back the urge to ask him for a hug. To beg him to hold me just long enough to let me catch my breath, to give me a moment's shelter from the horrible truths that were crowding in around us. I cleared my throat and reached for my pencil. 'Do you want me to start again from the beginning?'

'Take your time,' he said, and his voice was so warm with understanding that I almost broke down, almost turned to him and held out my arms. 'You don't have to—'

'I want to keep going. It's better that I do.'

'All right,' he said. 'Then no, you don't need to start afresh. But make a mark against the last one you checked, and I'll go back and look at those first ones again.'

Even with all my training, it took immense discipline to work as Teglio had instructed. I had to force myself not to double back and check this or that detail: to focus my whole concentration on just one item, and then move forward. But I did force myself, and with every new card it became a little more… no, not impersonal. This kind of work would never be impersonal. But every time I saw those eyes looking up at me, it got easier and easier to tell myself that this person needed me – was asking me, in fact – to be as calm and as methodical as I could be.

Finally, I checked the very last detail on the very last card and slid it towards Teglio, who applied the stamp and closed the ink pad with a firm click. 'Done,' he said. 'Thank you for your help. You did a terrific job.' He pushed back his chair and got to his feet, and I stood, too.

'Thank you for the talk.' My eyes were tired and sore; I rubbed them, making them worse. 'I'm sorry you had to do that.'

'Oh, believe me,' Teglio said. 'It was nothing compared to the talks I have to give myself.'

'What, really?'

'Truly. Like I say, I'm new at this, too.' He looked sad all of a sudden, tired and in pain. In the background, Bernardo's voice droned on in a steady, regular rhythm. Tonight's New Testament reading was obviously a long one. Perhaps we had a few minutes, I thought. Perhaps if I held out my arms now, Teglio would come to me, let me comfort him. Perhaps.

'Amen,' Silvia's voice rang out down the corridor, and Bernardo echoed her with a muted 'Amen'.

'That's our time up,' Teglio said. 'But will you help me again? Or was it too much, all this?'

I thought of the faces I'd seen – the people he was helping. The people I could help. 'No,' I said. 'It wasn't too much at all. I'm happy to do it.'

He smiled at me. 'Splendid,' he said. 'I think we work rather well together.'

14

From then on, Massimo Teglio and I were a team. He listened to Silvia's protestations and abandoned all talk of finding the stamp another home. Now he came to the house when he could manage it – most often after dinner, but sometimes just after lunch – and we'd sit side by side in the parlour or the kitchen, doing our shared work. I became used to acting as his second set of eyes. And gradually, I became used to seeing the faces – even familiar ones.

The first time that happened, it was a girl called Sara who had been one of my mother's English students. I'd known her as a bright adolescent with a passion for Shakespeare and a gift for asking the most disconcerting questions. Now she was grown up, a young woman, but unmistakably herself. The sight was an unpleasant shock: a reminder of the desperate situation that she, and I, and Teglio, and so many others had to face. I lost all my hard-won composure in that moment; I had to clap my hand over my mouth to stop myself from crying out.

Teglio understood, of course. He always did. 'Someone you know?'

I nodded, trying frantically to blink back the tears that were rising. I couldn't live without his comfort any longer. I held out my other hand and he took it, clasping it firmly between both of his.

'It's good,' he said. 'This is really very good, do you see? It means she's alive, and in Italy.'

'Oh,' I said, wiping my eyes. 'I hadn't thought of it that way.'

'Well, now you will,' he said. 'In fact, that is exactly how you *must* think of it. Every person we manage to help is a victory. We cannot change our situation, but we can do our best to improve it. That is within our power, at least. You must remember that.'

I promised that I would, and we went back to our work. But there was something about the way he'd said it, the note of determination in his voice, that dwelt at the back of my mind. We finished that evening's batch, and as he picked up his horn-rimmed glasses – ready to resume his Mr X persona – I found myself asking: 'Where in the city would you go right now, if you could? If it were safe, I mean to say.'

'Hmm.' Teglio set the glasses back down. 'That's a good question.'

'It's silly, I know.'

'No, it's not silly. Not in the slightest.' He leaned back in his chair, considering. 'Well, we wouldn't have the curfew, would we? So there wouldn't be any rush to get anywhere in particular. That would be quite restful in itself. I suppose I'd just set out and… walk.'

'Uphill or down?'

'Downhill, but not too far. In fact, I think I'd just go to the Spianata dell'Acquasola and watch the sun set from there. I like the idea of having nothing else to do with my time. How about you?'

I imagined the Spianata dell'Acquasola as it was when I last visited: the flat, elegant, tree-lined park carved into the hillside below via Assarotti. Standing at the wall with the city laid out before me, still undamaged and vibrantly alive. *I'll go there, too*, I wanted to say. *With you*.

'I might walk down to piazza Corvetto,' I said. 'Mutter a few insults at the statue of Victor Emmanuel. It's an old family tradition.'

Teglio laughed, as I hoped he would. 'Well, that does sound entertaining. I think I shall change my plans and come see that instead. But not tonight, alas.' He pushed back his chair and stood, reaching for his glasses. 'Thank you, Marta, for the help. And thank you for the distraction. It's much appreciated.'

'It's nothing,' I said. But it felt like a victory.

We often built castles in the air, after that. 'I feel like going to Spianata Castelletto tomorrow,' he'd say as he bundled up the cards ready for Silvia to pack. 'Let's assume the elevator's working. How about you?' Or: 'I think a quick hop over to Rapallo might be in order. We're going to have the weather for it, so why not?' And I'd briefly imagine sitting (with him) on a bench at Castelletto, or walking (with him) along the promenade at Rapallo; and then I'd push the image away and make myself come up with a completely different scenario, without him.

*

Much later, Teglio would explain to me that he preferred to move around the city at mealtimes, when most people were indoors and the Germans would be less vigilant. They had a price on his head by then, he said casually. A million lire, more than enough money to lure someone into betraying him – and indeed people in his network, important and well-connected people, had been betrayed by accident or design and had vanished into Marassi prison or the Gestapo cells at the Casa dello Studente. He never told me any of this at the time, though. He never gave me the slightest hint of the dangers he'd braved just to get to the house, or how he lived on the move between different locations. He was simply my refuge, and I did my best to be his.

I told myself that he and I were great comrades. I told myself that there could be no attraction between us; that our new complicity, as strong and surprising as it was, had to be something different. A working friendship, or a friendship rooted in work. I told myself all kinds of things, but the reality is that I was falling in love with him. I couldn't admit that then, but I know it now. I lived for his visits. I knew every detail of his face, every line of his hands, every fleck of his dark eyes. I could hold desire at bay while we were working, but in those brief moments where we were simply two people alone together, it flooded in and electrified everything; and when I woke in the night, in that liberated half-conscious state, I'd roll over and feel his arms around me, his body against mine.

But if I admitted all this, then it became real, concrete, a fact of my life. I would have to live with it all the time. I would have to let myself hope that he might want me, too, and that would be unbearable. And so I tried to shove my feelings down and be polite and cheerful, a help to everyone and a burden to none, even as I grew more restless by the day; even as pain bit deeper every time he left, and I had to face the long night ahead in that silent little room, alone.

I thought I was doing well, until Vittorio came to the house one morning with a new list of names for us to work through. I hadn't even picked up my pen before he said, in English:

'*I know it is difficult and painful to stay hidden. But this will change – I beg you, have faith. The war will end,*' he added as I stared at him, my heart racing. '*I have heard already that the Allies are close to taking Rome.*'

Teglio had told me the same thing the previous night; we had sat silently together for a while, neither quite daring to hope. I glanced over at Silvia. She appeared completely focused on her knitting. '*Thank you for telling me,*' I said. '*I do have faith, and I'm quite all right, I promise.*'

Vittorio shook his head. '*Are you? I shouldn't be. Had I to live so, I should be...*' he waved a hand as if feeling for the words '*...in the most frightful flap.*'

He spoke each word with such absolute gravity. I couldn't help but laugh. '*Where did you learn that phrase, Father Vittorio?*'

'*It isn't correct?*' He frowned. '*A colleague at Farm Street used to say this.*'

'*It's correct, as such; it's just... it's very charming.*'

'*Ah. Well. Anyhow, I understand.*' His ears were pink – I felt for him. '*Work helps with such things. Shall we continue with ours?*'

'*Yes, let's.*' I reached for my pen and pulled the latest list towards me. Vittorio gave a brief nod, stood and went to the window, where he lit a cigarette and smoked it with his back turned to me.

He didn't speak again until we had finished all that day's cards. I had long since concluded that I had offended him, and had given up being mortified by it. But as he was gathering up the forms to take downstairs to Bernardo, he cleared his throat and said: '*I shall be back already tomorrow. Stiff upper lip, now, Marta.*' And he nodded to Silvia and was gone before I could react.

Silvia looked at me with wide eyes. 'Whatever did you say to him? And more to the point, what did he say to you?'

'Oh, it was a sort of spiritual exhortation.' Laughter was threatening to bubble up: nervous, hysterical laughter. I couldn't give in to it. 'Silvia, have you any work for me? Really, anything at all. I need to keep busy.'

I thought she was going to protest, as she always did when I wanted to do something outside of the very few duties she allowed me. But then she nodded and said: 'Of course. Let me go and ask Bernardo what we have for you to do.' She got up and went out, giving my shoulder a sympathetic pat on the way. I can only think that I must have looked very bad.

From that day onwards, I had a new routine. The round kitchen table became my makeshift desk, and each afternoon I worked through everything that was brought to me: ledgers and records, bills and receipts, old letters to be filed or destroyed. I worked while Silvia bustled around me cleaning the kitchen, or did her knitting by the stove, or vanished downstairs to help Bernardo in the shop. I worked while Tiberio tried to get my attention, spreading his long orange body across my papers and trying to catch hold of the end of my pencil, mewing at me until I gave in and held him in my lap for a while.

I worked until six, and then I cleared everything away and helped Silvia to make dinner and cover the windows and light the lamps. We would eat our simple, early meal and I would hope, desperately by now, for Teglio to come. If he didn't, I would read silently while Silvia and Bernardo read aloud. We would put on the radio and listen to the clipped English tones of 'Colonnello Buonasera' telling us that all would be well and the war would soon be over, and then I would take myself to bed and make long, senseless lists in my mind until I was finally able to sleep.

The next morning, sometimes Vittorio would come to the house: always early, before the shop was open. I liked his visits, if not quite as much as Teglio's. I liked our work together; I liked our brief conversations in English while Silvia pretended not to hear. And I liked to observe him. He fascinated me. At first it was strange to look at him when he didn't often look directly at me, but as we grew easier with one another, I found myself watching him. I noticed how, at idle moments, his fingers went to the rosary at his waist – not fiddling with it, as I first thought, but methodically pressing each bead. He was praying when he did that, just as he was praying when he closed his eyes for a moment before picking up his pen, or stopped work to listen to the bells of the Immacolata. He was praying all the time. I noticed how he paused before applying the signature to each card, as if it were a new task rather than one he'd repeated hundreds of times already. I noticed how he paused to look at each one when it was created.

I observed other things, too. The dry wheezing cough that seemed a little worse each time. The fretted skin by his right thumbnail and the bruise-like shadows under his eyes. His wrists, bony and lost in overlarge cuffs that fell almost to the joint of his thumb; the gaping collar, the gaunt shoulders, the fabric bagging above the cincture of his cassock. The way his breath seemed to stick in his chest even when he sat still, and how he'd arrive sweating and winded as if he'd run, not walked, up the hill to the house. I noticed these things and they worried me more and more. I didn't have to pretend about my feelings when it came to Vittorio. He was my friend – not the friend I would have expected, but my friend nonetheless – and I wanted him to be well.

Every time he came around, I'd try to find a different way to ask if he was all right. And every time he'd rebuff me, reaching for one of his stock of eccentric London-acquired phrases. *Oh, mustn't grumble*, he'd say; or *worse things happen at sea*. Once, fantastically, he described himself as *fairly up to snuff* and then suggested we *crack on with it*.

I never pressed him any further. It scarcely mattered what he said, because the truth was written on his body. He was sick, very sick already. And he was getting sicker.

15

VITTORIO

When Vittorio next arrives at the Tipografia Guichard, he finds Marta waiting for him at the kitchen table and reading *Brighton Rock*. That pleases him, perhaps rather more than it ought. He's resolved so many times that he'll drop this frivolous habit of English chatter; that he'll stop dredging up silly little phrases to amuse her. But she looks up at him and smiles, and he finds himself saying:

'*Good morning, Marta. How do you like Graham Greene?*'

'*Not very much, I'm afraid,*' she says. '*It's all terribly exciting, as stories go, but... Well, I can overlook a certain degree of prejudice in an author. I rather have to, but Greene is proving too much for me. I hope that doesn't offend you, Father Vittorio.*'

'*Not at all.*' He sits down and casts a guilty glance at Silvia, who's looking steadfastly at her knitting, just as she always does. Sometimes, when Vittorio lies awake troubled by something he doesn't quite understand, he thinks that these conversations – however innocent they may be – go against the whole idea of having Silvia there in the first place.

'*You said someone donated it to your library*,' Marta says now. '*Does that happen often? Do people just drop off their old gangster novels for the Jesuits to read?*'

'*Well, in a way… I mean, some people – parishioners, kind ones – they do bring us books sometimes, if they think we might perhaps like them. We don't always like them*,' he adds, and she laughs. She's looking for distraction, he realises – she's hoping he'll say something to entertain her, to brighten her existence a little. And why should he hold back, when he has an entertaining story to tell? That it brings him pleasure is really neither here nor there. He looks down at the table, at the white cloth with its embroidered flowers.

'*Between you, me and the gatepost*,' he says, and – in his mind's eye – he sees her smile, '*I'm not certain how we ended up with* Brighton Rock. *I know only that I found my assistant librarian reading it, and I took it from him.*'

'*What, really?*' She's delighted; he can hear it in her voice, and that delights him in turn.

'*Really. Brother Carlo can be somewhat unserious. Besides, he was supposed to be weeding the books. I'm afraid he doesn't find library work as interesting as do I.*'

'*Then he's a fool, this… Brother Carlo, is it? Not Father Carlo?*'

'*Brother Carlo, that's right. He's what we call a…*' The translation eludes him. It seems an eternity before he retrieves it again. '*Temporal coadjutor. The brothers assist the priests, you see, taking care of the things of the house.*'

'*But they're not priests themselves? Or are they training to become them?*'

'*No, no. Being a Jesuit brother is its own vocation.*'

'*Perhaps that's just as well,*' Marta says, '*in Brother Carlo's case. Is he at least useful when he isn't reading Graham Greene? Does he have some talent for library work, even if he doesn't much like it?*'

'No,' Vittorio says. '*He's really quite awful at it. He doesn't help me at all.*'

He hopes she'll laugh again, but she doesn't. Instead she says: '*But that's all right, isn't it? Because then you have to go on doing everything.*'

He raises his head. Marta's looking at him. Her face is quite serious, but her eyes are merry.

'*I hope I didn't offend you, Father Vittorio,*' she goes on. '*It's just that if I had a library, then I should never let anyone competent help me look after it. I should want to take care of it all by myself.*'

Her mouth lifts just a little at the corner, her lips pressed together as if she wants to smile but is trying not to; and with a dizzying drop of the stomach, Vittorio knows what troubles him at night. He knows what sends his mind whirring even when his body is exhausted. It's her.

'*You understand,*' he says, and he watches her smile break like the dawn.

'*Of course I do,*' she says.

It's too much. It's painfully sweet, and he mustn't indulge himself. 'Let's start work,' he says brusquely, dropping into Italian, and he looks away. 'You take the first shift.'

'All right, I will.' Her voice is subdued; Vittorio suppresses a pang of regret. He goes to the window and stares out at the sky: it seems to him obscenely, irritatingly blue. After a moment, there's a discreet cough just behind him, and a cup of tisane is placed on the windowsill by his elbow.

'Thank you, Silvia,' he says, returning his gaze to the sky.

'Cigarette, Father?'

'Yes, please.'

A tin of cigarettes and a lighter appear next to the teacup. He waits until Silvia's footsteps have retreated and he hears the creak of her chair before he picks up a cigarette. His hands are shaking so badly that he has to make several tries at lighting it. But he manages in the end, and he takes a long drag, as deep as he dares, until his chest constricts and his diaphragm twitches and he has to slowly, slowly breathe out again.

It's happened to him before, this sort of thing. The first incident was in London, with a pretty young woman who used to accompany her grandmother to Mass at Farm Street. Of course, they didn't actually speak to one another. But he would see her shepherding the crotchety old lady around, being soft and kind and attentive in a way that made her seem even more like an angel, and after a while he started wanting to catch a glimpse of her. The day he found himself lingering before the statue of St. Thomas More, waiting for the two of them to emerge from the Calvary Chapel, he finally got an attack of conscience and took the matter to his spiritual director, Father Dominic. Father Dominic was an impressive man, about as old then as Vittorio is now. He took a strong line.

'The Adversary,' he proclaimed, leaning forward and looking Vittorio straight in the eye. 'You watch for him. A righteous man is a great prize for the Evil One. He seeks to attack us at our weakest point, and yours, it seems, is your chastity. You must fight him with everything you have. Confession, communion, fasting and mortification – and prayer, ceaseless and sincere prayer. That's the only way you'll rid yourself of this disordered lust.'

And Vittorio had been ashamed. He'd thrown himself into a regime of prayer and discipline that would have made a saint flinch. If he'd had the pastoral experience he has now, he would probably have recognised that this was itself disordered, that his soul was in greater danger from the sin of scrupulosity than the temptations of the flesh. But he was young and frightened, and whenever he wanted to break his fast or get up from his prayers, he'd hear Father Dominic's voice in his mind: *He seeks to attack us at our weakest point, and yours, it seems, is your chastity.*

This had lasted until one of the oldest members of the community – a tiny, wrinkled raisin of a man called Father Hugh – had found him sobbing before the tabernacle in the house chapel. Father Hugh, God rest his soul, had done the pastoral thing. He'd sat down next to Vittorio, waited patiently until his tears had died down, and he'd asked what was wrong.

'Well, that doesn't sound so bad,' he said, when Vittorio had told him – as he'd thought – all the dreadful facts of the case. 'You aren't *stepping out* with this girl, are you? So far as I understand, you haven't even talked to her. Unless there's something you aren't telling me.'

Vittorio shook his head. 'Of course there isn't. I've told you everything, Father, I promise.'

'I know, dear boy, I know. Well, then I don't see any reason to get in a flap about it. You're hardly an unrepentant sinner – you're all too repentant, as I see it. No, you're just a young man who noticed some attractive creature. And that does happen, I'm afraid. It may even keep on happening until you're too old to bother any more.'

'Then what do I *do* about it?' Vittorio asked, agonised.

'Accept that it's happened. That's the first thing you can do. And then don't act on it. Don't try to see her and, if you do cross paths, don't pay her any special attention. Stick with that for long enough and you'll forget all about it, I promise. And go a little easier on yourself, above all. Confide in God – confide in me if you like, but kindly drop all this self-flagellation business. It isn't doing you any good.'

'But Father Dominic said—'

'Father Dominic,' Father Hugh said severely, 'has many qualities, but he is rather a moral simplist. Look, far be it from me to undermine the authority of your spiritual director. But why don't you give my method a go, and then if it really doesn't work, you can go back to his?'

Vittorio had said that he would. And Father Hugh had been right, in the end. It hadn't been easy to train himself out of the habit of looking for the girl, and it was even harder to force himself to pay no heed when he did see her. But it got easier, and after a surprisingly short while, he discovered that his infatuation had faded. He was at peace again.

Father Hugh's method has carried him safely through twenty years and perhaps half a dozen pretty faces. As he stands at the window, listening to Marta's breathing and the steady scratch of her pen, he has the sinking feeling that it won't be enough this time around. Because it's happened to him before, yes, but he didn't know those women like he knows Marta. They certainly didn't know him like she does.

The scratching stops; Marta breathes out. 'Change,' she says.

Vittorio stubs out his cigarette in the saucer and lifts the cup of lukewarm tea to drain it. There's a gritty drift of leaves at the bottom and it makes him wince. 'Ready.'

In spite of it all, he manages. He and Marta work in silence, bar the odd polite word. He doesn't look at her, but spends his breaks at the window, smoking or else reading in his breviary. By the time they've worked through all the cards, he's starting to think that he might be able to apply the usual method after all. If he can only stay detached like this for a while longer, then perhaps he'll grow used to it.

He's packing up his bag when Marta speaks. '*Father Vittorio*,' she begins, and he knows what she's going to ask because she always asks it, won't be deterred from asking it. '*Father Vittorio, how are you feeling? You're very quiet today. Are you all right?*'

Vittorio looks down at the stole in his hand, and he mentally apologises to Father Hugh: for lapsing in his discipline, and for borrowing his words to do it. '*Of course I'm all right*,' he says. '*I'm positively top-hole*.'

16

Anna

'We have to do something,' I said to Silvia one afternoon in the kitchen. I had been trying and failing to concentrate on my administrative work for at least an hour. Even Tiberio had given up trying to engage me and had slunk away to lie upside down in front of the stove.

She put her knitting down in her lap. 'What about?'

'About Father Vittorio. He isn't well at all,' I said. 'I mean to say, he's getting worse. It seems like he's worse every day and I don't know what to do about it.'

I knew even as I said it that I was being foolish. But my heart still sank a little when Silvia shook her head and said: 'I know, dear. And it's very painful to see, but there simply isn't anything we *can* do about it. Believe me, I've thought about it plenty. But he's a grown man and besides, he wouldn't listen to us. I don't think he'd even listen to Mr X.'

'No, he won't,' I said, unthinking, because I'd had this same conversation with Teglio a couple of evenings before.

Silvia raised an eyebrow but kept her counsel. 'But maybe,' I went on, 'if we could find a way to talk to him, the right way—'

'Marta, there *is* no right way.' Silvia sounded almost angry. 'Do you think for a moment that he'd take orders from you or me? It's a miracle that he lets me put honey in his tea. No, all this is between him and his superior, or whatever they call the Jesuit-in-charge. So long as he's able to stand, I dare say he'll be made to keep standing. He knows he's sick and they know it, too – you can be quite sure of that, and you can be sure that he won't stop and rest until they say he can. No doubt he's been told to *offer it up for the Lord*,' she added, with a roll of the eyes.

'I don't understand why anyone would choose to live like that,' I said. 'It isn't human.'

'No, it isn't, but that's the path he's chosen. I know you've made a friend of him, or as close as you can get with a man like that.' Silvia's face softened. 'He likes you, I can tell. He likes talking to you. But—'

The wail of an air-raid siren cut across her words. We sprang into action – we'd done this a few times by then. I went to get my bag with my false papers while Silvia wrestled Tiberio into the wicker basket that always stood ready in the corner. Then we hurried downstairs, where Bernardo was already outside and holding the door for us. He had a pair of binoculars around his neck.

'Looks like the Americans,' he said. He was terribly pale.

And we practically ran across via Assarotti, me clutching Tiberio in his basket, Silvia and Bernardo on either side of me like a protective barrier as a growing stream of people jostled and pushed alongside us. I had that strange sensation

I always did when we had to go outside to the shelter. All around, the crowd pressed in as if it might crush me; up above, the sky was oppressively vast and full of danger. I felt small and terribly vulnerable. I put my head down and tried to block it all out, but part of me wanted to bolt back to the relative safety of the flat and my room. As we crossed the road, I glanced down the hill towards the city and saw planes on the horizon.

The air-raid shelter was a dead end, a semicircular tunnel cut into the side of the high terrace that rose above corso Armellini. It was higher, wider and less crowded than the tunnel under Galliera Hospital, but without that through-current of air it quickly grew humid and stifling. The echo was nearly unbearable, and I could only imagine how scared Tiberio must be in his cage-within-a-cage. When the guns began to sound, I took off my coat and draped it over his basket, which I held in my lap, so that he could at least hide in the dark.

Since it was a daylight raid, we were released relatively quickly. We emerged into the fading light, crossed the road and went down the steps that led back to via Assarotti. I looked down the hill as we emerged into the street, hoping against all reason to see the city still intact, or as much as it had been. But it was covered by a thick, hanging cloud of smoke and dust. I stood transfixed with fear. What had been destroyed this time? And where was Teglio, among all this destruction?

Silvia took my arm. 'Marta, let's you and I get Tiberio back to the house. He'll be very shaken up, poor boy.

Bernardo will find a good viewpoint and see if he can't get a sense of the damage before we go worrying about it any further. Won't you, Bernardo?'

'Yes, love.' Bernardo tried to smile. 'I'm sure it's not as bad as it looks.' He patted my shoulder and gave Silvia a quick, husbandly kiss before walking away, uphill in the direction of piazza Manin.

When he came back to the house, he was clearly shaken. 'The university's been hit, and the San Martino Hospital.' He swallowed. 'And the Curia.'

Silvia breathed in sharply. 'The Archbishop's Palace?' Now my heart sank further. The Archbishop's Palace was only a short distance from the Jesuit church and its community house, where Vittorio must have lived.

'Yes. It took a direct hit. It's... it's gone,' he said bleakly. 'Nothing but rubble.'

'But the cathedral is still standing,' Silvia said. 'Isn't it? The big bell tower's still there?'

Bernardo nodded. 'Yes, thank God.'

'Then that's fine.' Her voice was firm, her expression determined. 'There's a shelter at the bottom of the bell tower – do you see, Marta? As soon as those sirens went off, they'll all have gone there directly. Cardinal Boetto and his people and all the Jesuits, too, from the Gesù. You'll see, he'll... they'll all be fine, all of them. Father Vittorio will be with us again tomorrow, safe and sound.'

She didn't say what all three of us knew: that Vittorio might not have been at the Gesù with his brothers, or even at the Curia with the archbishop. He had other duties, other people in his care. He could have been anywhere when the bombs fell, as could Teglio.

There was a silence, and then Bernardo said: 'We can't 'phone them up, can we? I mean to say, there must be somebody at the Jesuit house whose job it is to answer the telephone. I suppose we couldn't...'

'What, ring up and ask for Father Vittorio?' Silvia shook her head. 'I don't think we can. We don't know who'd answer and what questions they'd ask us and besides, we don't even know his surname. For all we know there's some other Father Vittorio, if that's even his real Christian name. There could be half a dozen of them. And as for Mr X...' She cast me a quick, sympathetic glance. 'I can't imagine how we'd even start tracking him down. No, we shall simply have to wait and trust in the Lord.'

She said it in such a definite manner that neither Bernardo nor I had the heart to argue back. But that evening's reading was a subdued affair. Tiberio came out from his hiding place under the sofa and crept up into my lap, and lay there in a dense, unhappy ball while I looked at the same page of *Brighton Rock* and tried not to imagine the most dreadful scenarios involving Teglio or Vittorio or both, but those were all I could imagine. I sat there enveloped in horror, Silvia and Bernardo's voices a muffled hum in the background. I didn't even realise they had stopped their reading until someone shook me by the shoulder.

'Marta, dear.' Silvia's kind, worried face was looking down at me. 'You really should go to bed.'

She was wearing her nightdress and robe. The light was dim now, with a single lamp burning low on the table. Tiberio was gone and my lap was empty, except for the book I'd dropped there I didn't know how long ago. 'Sorry,' I said rather stupidly.

'There's nothing to be sorry for, but you mustn't sit up in the dark any longer. At least go and lie down, close your eyes for a while. It will be morning before you know it – and come morning, we'll be able to find something out. We can even 'phone up the Gesù if you like. Bernardo can put on a silly voice. Well, sillier than the one he has already.'

I tried to smile, but I'm afraid I looked ghastly. Silvia sat down opposite me.

'Poor thing,' she said. 'I'm sorry. After all you've been through, and now you have to worry about your friend and your… your other friend. It's a lot for anyone to bear, never mind a young thing like you.'

'I'm thirty,' I said.

Now Silvia smiled. 'And I'm more than twice your age, but I'm not ancient yet. You're young. I hadn't even got married when I was thirty.'

'Really?'

'Really,' she said. 'I shan't bore you with the details, but…'

'No, please do. I mean, tell me all about it.'

'Very well.' She sighed. 'I was the only child and my mother was fragile, so I had to look after her. My father was so taken up with his business. And after Mamma passed away, just when I thought I might finally get a little freedom – I know that's awful, dear, but that's how it was – my father fell sick, and so I had to look after him. By the time that was over, I didn't think I'd ever marry.'

'But then you met Bernardo.'

'And now I have to look after *him*.' But she was smiling as she said it. 'He was a widower, as it happened. That was before the war, of course – I mean the Great War. It all seems idyllic now, although I'm quite sure it wasn't. Being a widower was rather a romantic thing. Not for him, of course.'

'Right,' I said, thinking of Stefano.

'But you can't imagine the fuss people made when he showed up to our church. A widower, and a fairly young one – and from the valleys, too! A sort of committee was formed to find him a wife. But luckily, Bernardo chose me all on his own. And he'd taken his time to mourn. He'd even moved down here especially to... well, make a new start of it, I suppose. That's a luxury you wouldn't have these days.'

'No,' I said. 'You simply have to get on with it. You don't really have time to mourn at all.'

Silvia looked at me for a moment. Then she reached across and patted my arm.

'I think perhaps I'll sit up for a little while after all. Would you like a brandy? I'm having one. Not that awful stuff I keep for visitors,' she went on, with a grimace. 'I'll get the good bottle out. And then when Mr X next comes – and we must believe he will, Marta, until we're told otherwise – you and he can drink a glass together. How about that?'

The next morning, I sat at my usual place with a pile of forms in front of me. My head ached and I was nauseated: whether from the late night or the brandy or sheer nerves, I don't know. Bernardo had eaten breakfast and gone down to start work, and Silvia was sitting by the stove with a book. ('No point trying to knit anything today. I shall only have to unpick it all again tomorrow.') And both of us were trying not to look at the clock, although the shop was already open; although the bells of the Immacolata had long since tolled nine o'clock. Vittorio was late.

Vittorio was never late.

'It will be terrible out there, you know,' Silvia said. 'No trams running – not from where he is, anyway. And God knows how many people out on the street.'

'He might not even get to us at all,' I said. 'He might be helping people.'

She nodded a little too vigorously, then winced. 'I dare say. What is a priest *for* if he isn't helping people? So we mustn't be alarmed if we don't see him today. It doesn't mean anything bad. It just means that he's doing his job.'

'Of course.' I was squeezing my hands together, I realised, pushing my right thumb into my left palm as if I could stop the pain somehow. I tried to take a breath to calm myself, but it caught in my chest.

And then there was a shout of joy from downstairs, and footsteps coming steadily up towards the kitchen. I just had time to take it in before Bernardo appeared in the doorway, beaming, his arm around Vittorio's shoulders. 'Here he is,' he proclaimed. 'Safe and sound!' And he dealt Vittorio such a slap on the back that he almost knocked him over.

'Leave the poor man in peace,' Silvia reproached him. 'Come on, Father, sit down. Are you all right? Have you eaten? You must eat something – I insist.' She was already bustling around, pulling out a chair, putting things in place: a cup, a plate, a napkin. 'Sit down, Father,' she repeated – but Vittorio didn't sit. He simply stood there, looking. Looking at me. I stood without thinking.

'Oh, for heaven's sake, Bernardo,' Silvia said, waving a tea towel at him. 'Stop clogging up the doorway and get back to work. Go on, go! Father Vittorio will come down and see you later. Now, where is that cat?' And she hurried out into the corridor, leaving the door open behind her.

For a moment I feared that Vittorio would walk out after her; that he would refuse to be alone with me. But instead he smiled a weary smile and said: 'I'm sorry. I must have given you all a dreadful fright. As a matter of fact, I can't stay very long – I don't have the list with me anyway. Mr X handed it to me yesterday, but I'm afraid it was a casualty of the bombing.'

'But is Mr X all right?' I asked. 'Is he safe? Tell me he's safe, Father Vittorio, please.'

'He is, but it was a close thing.'

'Oh, God!' I blurted out, and then clapped a hand over my mouth.

'We had actually met at the Curia for the handover,' Vittorio went on, unruffled by the blasphemy. 'He gave me the list and I locked it away in a drawer to keep it safe. We went through a few more things we had to discuss, and then the alarm went up and I ran for the shelter. I didn't think for a moment that the palace would actually be hit, not directly; I just put my own safety first. I assumed that Mr X would do the same and go with me.'

'But he didn't?'

'No.' He paused, just long enough to let the unspoken filter through. Teglio hadn't gone to the shelter because being underground, trapped in a small space with people who may well recognise him, was riskier than staying where he was. 'When I realised he wasn't there, I was horrified. And when the impact came…' Vittorio swallowed. He was pale, and I could see that he was reliving it. 'I thought the cathedral itself had been hit – that the bell tower would come crashing down on our heads. And when it didn't… well, I was quite certain that Mr X was dead. If he was anywhere above ground, he had to be. I – and those who were with me – decided that once it was safe, we'd form a search party and try to look for his body. We wanted to be the ones to find him, to give him a decent burial – we'd dress him in a cassock, we decided, make him pass for a priest. And as we were in the middle of all these deliberations, he walked up to us, covered in plaster dust. He must have run down just in time. It was miraculous – I thought I was having a vision. I asked if he was all right – stupid question, I know – and he said…' Vittorio gave a nervous, abrupt laugh. 'I can scarcely believe he had the presence of mind to come up with it. He said: "You know, I'm the last man on earth to see the archbishop's frescoes."'

Now I laughed too, relief finally flooding in. Teglio was alive and safe. I wanted to laugh and I wanted to cry and I needed to sit down. So I did, without ceremony, and buried my face in my handkerchief.

There was the squeak and creak of a chair as Vittorio sat down next to me. '*There's no harm done*,' he said in English. '*Don't take on so*.'

I couldn't speak. I could only nod, keeping my handkerchief firmly clamped in place as my eyes grew treacherously hot. I felt so alone in that moment, even with him right there beside me. All I wanted was to be held. I knew, though, that Vittorio would never hold me.

'Marta,' he said softly. And before I could think, I put my hand flat on the table, palm up, towards him. There was a hesitation – I thought I had done something wrong –

and then he took it and twined his fingers through mine. I cried then, sobbing out my pain and my fear as he held tight to my hand, rubbing his thumb along the side of my own in a firm, soothing rhythm.

Once my tears died down, Vittorio let go, gently pushing my hand away as if he were returning it to me. 'I'll get you some water,' he said. 'Where does Silvia keep the glasses?'

'Top left cupboard.'

'Oh, yes, I see.' He turned on the tap and began to fill a glass while I quickly mopped at my eyes and nose. My cheeks were hot and sticky with salt. I couldn't imagine what I must look like. Vittorio sat down – next to me again, and not safely across the table as I half-thought he might – and put the glass in front of me.

'There you go.'

'Thank you.' I picked it up and tried to take a sip, but my hand was shaking and my mouth trembled, too. I had to take the glass in both hands, like a child, and even then I spilled a little down my chin. 'Sorry,' I muttered as I wiped it away.

'Please don't worry. Anyone would be shaken.' His voice was calm and steady. But when I glanced at him he looked away, and his hand went to the rosary at his side.

'Here he is!' Silvia's voice rang out, making me start. She was standing in the doorway, brandishing Tiberio in her arms. 'He was on top of the bookshelves in the parlour. The Lord alone knows how he got up there.' She placed the cat on the floor and he sauntered over to his place by the stove. 'Now, Father Vittorio, how about some breakfast?'

'Thank you, but I'm afraid I can't stay,' Vittorio said, getting to his feet. 'I have much to do. We have the archbishop staying with us at the community,' he added. 'He's a Jesuit, of course.'

'Of course,' Silvia said.

'But I'll come back once I've had a chance to see Mr X again. Our handover yesterday didn't quite come off as planned – Marta will tell you the details.'

'I'll make sure she does. Thank you, Father, and thank you so much for coming by. Take good care.'

'You too,' Vittorio said. 'Both of you. Good day.'

When he'd gone, Silvia went over to the sink and turned on the tap. Taking out one of Bernardo's handkerchiefs, she drenched it in water, wrung it out and handed it to me.

'Thank you.' I pressed the handkerchief to my face – it was wonderfully cool.

'So he's all right then, is he, our Mr X?' Silvia poured out two cups of tisane, one for each of us, and sat down opposite me. 'Don't worry – I won't make you tell the whole story, or at least not yet. But I had a dreadful fright for a moment. You all in a state, and Father Vittorio looking like he didn't know what to do. I thought the worst had happened.'

'Oh, no.' Shame washed over me. 'Did Father Vittorio look very uncomfortable?'

'He looked like a stricken haddock,' Silvia said, and I snorted with laughter. 'Poor man, I can't imagine he often has young women weeping all over him. He must have been cold comfort for you, I'm afraid.'

'No,' I said, remembering his fingers slotting through my own. 'No, he was very kind. He knew just what to do.'

'Someone write to the Pope,' Silvia said, smiling. 'A miracle has occurred.'

She meant to cheer me up, I know, but the word 'miracle'

made me think of Teglio – how close he'd been to dying, the choice he'd had to make – and I hid my face in the damp handkerchief and cried all over again.

'It's a good thing Father Vittorio is a priest,' Silvia said gently, once I'd managed to get myself under control. 'If he were a man, the ordinary sort of man, he might have been quite put out. Having to console you while you went to pieces over someone else.'

'I'm not in pieces over anyone.' I pressed the handkerchief to my eyes so I didn't have to look at her. 'I'm just... I'm tired. And shaken. Anyone would be shaken,' I said, echoing Vittorio's words.

'That's all perfectly true. But, Marta, really...' Silvia sighed. 'All these tears – they aren't for Father Vittorio, are they? I know you were very happy to see him alive and well,' she added. 'He's your friend, like he's my friend and Bernardo's, and we all care about him very much. And the good Lord knows that your private concerns are your own, and the last thing I want to do is poke my nose in where it doesn't belong. In another world... well, you wouldn't be living here at all, and all this would be quite irrelevant. As it is, we're all here together under one roof, and I know you've been keeping busy and trying not to fret about it, because you're a good, conscientious girl who doesn't like to be a bother. But it might just be time to admit the perfectly obvious: that Mr X is someone very special to you. And that's really quite all right,' she went on as I stared at her. 'It could hardly be otherwise.'

For just a moment, I wanted to confess everything. It would have been such a relief to tell someone how I felt about him; to confide in Silvia like I would confide in any woman friend. But once I spoke the words out loud, I'd never be able to take them back. It was a big secret to unleash in such a small house.

Silvia took pity on me. 'Look,' she said, 'you're a bright young woman and he's a clever and charming man, and the two of you spend all that time together doing work that affects both of you, and everyone you love. You're bound to trust one another in a way you just can't trust me or Bernardo or Father Vittorio – because we all want to help, but when it comes down to it, we're not in your situation. It would be a wonder if you didn't fall in love with him at least a little.'

'Really?'

'Really,' Silvia said. 'You're much too young to remember the last war, but you can't imagine how many love affairs started up then. It's a very powerful thing, facing a great danger together. It creates all kinds of intimacies: some of them survive, many don't, but they all feel quite real in the moment.'

'Yes.' I hesitated, caught between relief and a sad, painful longing. 'Then perhaps it isn't anything... I mean to say... Perhaps it's just the circumstances, then.' I said it as firmly as I could, but I felt a sharp pang of disappointment deep down. 'I'm sure it will pass. And I'm sure... I'm sure he doesn't feel like that about me.'

'Well, I don't know, dear,' Silvia said. 'I haven't seen the two of you alone, obviously, and he's only ever his usual self around me. Ever so gallant, of course, but he doesn't exactly give much away, does he? Only you know how he is with you in private – and I'm not asking you to tell me anything, by the way.' She raised a hand as if to ward off confidences. 'That's between you and Mr X. But, Marta, you're a clever girl. If you think about how he is with you, if you really think about it, then I'm sure you'll figure it out for yourself.'

I thought about how Teglio looked at me. I thought about how he always seemed to know what I needed. I thought about his eyes crinkling at the corners, the kindness in his voice, the warmth in his touch when his hands held mine. And I knew, as I'd never allowed myself to know before, just how badly I wanted each and every one of these things to be a sign that he had fallen in love with me.

'I don't know,' I said, twisting the handkerchief around my fingers. 'I wish I did, but I don't.'

'Well, perhaps you'll find out,' Silvia said. She drained her tea and set the cup down in the saucer. 'Maybe you're not the only one who's had an epiphany. Anyway, I expect he'll come past at some point. Probably not soon,' she added, 'so there's no need to look so startled. I'd be surprised if he gets here today.'

'And what then?' I asked, though I knew she wouldn't tell me. 'I don't know what to say to him, Silvia. I don't know what to do.'

Silvia got to her feet. 'Well, that really is up to you. I'm sure you'll know when you see him. And I know you're a well-brought-up girl who won't do anything rash, but still…'

'Leave the door open,' I said.

'That's right. Now, at the risk of sticking my nose in again, I think you'd better have a little sleep before lunch. Take this one with you.' She scooped up Tiberio from his bed and put him into my arms where, docile as ever, he settled against my shoulder and started up his rumbling purr. His trust was so touching that I felt myself tear up again.

'Thanks,' I said, and my voice wavered. 'Thanks for… for all this.'

'It's quite all right. Now go!' Silvia commanded. 'Go and get into bed. I don't expect to see you for another hour at the very least. Preferably two. And if Mr X comes during that time, which I shouldn't think he will, he can bloody well come back again later.'

17

Vittorio

Vittorio commits his first great act of disobedience that day.

He's been sleeping badly. He's never slept well, but these last nights have been torture. He can't ease the tightness in his chest by lying on his side any more. Now he has to get out of bed and sit at his desk, where he leans forward with his head on his arms and tries to breathe – not too deeply, or it hurts – and the sweat rolls down his sides, down his back, between his legs until his nightshirt is drenched and his skin starts to itch. The sweating's new, too, and it isn't good. None of it's good.

What he ought to do is go to the infirmary, at last, and ask to be seen. It's a miracle someone hasn't told him to go already. Vittorio spends a lot of his time in the library, or else outside, taking advantage of the dispensation he's been given. But there are still the fixtures of Jesuit life: meals and Mass, spiritual direction, confession. Recently, his coughing has disrupted all of them. It's getting harder and harder to hide just how ill he's feeling – both from other people and from himself.

Yes, he ought to go to the infirmary. But first, he ought to go and speak to don Francesco. He's bound to have noticed that the supposed 'cold' of a few weeks ago hasn't improved but has only lingered, worsened. He's bound to be wondering whether Vittorio can manage even the restricted duties he's been given. Wouldn't it be better to talk to him first, before he's forced to raise the question? Don Francesco has been good to him. Doesn't he deserve the truth?

By the time Vittorio has struggled up the hill to the Tipografia Guichard, he's almost resolved to do it: to go to don Francesco, admit everything, and accept that what happens next will be out of his control. That he might very well be stripped of his duties, returned to the authority of his superior, confined to the infirmary or even sent away to a hospital somewhere. That he won't be able to do his work, or be useful to anyone any more. But when he leaves a short while later, exhausted and shaken – from the bombing, the sleepless night, Marta's distress, all of it – Bernardo is waiting for him downstairs in the empty shop.

'Look, Father, I don't like to interfere.' He looks as uncomfortable as Vittorio feels. 'But have you seen a doctor about that cough of yours? Seems like something you ought to get looked at.'

Vittorio's heart sinks. He's grown used to worried questions and honey in his tea; those he can dismiss, but this is something else. If Bernardo has been moved to speak up, he must look very sick indeed. 'It's in hand,' he says. 'The Society of Jesus provides all the care I need.'

Bernardo shakes his head. 'Forgive me, but that clearly isn't true. I understand that you have to live in a certain way – and that's your choice, I'm sure, but there's a limit. I know a doctor,' he forges on before Vittorio can protest. 'An elder of our church. He helps anyone who needs it, no matter who they are. He wouldn't ask you for money and he wouldn't tell anyone. I can 'phone him up now and ask him to see you.'

Vittorio must say no. But the devil is whispering in his ear. If he did go to see this Waldensian doctor, then he'd know what exactly it is that's causing him these problems. He'd have a sense of what might happen next. He'd have time to take action, if need be; to disclose everything to don Francesco and give him a chance to find someone else, someone stronger and more capable.

He'd have time to say goodbye to *her*.

'I'm 'phoning him up,' Bernardo says. 'I'm sorry, Father, but I won't wait for you to make up your mind.' He lifts the receiver and recites a number to the operator. Vittorio just watches him, willing himself to do the right thing and protest. 'Good morning, doctor. I have someone who needs to see you. It's urgent… A bad cough. Very bad, yes… No,' he says, and rubs the back of his neck. 'No, as it happens, he's a Catholic priest. But he's a good man, I can vouch for that… All right, then, I'll tell him. Thank you.'

'I really mustn't—' Vittorio begins, but Bernardo cuts him off.

'You can go now. He's not receiving patients, so you won't be disturbed. His surgery's at via Assarotti 39B, practically on piazza Manin. The doctor's name is Rostan. He won't call you Father, I'm afraid. We do it out of respect, Silvia and I, because you're our friend, but he won't. He'll insist on calling you Brother.'

'I understand,' Vittorio says. He's touched, almost painfully touched by all this.

'Shall I walk you there?' Bernardo asks.

'No, no. I can make my own way. But thank you,' he says, and means it. 'Thank you for your care.'

Bernardo pulls at his moustache. 'It's nothing. You'd better get on – he'll be waiting.'

Vittorio thanks him again and goes out. He knows that Bernardo is watching him, and so he turns left, exactly as if he were planning to go directly to the doctor's office. He'll follow the road until it joins via Assarotti, and then he'll turn left again and go down the hill to the Gesù; and he'll do what he should have done long ago.

But when he reaches via Assarotti, he hesitates. Would it be so very bad to go after all – to find out what's wrong, and have it over with? Does he really need to reject Bernardo's gesture of friendship and leave the doctor waiting for him in vain? Perhaps it's even better this way, the devil whispers. Perhaps he'll find it easier to obey, to accept what's coming to him, if he takes this chance to prepare himself.

His mind goes to Marta, as it too often does. He thinks about her clinging to his hand, weeping her heart out for another man: a man who can love her, a man who very well might. He'll remember that forever. Can he bear for it to be his last memory of her?

He turns right, and begins to walk up the hill.

Dr Rostan answers the door himself. He's a short, stocky man with abundant grey hair, and he sticks his hand out for Vittorio to shake. 'Come in, come in. You are Brother…?'

'Vittorio. Bernardo and Silvia's friend.'

'So I gathered. Well, Brother Vittorio, you caught me at a good time. I just came in to catch up on some work.' He shepherds Vittorio into his office and closes the door after him. 'Now, what's the problem? Bernardo said that you had a bad cough.'

'Yes,' Vittorio says, and he outlines his symptoms: the shortness of breath, the night-time sweats, the dry cough that comes and goes, the chest pain that nags more and more. 'I can't even lie down to sleep,' he says, suddenly desperate. 'I feel like I'm suffocating.'

'I see. And how long has this been going on? Be honest.' The doctor fixes him with a steely blue eye.

'It's only been like this for a few days. But I haven't been feeling very well for a while.'

'And when you say a while, you mean…'

'Weeks. Months, I suppose,' Vittorio admits. 'But it hasn't been all that bad. I could manage. I've always had weak lungs – I seem to get any cold or flu going around, so I rather thought it was something like that. And my work… my work is stressful, and I spend a lot of time walking. I was away from Genoa for twenty years – I'm not used to hills any more.'

'Right.' Dr Rostan looks sceptical, but he doesn't push any further. 'Well, if you'd strip off – down to the waist, if you would – I can have a look at you and we'll see what's going on.'

Vittorio can't remember the last time he had to strip in front of anyone. Since becoming a Jesuit, he doesn't even look at his own body; he's adept at dressing and undressing without touching any part of himself, as his discipline demands. The discipline he's traducing simply by having come here. Dr Rostan is looking at him with wide eyes.

'You're very underweight. Dangerously so, I'd say. Haven't you been eating?'

'I haven't wanted to eat much. And there was Lent, of course, and...'

'Lent shouldn't do this to anyone, much less a man of your age. But now we're getting into theology, and I think we'd better stay out of *that*. Sit up on the table and breathe as normally as you can.'

Vittorio hoists himself up onto the table that stands behind him, and Dr Rostan begins examining his chest, methodically placing one hand in a particular spot and then tapping at it with the other. A memory comes rushing back, so vivid that he might be there: his childhood bedroom, sitting up in bed with his blue-striped pyjama jacket open and kindly, bald Dr Parodi, the family doctor, tapping his small chest with large, warm hands. He'd given Vittorio a big smile and said that he'd been ever so brave and it was all perfectly in order. Then he'd ushered Vittorio's mother out of the room, and a moment later he'd heard her start to cry, a sharp, keening cry that made him feel alone and scared.

Dr Rostan is listening with a stethoscope now. The feel of the cold metal on his skin is horribly familiar. Vittorio tries to breathe, to force down the fear that's rising up within him. The doctor must notice, because he puts a steadying hand on Vittorio's shoulder as he removes the stethoscope.

'All right, Father. You can get dressed now.'

Father. It doesn't feel like a term of respect; it feels like an act of indulgence, a sop to a patient in dire straits. 'What is it?' Vittorio asks, pulling his clothes back on with shaking hands. 'What's wrong?'

'You have a pleural effusion: in other words, your chest cavity is full of fluid. It's pressing on your lungs and that's why you can't breathe comfortably. You need to get a chest X-ray and have some of the fluid drawn and analysed. In fact,' Dr Rostan adds, 'you should do so urgently.'

'Why? What's causing it?'

'There's no sense in my frightening you with a list of potential diagnoses. Get the tests done, and if you want to talk over whatever you find out, then you can come back and see me.'

'But I need to know,' Vittorio says, frantic now. 'I'm not asking for a precise diagnosis. I just need to know what kind of thing it might be – how serious it is. I need to know what's going to happen to me. It's important. Please, doctor.'

Dr Rostan considers him for a moment. 'Fine,' he says at last. 'You are a friend of my good friends, and so if this is an extraordinary situation – which I can only assume it is, since you've come to me in the first place – then I can tell you something in general terms. But I think we'd better sit down.'

18

The doctor is talking in a low, soothing voice. But the words he's using aren't soothing at all. Cancer – that's one thing it could be, with the weight loss and the night sweats. Lung cancer, perhaps, or another type that's spread to the lungs. Heart failure. Tuberculosis.

'But it can't be that,' Vittorio protests. 'I haven't been coughing anything up.'

'TB can take root outside the lungs,' Dr Rostan explains. 'It's much less common, but it happens. When it does, it can infect more or less any part of the body – and in that case, you won't have the classic productive cough. It's just one possibility and not even the most likely one, but it's something to consider. Especially given your risk of exposure. I expect you've done missionary work in the past? Ministered to the poor and the sick, that sort of thing?'

'Yes, but I…' Vittorio has to pause for breath. The fear is at his throat, strangling him. 'I had TB as a child,' he says.

'Ah.' Dr Rostand gives him a sympathetic look. 'In that

case, I'm afraid the probability is rather higher. The disease can recur, even in patients who make a good recovery. I'm sure you're aware of that already.'

'Yes. I knew it might come back, but I didn't know...' He's been making bargains with himself all this time – stupid, wrong-headed bargains. *If I cough something up, I'll go. If I taste blood, I'll go.*

'Well, you know now,' Dr Rostan says. 'So the important thing is to get the tests done, find out what you're dealing with and go on from there.' He reaches across and pats Vittorio on the arm. 'You've asked me to tell you what's going to happen, and so I shall be honest with you. If it's cancer or TB, you should be prepared to hear that it's terminal. That means you might have a few months left. If it's heart failure, you could go on for a bit longer – an additional year or two, with good care and a following wind. But in any case, treatment can only be about managing your symptoms, not curing them. I'm very sorry, Father. I know this is hard to hear. If there's anything I can do...'

But Vittorio isn't thinking about dying. He's thinking about all the time he's spent sitting in closed rooms with the people he's supposed to be helping. The shared meals, prayers, conversations with his fellow Jesuits. The mornings spent with Marta, working together at the kitchen table, filling the air with frivolous, unnecessary words.

'If it is tuberculosis,' he says, 'does that mean I'm contagious?'

The doctor shakes his head. 'No. If there's no infection in the lungs – if you're not coughing up sputum – then you're not going to be infecting anyone else. The one you need to worry about is yourself. You must get those tests done right away.'

'All right.' Vittorio is starting to feel very strange: numb and detached, as if he's been dropped into a conversation that doesn't concern him at all. 'I will.'

'Good man. Now, if you want, I can draw off some fluid just to make you more comfortable. It isn't a pleasant procedure – I have to use a big needle. But it will give you some respite.'

'Yes,' Vittorio says. 'Yes, please.'

When Dr Rostan shows him out, he shakes his hand warmly and says: 'I wish you the very best, Father. And if you have any questions or you need help, then you must come back to me any time. All right?'

'I will,' Vittorio says. 'Thank you.'

'I must say, you were very good about the needle,' the doctor adds. 'I've seen stronger men than you make a fuss about it. No offence, of course.'

'None taken. It was a relief to get some of that fluid out.' The truth is that he's used to enduring discomfort for the sake of improvement. If he told this good Waldensian about the thin seven-corded whip he uses to flog himself three times a week, or the barbed chain he sometimes wears around his ankle, he knows that the fragile understanding between them would instantly vanish.

Outside, the sun is high in the sky. Vittorio stops and takes a tentative breath, and then another. He's still aching and the tightness is there, but now his lungs expand just enough to let in a thin stream of sweet air. It's such a sudden pleasure that he feels almost faint. Perhaps he'll sleep tonight. He could happily sleep now – fatigue is dragging at him, but that's unthinkable. He has to get on with his day, and that means going to talk to don Francesco. He can't conscionably put that off any longer.

As he walks down via Assarotti, the devil starts up his assault. *You don't need to rush to do anything. You're feeling so much better as it is. And you're not going to hurt anyone, are you, if you keep on as you are for a little longer? See how you go. See* her *again, spend a little more time together – just working, of course – before you do the right thing and let them send you away. It wouldn't be a sin. God would understand.* And the more the sun shines on him, the more his body begins to relax with the steady flow of his new, easier breathing, the more appealing it all seems.

He gets as far as piazza Corvetto before he realises that he's going to die.

His knees buckle. He sits down abruptly on the nearest bench, cold nausea washing over him, and prays that he isn't about to vomit. Just as he's pulling out his handkerchief to wipe his face, a hand descends on his shoulder, making him start.

'Are you all right, son? Father, I mean to say.'

Vittorio turns his head. There's a man sitting on the bench next to him: as old as Methuselah, his broad, wrinkled face dotted with brown spots. He blinks his watery eyes and says: 'You don't look too well, if you don't mind my saying. Something up?'

'Yes,' Vittorio says. It seems useless to deny it. 'I had some bad news. I'm sorry to disturb you.'

'Oh, you're not disturbing me. I like company. But I'm sorry for you,' the old man says. 'All upset like that. I'd say you had girl trouble if you weren't wearing this thing.' He reaches over and tweaks the skirt of Vittorio's cassock, letting out a throaty chuckle. 'Sorry, Father, didn't mean to shock you. Whatever's wrong, I'm sure it will all pass over. In the meantime, have some of this.'

He reaches into his jacket – a smart English-looking tweed jacket, the kind Vittorio's father used to favour and perhaps still does – and brings out a silver flask. Vittorio starts to shake his head, but the old man insists.

'Have a drink. You need it – and you won't offend me by refusing, will you? Good lad.' He nods approvingly as Vittorio takes the flask with a trembling hand and brings it to his lips. The brandy inside is fiery and good. 'Go on, drink.'

Vittorio takes a big draught of the brandy, much more than he would usually allow himself. He wipes the neck of the flask with his handkerchief and hands it back. 'Thank you, signor…'

'Fulvio. That's my name – I don't bother with formalities. What's your name, Father?'

'Vittorio.'

'Like him,' Fulvio says, and nods at the old king's statue. 'I don't suppose you have a brother called Emanuele?'

Vittorio laughs. 'It so happens that I do. And another called Umberto.'

'Well, that tells me quite enough about your family,' Fulvio says. 'Look, Father Vittorio, why don't you sit here with me for a little while? I won't bother you. But I can't let you go yet, not while you still look so bad.'

It's been so long since Vittorio sat in the sunshine: not praying, not helping anyone, not listening or confessing or working. 'All right,' he finds himself saying. 'Thank you, I will.'

19

Anna

I slept for an hour with Tiberio cuddled up in my arms and woke feeling distinctly better. For a while I lay there holding him, listening to the familiar sounds of the house – Silvia bustling around in the kitchen, Bernardo's gruff voice from the shop downstairs – and I thought over everything Silvia had said. Of course, she was quite right that I felt something for Teglio, something beyond comradeship or even friendship. It would be foolish to deny that now. But she was equally right that people formed attachments in wartime: the kind of attachments that might seem very strong in the moment, but that would never survive once the danger was past. If Teglio and I had anything, then surely it was that. We'd spent so little time together, and when we were together then we were usually working. Really, what else could it be?

The fragment of a dream filled my mind, desire flooding in with it: Teglio holding me close, my head resting on his shoulder. Cedarwood and tobacco and warm, clean skin.

'No,' I said out loud, and I tipped Tiberio out of my arms and sat up. 'No, this won't do.' And I went to wash my face.

All through lunch, I was perfectly collected. Silvia seemed anxious – she fussed over me as she doled out the soup, giving me an extra share of bread and promising me an egg for breakfast, if not the next day then the day after, or the one after that. 'One of Bernardo's cousins is going to be visiting Genoa, and she'll certainly bring some with her. Won't she, Bernardo?'

'If we're lucky,' Bernardo said, and took another slurp of his soup.

'I'm sure she will,' I said, wanting to reassure Silvia. I hadn't seen her worried like this before, and it worried me in turn. 'But even if she doesn't, it's quite all right. I'm all right,' I said, casting a quick glance at Bernardo – but he was absorbed in his meal.

'Are you sure?' Silvia asked. 'Because I know you weren't feeling too well earlier. With a headache,' she added for Bernardo's benefit, although he was clearly deaf to nuance.

'Really, I'm fine. It felt bad at the time, but it's just a passing thing. As you said,' I added. 'I just needed to rest and get over the shock of last night. It all looked quite different when I woke up.'

'Well, that's good,' Silvia said, although she didn't look entirely convinced. 'That's very good news, if you're feeling better. Do you feel like working this afternoon? Because I'm sure I can dig out something for you to do, if that would help. Or maybe you'd rather rest up, or do some reading—'

'The poor girl's going to get another headache if you keep on at her,' Bernardo cut in.

'I'll read,' I said quickly, before Silvia could respond. 'I'd like to catch up on my reading.'

'All right then,' Silvia said. We finished our soup and I helped her to clear up, then drank a cup of tisane while Bernardo smoked his pipe before going down to reopen the shop. Once he'd gone, leaving a fug of tobacco behind him, Silvia turned to me.

'I don't think Mr X is coming for now. I wouldn't have expected him anyway, not today, but—'

'It's really all right.' I said it as brightly as I could, as if I hadn't been listening for the doorbell myself. 'I mean it. I'm sure he'll come around at some point, and just like you said, I'll know what to do then. Until then, I'm not going to fret about it.'

'Good girl.' Silvia gave me a quick hug. 'Sensible. I knew you'd manage, if you would only be honest with yourself.'

'That's all I needed to do,' I said. 'Be honest with myself.' And as I headed down the corridor to my room, I found myself almost believing it.

Once I was alone, I was tempted to lie down and give in: to weeping, to dreaming, to I don't know what, but I didn't. Instead I sat on my bed, propped up on the pillows, and picked up *Brighton Rock*. I'd decided to finish it, loathsome as it was, just for something to read. I'd just reached the death of Spicer when I heard noises: a single set of footsteps ascending the stairs. Still clutching the book, I slid from the bed and crept silently towards the door, performing frantic calculations in my mind. It was probably Silvia. It really *had* to be Silvia, alone and at this time of day, but what if it wasn't? Should I hide in the wardrobe, or fling the door open and make a run for the bathroom instead? I pressed my ear to the door and tried to listen past the thump of my own heartbeat.

'Oh, damn it,' came a low voice from the other side. Teglio. I dropped the book. 'Marta?' he called softly. 'I can't find you. Where are you?'

I opened the door and there he was, standing in the corridor, looking lost. Looking for me. For a moment, all I could do was stand there and stare at him. And then he smiled, a warm slow-dawning smile that illuminated everything.

'There you are,' he said, and held out his arms. There was no need to think. I went to him and nestled in, breathing his scent, marvelling that he was alive and here and with me. His heart was beating hard and fast – it sent mine racing.

'You're all right.' It was a stupid thing to say, but I didn't care. 'You're really all right.'

'Yes, thankfully, though I had a hell of a scare. I think I scared a few people myself.'

'Father Vittorio told me,' I said. 'He thought you were dead.'

'So did I, for a moment,' Teglio said with a wry laugh. 'I've had some close calls in my time, but that—'

'Don't joke about it!' The words burst out of me before I could stop them. My throat was tight, and I willed myself not to cry – not now, not again. 'I'm sorry,' I said. 'I'm sorry, just… don't. Please.'

He sighed. 'You're quite right,' he said frankly, and held me tighter. 'I oughtn't to do it. It's in awfully bad taste and, besides, it isn't honest. I really did think I was finished. I've been in plenty of scrapes, but I've never experienced a thing like that before – and I hope I never will again, because it was terrifying.'

'That's better,' I gasped. The tears were flowing now of their own accord, rolling down my cheeks and soaking the lapel of his very nice jacket.

'Oh, my darling.' Teglio's voice was unbearably tender. He stroked my back as I shivered in his arms, hiding my face in his shoulder. 'I'm sorry. I didn't meant to upset you, dearest Anna.'

That shocked me back to myself. I blinked up at him and he looked steadily back, those dark eyes fixed on mine. 'You called me Anna,' I said.

He looked as surprised as I was. 'Ah. Yes, I suppose I did. Is that… is that all right?'

'Yes. I think… I think you probably should.' He was still looking at me – I was very aware of my flushed, tear-stained face, my nose that was perilously close to running. I almost reached for the folded handkerchief in his breast pocket, and then caught myself just in time. 'May I…?'

'Absolutely,' he said. 'What else am I for?' He shifted his grip and, resettling me in the crook of his arm, took out the silk square and handed it to me. I dabbed at my face and tried to breathe slowly, to calm the nervous energy that was bubbling up inside me.

'If we're going to use our real names…' I hesitated. 'I mean to say, if I can call you by yours…'

'I should say so.'

'Well, then.' I couldn't look at him, couldn't bear to see his reaction. I studied the diagonal stripe of his tie: dark green, lighter green, over and over. 'If we are, then perhaps we ought to go somewhere private.'

'Private,' he repeated. 'Private like the parlour?'

'Like the parlour, yes. Or my room.' I was blushing fiercely now. As if I weren't thirty years old, and a widow; as if I'd never been with a man before. Perhaps it was simply that I hadn't been with *him*. 'We would be quite private there.'

'Yes, we would.' He seemed to be considering it. *Maybe I've embarrassed myself*, I thought. *Maybe he's working out a diplomatic way to let me down.* I stood there in his embrace, tucked against his shoulder, and fought the urge to flee.

'I want to take up your invitation,' he said, and there was a new tone in his voice: something low and serious that made me thrill with hope. 'I do. It's just that I'm not sure when Silvia's supposed to be back.'

I'd forgotten about Silvia. I'd forgotten about everything but him. 'She's gone out?' I asked. 'Do you know where?'

'A meeting of some kind, Bernardo said. Church council? Youth group? One of those.'

'Oh, *good*,' I said, without thinking. 'Those go on for ages. But what does Bernardo think you're doing up here?' I forged on. I was blushing all over again. 'What did you tell him?'

'As far as he's concerned, we're stamping forms. I asked if he wanted to come up and keep an eye on us, and he looked very uncomfortable and said that there was no need for that. Which was a relief, I must confess. But I don't want you to think that I presumed…' He cleared his throat. 'I hoped to see you, of course. But you could have given me a brisk handshake and told me to go, or refused to have anything to do with me at all, and I'd have gone like a lamb. I still can, if you like. Or we can sit in the parlour, ten feet apart with the door open, and be terribly respectable. We can drink tea in the kitchen and play with the cat, and I shall be as happy as anything if that's what you want.'

He was looking down at me: tender, worried. I knew then that I was lost.

'I don't want to sit in the parlour,' I said. 'Truly I don't. I don't want to sit in the kitchen and drink tea, either. I don't want to send you away, and I certainly don't want to be respectable. I can assure you of that.'

He broke into a wide, irresistible grin. 'Right, then,' he said. 'Lead on.'

Once we were inside and I'd closed the door behind us, my courage faltered. I was suddenly very conscious that I hadn't even kissed another man since Stefano died. I'd thought about it, of course. I'd thought about kissing Teglio often – thought, dreamed, fantasised – but now he was here in my bedroom, standing close to me, it was all intimidatingly real.

'All right there?' he asked.

I forced down my nerves and smiled at him the best I could. 'Yes, of course.'

'I wondered if we might not be feeling the same sort of thing.' He smiled gently back at me. 'How long have you been widowed, if it's not too painful a question?'

'Five years,' I said.

He nodded. 'Two, for me.'

I knew he was a widower; he'd said as much the first

time we spoke. But it was still a shock. 'That's very new,' I said.

'Yes, it is. It feels new, sometimes. And yet... You know, I'm not sure I could say this to anyone but you. But in another way, it's a very long time indeed.'

'That's it,' I said, and he reached for my hand and squeezed it. 'That's it exactly. You miss the person, of course you do. That's the part that's fresh. But if you're used to being married, to having someone, and then suddenly you're alone all day and all night...'

He raised an eyebrow. 'It gets old fast, doesn't it?'

'It really does. And the idea of having someone again, that closeness...' He was still holding my hand, and his eyes were fixed on mine. I swallowed convulsively.

'Go on,' he said.

I made myself hold his gaze. There was no sense now in being anything but honest. 'It's wonderful. It's everything I want. And it scares me. I don't know whether I want to leap in or run away.'

'Yes,' he said quietly. 'Then we're feeling very much the same sort of thing.'

My mouth was dry. I knew in that moment exactly what I wanted. I wanted to leap, if he would leap with me. I wanted him, all of him, and the idea that he might pull back now was almost unbearable.

'Then I shall leave the next step up to you,' Teglio went on. 'Everything I said before still stands. You can send me packing, or we can sit in the parlour and talk about the weather. Although personally,' he added, 'I'm a great proponent of leaping in.'

Relief coursed through me. I beamed at him, all shyness forgotten. 'Yes, so am I.'

'Oh, good,' he said, and he leaned forward and kissed me.

It was the most natural thing in the world. His arms wound around my waist; mine slipped around his neck. Our bodies settled together and we kissed one another until we were breathless with need, until we had to sit down on the bed – it was the only place to sit – I tilted my head away so he could kiss my neck and oh, thank God, he did, the touch of his lips sending a fierce throb of pleasure through me. I was shameless, then – I took his hand from my waist and brought it to my heart so he could feel it beating, so he could know what I wanted him to do next.

'You're sure?' he murmured into my ear. His fingers found the top button of my blouse and played with it, teasing, promising.

'Yes,' I said. 'Yes, Massimo.'

20

When I went into the kitchen that evening to help Silvia with dinner, she gave me a knife and a board with some pieces of stale bread: the remains of various perished loaves, hoarded over several days.

'Pancotto tonight. I'm sorry, Marta dear, but needs must.'

She knew that I hated pancotto: that hot mush of old bread and vegetables we ate whenever there were loaf-ends that needed to be used. I always helped to make it and I always finished it without complaint, because I didn't want to offend Silvia, and because turning it away meant no dinner at all. But the texture made me want to gag, and I simply couldn't be cheerful while I was eating it. Today, though, I felt that nothing could ruin the happiness pervading my body. Not even pancotto.

'That's all right. It had to come round again some time.' I sat down at the table and started to cut up the bread. Silvia sat opposite me and began to prepare the vegetables.

'Bernardo tells me Mr X came past this afternoon,' she

said, peeling a carrot and setting the peel aside, as she always did, in a little pile to use for stock.

I nodded and kept my eyes on my task. Massimo and I had spent perhaps half an hour together, making love in taut and breathless silence, before he'd reluctantly said goodbye. The goodbyes had gone on for a little while after that, and he'd finally left just a few minutes before Silvia arrived home from her meeting.

'I shan't ask you to tell me anything,' Silvia went on. 'In fact, please don't. The less I know, the less I have to worry about. But by the looks of you, I'm assuming that it all went just fine and that you're not going to be moping around the house any more. Is that about right?'

'Yes,' I said, and blushed to the tips of my fingers.

'Then that's an improvement. And it's as well you have something that makes you happy,' she added. 'Heaven knows you deserve that. And so does he.'

'He does. He's a good man.'

'Oh, I know that. He's a thoroughly decent soul, for all he's a bit of a charmer. That face!' Silvia shook her head. 'As far as I'm concerned, you couldn't do better. And I like to think I have good taste.'

I thought of Bernardo's quiet, constant care for his wife; his steadiness and patience. The tenderness in his expression whenever he looked at her. 'You do,' I said.

'It's just… oh, Lord, I do hate to interfere. But you'll take care, won't you? Of your heart, I mean,' she continued, before I could wonder whether I was going to hear another talk about respectability or worse. 'I don't think he'd do anything to hurt you, not for a moment. Not deliberately. But it's bound to be hard when you love someone who takes the kind of risks he does. In fact, I don't know what's worse – the risks you know about, or the ones you can only imagine. Oh, I'm sorry,' she said as I looked at her, stricken. 'I shouldn't have said that. It's not my place, not at all.'

'It's fine,' I said, trying to sound as cheerful as I could. 'Don't worry about it.' But I was worried, of course, because she was right. Even in the warm haze of new love, I knew it all too well.

'No, no, it isn't fine, not at all. I said I wouldn't interfere, and then I did. What must you think of me?' Silvia shook her head and stood up, pushing back her chair. 'Besides, I'm sure he'll be just fine. I must nip downstairs and see to something, dear. I'll be back in a moment.'

She turned and went out of the kitchen before I could try to reassure her again. Tiberio, roused from his sleep by the stove, stalked out after her.

By the time Silvia returned, I'd finished preparing the bread and chopped the rest of the vegetables for the hated pancotto. I braced myself for a telling-off, but she thanked me profusely, added everything into the pot, covered it with water ('We'd have a nice meat stock, you know, if we could'), set it simmering and then handed me a wooden spoon.

'You stir this and keep stirring. All right? Just gently, mind – it's not risotto.'

While I stirred the pancotto, Silvia talked to me, asking me what I'd read lately and what I thought of it, what I reckoned to Colonnello Buonasera's last speech, and various other harmless matters. I knew that she was being extra kind, and I wished I could tell her that she needn't try to keep me distracted. Her determined cheer was far worse than any amount of awkward silence. But I felt wretched and ungrateful for even thinking it, and so I did my best to play along, answering her questions with all the goodwill I could summon.

'You know, this can actually be a very nice dish,' Silvia said, once the table was set and Bernardo had taken his seat. She set out three bowls and started doling the awful stuff into them. 'If I only had the ingredients to make my own pancotto, Ligurian style with garlic and oregano and cheese, then you'd see just how different it can be. You might even find you enjoy it, though it's still frugal food, of course. But Bernardo's had my pancotto plenty of times and loved it. Haven't you, Bernardo?'

'Hmm,' Bernardo said. 'Shall I say grace?'

Over dinner, I sat as quietly as I could while Silvia continued to talk. She was bright-eyed, apparently set on making up for my and Bernardo's taciturnity, and she regaled us with stories from that afternoon's church council meeting. Pastor Peyronel had made a stern appeal for donations from all those who could afford it. Dr Rostan had been asked to speak to the youth group about the dangers of dancing, but had refused on the grounds that it was a delicate matter and should best be addressed by someone with a speciality in adolescent development. In Silvia's personal opinion, he simply didn't want to do it. But his reasons had been accepted, eventually, and the council had decided to send for a lady doctor from Turin who was known for giving brisk talks on such matters.

'What's wrong with dancing?' I asked.

'You have to be *close together*,' Silvia said, as if it were obvious. 'It stirs up the passions.'

I remembered the dances I'd gone to as a girl – some quite lovely memories, in fact. Silvia definitely had a point. 'I see.'

'It's very dangerous for the young, it's true,' Bernardo said. 'They need a lot of guidance. Grown-ups, of course, can make their own decisions.' I shot him a quick glance, but he was focused on his pancotto.

When we'd eaten and washed up and the evening was over, I went to my room and got into bed. I hoped to find some trace of Massimo, some lingering scent of cedarwood or shaving soap, but of course there was nothing. We'd had only a little time, and we'd had to be so quiet, so careful. He could scarcely have left an imprint. But the memories were there, so fresh and vivid I could live them all over again: holding tight to him, stifling my gasps in his neck as he brought me to ecstasy; his mouth seeking mine, kissing me fervently as the world fell away. I missed him. I had only just found him, and now I had to wonder where he was and what danger he might be in, and when – if – I would see him next.

21

Vittorio

For the first time in weeks, Vittorio doesn't wake until the morning bell rings. He's lying in bed, on his back; he's kicked off the covers and his nightshirt is clinging to him, soaked through with sweat. He's aching and clammy and itchy, but he's slept for once. He's really slept.

He sits up slowly and perches on the edge of the bed, waiting for the usual coughing fit. But it doesn't come, and when he breathes in he can feel his lungs expand, steady and serene. He does it again and again, wondering at the rise and fall of his ribcage, before he comes back to his senses and forces himself to his feet. Peeling off his nightshirt, he goes over to the washstand, drenches his washcloth in the water he put out the night before – it's cold, of course, but that's the point – wrings it out and lathers it with soap.

And then Vittorio does something he never does. He looks down.

It's an unpleasant shock. His chest is sunken, his ribs and hipbones jutting out. Below his concave stomach, his penis lolls awkwardly, half-engorged; he must have had a shameful dream. The creases of his groin look angry, red and prickly, like the heat rash he once had as a boy. His arms are wasted, bones and veins horribly prominent. He lifts one experimentally and catches sight of a red patch of inflamed skin in the hollow of his armpit.

And there, affixed to his side a few inches down, is the dressing Dr Rostan applied yesterday. He's supposed to have it removed, or changed – today? tomorrow? He can't remember. But he knows that he can't do it himself. And if he goes to the infirmary, he'll have to explain; it will all be over then, and he hasn't even spoken to don Francesco yet. He meant to yesterday, of course, but he ended up sitting with Fulvio on the bench at piazza Corvetto until the Angelus rang at noon. They'd prayed it together, Vittorio leading and Fulvio responding, and Vittorio had got back to the community just in time for lunch. After that there was work to do and meditation and dinner and the steady, constant demands of the Liturgy of the Hours, and the day had ticked past until it was gone.

He can't go back to Dr Rostan and ask him to see to the dressing. That would only compound one act of disobedience with another. No, he must go today and tell don Francesco everything. Then he'll be given proper treatment, and can go to his end in good standing with the Lord. He begins to wash with the cold wet cloth, his eyes fixed ahead and upwards, towards the crucifix that hangs on the wall.

That morning, Vittorio assists Cardinal Boetto in celebrating Mass at one of the side altars of the church: a job usually reserved for a student or a Jesuit brother, but both are in short supply. Cardinal Boetto offers to assist, in fact, and let him preside; but with so much on his conscience, Vittorio does not feel confident enough in the state of his soul to say Mass himself. He's likely doing wrong even by assisting. After a brief and extremely polite argument – because if he admits that he has sinned, Vittorio fears that this kind, pragmatic man will offer to hear his confession right away – the cardinal accepts and says nothing more about it. He doesn't even raise an eyebrow when Vittorio refrains from Communion.

Afterwards, just as Vittorio is finishing breakfast in the refectory – not that he's eaten much, but he's managed something, at least – don Francesco comes bustling up to him.

'Good morning, Father Vittorio. May I speak with you for a moment? Have you got time?' It's a genuine question. Vittorio feels a sudden pang of guilt at having wanted to lie to this thoughtful man, even by omission.

'Of course. As a matter of fact, I was hoping to talk to you.'

'Oh, well, that works out nicely. The Holy Spirit in action.' Don Francesco beams at him. 'Where can we go that's private?'

'This way,' Vittorio says, and leads him to one of the small parlours the Jesuits use for spiritual direction. As they walk along the corridor, he rehearses the conversation in his head. *Don Francesco, I have something to tell you. Don Francesco, I'm afraid I had some rather bad news...*

But as soon as the door is closed behind them and they're alone in the spartan parlour with its two chairs and its plain table and its portrait of St. Ignatius, don Francesco begins to talk. With more than even his usual urgency, because it's urgent. There's a family arriving this morning on the train from Lucca. A mother and her three children for expatriation to Switzerland, all organised by Mr X. The father should have come, too – the move was originally planned for the following week, but he was arrested last night. The children speak Italian fluently, the mother less so: they are Polish Jews, part of the great wave of refugees who arrived after 1933 only to find themselves, a few years later, plunged back into the same hell they had tried to escape. Someone from the Lucca organisation will have seen them onto the train; he or she may even be travelling with them, but once they arrive in Genoa they will need a new, safe pair of hands. Will Vittorio meet them at Brignole station and walk them to the safe house in via Peschiera?

'Of course I will,' Vittorio says, and don Francesco looks profoundly relieved.

'Oh, good, good. I told my contact in Lucca to expect a priest: a slim dark-haired priest with round spectacles and a Jesuit cassock and a breviary in his left hand. If you hadn't been free, I would have swapped my own cassock for a Jesuit one and found a way to go myself. But I can't go, not really. I never can do quite enough.' Don Francesco shakes his head in self-recrimination. 'It's very frustrating,' he says. 'Anyway, you wanted to talk to me, didn't you, Father Vittorio? Let's do that before we get into the details. Is there something wrong?'

He's looking at Vittorio in the way people tend to look at him these days, head cocked to one side, eyes full of concern. This would be the moment to say it all out loud. *Don Francesco, I'm dying.*

'It can wait,' he says. 'Tell me about the family. How will I find them?'

The strategy works. Don Francesco begins telling him all the details: when they're expected, by which train and on which platform; how old the children are, two girls and a boy. 'I shall give you some money and ration cards to take along for them, if that's all right. Or if you'd rather have someone else deliver those, share out the risk, I can ask Mr X to arrange—'

'No,' Vittorio almost snaps, and don Francesco looks faintly startled. 'I mean to say, it's quite all right. I don't mind carrying them.'

'If you're sure, then that does make things much easier. Shall we go and fetch those now?' He's already getting to his feet. Don Francesco is always on the move. He has so much to do, and his entire work – the whole operation of the Curia, of DELASEM and the many people who depend on it – has been drastically affected by the destruction of the Archbishop's Palace. Vittorio's state of health isn't that kind of emergency. So long as he's feeling all right, it can continue to wait.

'Yes,' he says. 'Let's do that now.'

22

By the time Vittorio has met the lady and her children at Brignole and walked them to the apartment at via Peschiera – a mercifully short distance, but uphill all the way – he's starting to suffer again. Not from shortness of breath; that, thankfully, seems to be staying away. No, what's paining him this time is the fiery itching under his arms and elsewhere, which only grows stronger the further he climbs and the more he heats up. It's as if he has been relieved of one torment only so that he can more fully experience another.

Via Assarotti is just around the corner. Couldn't he call in on Dr Rostan just once, have him deal with the dressing and look at the skin problem, too? How wrong would that really be? He stops right there on the pavement and briefly closes his eyes. He knows the devil is tempting him, and he tries to fight it, to recollect himself. But blocking out the outside world only leaves him at the mercy of the itch.

There's a bar up ahead. Before he can think, Vittorio goes

in and asks the man behind the counter if he can make a telephone call.

'Of course, Father,' the man says. He nods to the telephone that hangs on the back wall. 'It's all yours.'

'Thank you,' Vittorio says, so fervently that the man gives him an odd look. The card Dr Rostan gave him with his office and private numbers is tucked into his breviary; he thanks God he thought to put it there. He lifts the receiver and places it to his ear.

'Number, please,' the operator says. He gives the office number, and thanks God again when the doctor answers on the second ring.

'Rostan here.'

'Good morning, this is Father Vittorio. May I come and see you today?'

'Certainly. Come by in an hour,' the doctor says, and rings off.

An hour seems interminably long, but at least he'll be seen. Vittorio replaces the receiver. 'Thank you,' he says to the man behind the counter – the owner, it must be.

'It's no problem, Father. Though if you wanted to buy something…'

'Oh,' Vittorio says, stricken. Of course, it's only good manners to buy a drink when you've been allowed to use the telephone. But he hasn't any money. He never carries any, except to pass on to others.

'He'll have a drink with me,' a frail voice pipes up. Fulvio, the only customer, is sitting at a table by the window. 'Give him a glass of that Vermentino, and another for me, too. Sit down, Father Vittorio, and let's talk for a little while. If you've got time?'

He has time. He can't deny that he has time, and some conversation might keep his mind off the itch. 'Thank you,' he says, and sits down.

Fulvio gives him a wide, rather gummy smile. He's genuinely pleased, Vittorio realises – he wants the company, perhaps even needs it. The bar owner comes over with two small glasses of white wine and removes Fulvio's empty one. The moment he's gone, the old man says: 'Well, now, how's it going with you? Still got girl trouble? Oh, don't take offence.' He chuckles. 'I'm only saying that to tease you, friendly-like. I don't mean to suggest anything.'

But Vittorio isn't offended. He's imagining what it would be like if he spoke to this kind, lonely old soul as if he really were a friend, the sort of bosom friend Vittorio has never had. If he said: *As a matter of fact, yes. I think I've fallen in love with someone and even if I could do anything about it, which I can't, I'm fairly sure she's fallen in love with someone else*. He longs to say it. For a moment, he fears that he really will.

Fulvio's looking at him. Not like other people do, not with concern or alarm, but with dawning compassion. 'Oh, Father, the look on your face. I'm sorry. I shouldn't have said it.'

Vittorio picks up his glass and takes a gulp of wine. He feels hot and sullen and there's an ominous pricking behind his eyes. Fulvio leans forward.

'Look,' he says quietly. 'You don't know me and I don't know you. We're first names only, right? So if you want to tell someone about it – about her – without being judged or made to do penance or whatever else, then you can tell me. I don't go to church. I haven't been to church since

1871. I know the Angelus because it was drilled into me as a boy, and I like you, Father Vittorio, so it gave me pleasure to say it with you. But with all respect, I won't set foot in a church until I'm dead, and maybe not even then. So if you're thinking that you could spill your guts to me and then find me on the other side of the confessional grille or staring back at you from the front pew at Sunday Mass, you can lay that worry to rest right now. Whatever you say to me, I'll take it to the grave, and I shall be there soon enough.'

So will I.

'Her name's Marta,' Vittorio says. It's a common enough name, so why not allow himself to say it? 'She's... she's clever. She reads everything.'

'Ah.' Fulvio sucks his remaining teeth. 'Bluestocking, eh?'

Vittorio ignores this. 'She loves to work,' he says. 'She loves to work, and be useful, and help others, even when she's in difficulty herself. That's one of the things I... it's one of the best things about her.'

'Is she pretty, though?' the old man asks.

'I think she's beautiful.'

'And what does she think of you? That's the question.'

'It doesn't matter,' Vittorio says, feeling very bleak all of a sudden.

'Oh, but it does,' Fulvio says. 'For all you know, she's secretly pining over you. Some girls love a man in a cassock.'

'Not her.'

'You don't know for sure.' Fulvio gives him a broad wink. 'Believe me, you can't know what's going on in a woman's head. You might find that she's very interested indeed if you ever decide to kick over the traces.'

It's a dreadful affront to his priestly dignity. Vittorio should object, but he's too busy thinking about it. Just for an instant, of course, before he remembers his vows, and Mr X, and Marta's desperation. *Tell me he's safe, Father Vittorio, please.*

'I won't do that,' he says.

Fulvio sighs. 'I know. You're a good man – too good, in my opinion. But I hope it feels better to talk about it, at least.'

Vittorio manages to smile and say that it does. And in a certain sense, that's true. Talking about Marta out loud to someone feels like that first moment when his lungs opened and took in air. He's alive and in love. And he tries to see that love as sinful and misdirected – a disordered attachment, Ignatius would call it – but he can't. Not now, not any more.

But talking about her has also made it all real. He can't unsay what he has said; he can't force it back into the depths of his awareness. He'll have to live with it, carry it, for what remains of his life.

He and Fulvio lapse into silence after that. Vittorio is used to silence as a particular, set-apart thing – a spiritual practice, a form of deprivation, the place where he meets God – or else as the natural corollary of living in a community of self-contained men, dividing so much of his time between the library work he does alone and the clandestine work he can't talk about even with his spiritual director. But this silence is different: companionable, undemanding. It's a friendly silence, and he's grateful for it.

When he finally gets up to go, Fulvio says: 'Be nice to yourself, Father Vittorio. Won't you?'

'I'll try,' he says, as much to reassure the old man as anything.

'Good lad.' Fulvio nods. 'And if I don't see you again, good luck.'

'Intertrigo,' Dr Rostan says, inspecting Vittorio's left armpit. He's already removed the dressing on the puncture wound and pronounced it satisfactory. 'You can put your arm down now, Father.'

Vittorio gratefully lowers his arm. It aches from being held aloft even briefly; his right one is still aching. 'What is that exactly?'

'It's a very common condition – don't worry. Essentially, you sweat, and that makes your skin stick together. Then you move around, creating friction.' Dr Rostan rubs his palms together to demonstrate. 'And that's what makes this nasty, prickly rash. If you're unlucky, you get a nice infection to go with it – but in this instance, you've been lucky. Yours doesn't look infected, only angry. I know that doesn't count for much in the current situation…'

'It does, believe me,' Vittorio says. He can't imagine what *that* itch would be like.

'It's not surprising you've got it,' the doctor says. 'If you're sweating at night, and your system is under stress, it's easy for something like this to crop up. Add in this warm weather and that… thing you wear all day—' he gestures to Vittorio's cassock, which lies draped across the end of the table '—and it was pretty much a certainty. The only thing I cannot understand is why you didn't tell me about it yesterday. Were you embarrassed? Afraid?'

'It didn't seem too bad,' Vittorio says. 'I was in too much discomfort with my breathing. Now you've fixed that, I'm noticing other things more.'

'I didn't fix anything,' Dr Rostan says sternly. 'I gave you some temporary respite from just one of your symptoms, but you need diagnosis and proper care. You know that perfectly well, so I shan't keep bludgeoning you over the head with it. But I can't believe for a moment that a rash like this didn't bother you until today. Wasn't it driving you mad?'

'No. It did bother me – I was uncomfortable, but I managed to ignore it.' Vittorio can't begin to explain just how divorced he is from his body and its sensations; how two and a half decades of strict discipline have made him not just able, but inclined to disregard all but the most urgent physical signals. He's only just starting to realise it himself. 'It didn't start driving me mad until I looked at it.'

'Until you looked at it,' the doctor echoes. 'I see. And have you got it anywhere else? Or is it just under the arms?'

'Just under the arms,' Vittorio says. It's another lie for the list, he knows, but he can't strip off below the waist and let this man look at his intimate parts. He simply can't.

'Right. Well, if you did have it anywhere else, assuming it wasn't infected, then the treatment is the same and it's really very simple. Keep the area clean and as dry as you can. Wash at least twice a day, and certainly before you get into bed. Don't scrub or scour yourself, and dry the skin by patting, not rubbing. Apply some medicated talc each time – I'll give you some of that – and petroleum jelly, to help with the friction. I'll give you a cream to leave on overnight, too. Ideally you'd start wearing nice, light, breathable summer clothing instead of that get-up of yours, but I expect that's out of the question.'

'It is.'

Dr Rostan makes a regretful face. 'Worth a try. But if you do everything I've told you to do, it should improve quite quickly. If it doesn't, of course, let me know. Have you any questions?'

'May I put my clothes back on?' Vittorio asks, and the doctor laughs.

'Yes, of course, unless you've got any more surprises in store.'

That night before bed, Vittorio carefully washes, dries and powders himself, then smooths on cream. He makes himself look as he does it, taking care to find and cover every bit of red, itchy skin, and it feels wrong to pay such close attention to his body. It feels like a breach of every rule he's absorbed since he entered the novitiate at seventeen. But he knows that if he wants to keep going for as long as he can, to wring every bit of use out of these last months of his life, then he must learn to pay attention; to be nice to himself, as Fulvio put it. And there is no question now that he wants to keep going.

When he wakes up the next morning, he's drenched in sweat as usual. But the rash has already started to fade, and the itch has dulled to a nagging hum. It feels like a sign. He rises and prepares for his day.

After breakfast, don Francesco asks to see him again. 'Excellent news,' he says, once they're alone in the parlour. 'It's taken a certain amount of legwork, but between us,

Mr X and I have managed to reconstruct the list that was lost the other day.' He takes a folded piece of paper from the breast of his cassock and hands it to Vittorio. 'If you'd be happy to start work on those...'

'Of course I will. I'll go right away. I'm sorry I left it behind,' Vittorio adds, hot shame rising. 'I should have thought—'

Don Francesco raises a hand. 'Please, Father Vittorio, don't you start excoriating yourself. I already had to reassure Mr X in that regard. We can remake a list, but we can't replace either of you. As far as I am concerned, the discussion ends there.'

'But—'

'No buts. *Ego te absolvo*. Go forth and continue your work.'

As he sets off towards via Assarotti, Vittorio feels his spirits rise. He's been forgiven – at least, for the mistake he's admitted to – and the damage repaired. The morning sun is warming his limbs, his breathing is easy and rhythmic and, for the first time in weeks, he feels comfortable in his skin. And beneath it all is the knowledge that he'll get to see *her*. He can't even bring himself to feel guilty about it.

23

Anna

When Vittorio walked into the kitchen that morning – only two days, by my calculation, since I had seen him last – I almost exclaimed out loud. The difference in him was striking. He was still pale and painfully thin. And yet he seemed taller, broader, more… present, somehow, in a way I couldn't quite put my finger on.

'Good morning, Marta, Silvia.' He put his black bag on the table and took out a little prayer book, slipping a piece of paper from between its pages. 'I'm sorry I didn't have time to find you something exciting to read, Marta. I only just got this list. It's the reconstructed version of the one that was lost – I told you about that, I think – and it took time to put together. So I thought there was no sense in messing around looking for a suitable cover. Best just to come straight here and get on with it.'

He wasn't coughing, I realised; wasn't sweating or gasping or struggling for breath. I looked at Silvia and she raised her eyebrows as if to say: *Yes, I see it too.*

'Silvia,' Vittorio went on, 'could I possibly trouble you for a cup of tea? And the blank forms, if you would. I don't see them here. But then I didn't give you any warning I was coming, did I? I hope Bernardo will forgive me.'

'Tea,' Silvia muttered. She seemed to be in a daze. 'Forms. Certainly.' She went to the stove and poured out a cup of tisane, then hesitated. 'A spoonful of honey, Father?'

'Yes, please. It's not the same without honey.'

'There you go.' Silvia put the cup in front of him. 'I'll have to go and fetch the forms – we put them somewhere safe. I'll be back in a moment.'

'Thank you so much.' He picked up the cup and took a sip, with positive enjoyment.

I sat down in my place and looked at him. He had a little colour in his cheeks now, I noticed, and the marks under his eyes were fading.

'*You're better*,' I said.

'*I saw a doctor*.' Vittorio shrugged. It was a strangely casual action from him. '*I had an infection of the chest. He made a procedure – it was unpleasant, but it worked and now everything is tickety-boo*.'

Tickety-boo. I didn't think he had any funny English words left to spring on me, and yet he'd managed it. '*I'm glad it's… I mean, I'm very happy you're well. Did the doctor say what caused the infection?*'

A shadow crossed his face. Just for the briefest instant – if I hadn't been watching him, I'd never have noticed. '*It's nothing*,' he said. '*An old trouble. I should have gone earlier, but it's fixed now*.'

'Here they are,' Silvia proclaimed, all but bursting into the kitchen. She was breathless herself – it seemed like she'd run down the stairs and back up again. 'Bernardo had hidden them rather too well,' she said as she set the stack of forms on the table. 'And here are pens, and ink, and I shall get on with my knitting.'

She collapsed into her chair by the stove, and Tiberio hopped up into her lap. He knew the routine. My mind was boiling with questions: What old trouble, exactly, did Vittorio mean? Was he really completely back to health? Why *hadn't* he gone to the doctor before? I looked over at him again, hoping to catch his eye and resume our conversation, but he pushed back his chair and stood up.

'I'll drink this by the window as usual,' he said, switching back into Italian. 'Marta, tell me when you're ready to change over.'

I took the hint and started work. For the first few minutes, it was strange. Tiberio's purr and the click of Silvia's needles, Bernardo moving around in the shop downstairs, the distant sounds of the city that drifted in through the open window – all these noises were suddenly very loud and intrusive. I couldn't understand why, and then I realised that I couldn't hear Vittorio's breathing. It had been the invariable background to our mornings together – strident and rasping, catching in his chest so that I felt an echoing catch in mine – and now that background was gone. Whatever unpleasant thing the doctor had done, it had clearly worked.

Soon enough, habit took over, and I was focused again. I filled out a dozen or so cards before I started to tire. I could have managed more if I'd pushed myself, but I never liked to risk it. The repercussions of any error that might creep in were simply too vast. When I looked up, Vittorio had resumed his seat at the table and was reading his prayer book.

'Change?' he asked without looking up.

'Yes, please.'

He closed his eyes for a moment, murmuring something under his breath. Then he crossed himself, set the little book aside and gestured for me to pass him the completed forms. 'Thank you,' he said, and picked up his pen.

I suppose I might have got up at that point. Stretched my legs a little, had a cup of tea, trailed a piece of wool for Tiberio to follow. But I was exhausted, worn out by it all. I'd been keeping myself relentlessly distracted since Massimo had left, trying to drown out the echo of his words. *I'll be back soon*, he'd said, and kissed me softly on the lips. *As soon as I can. I wish I could make you a promise.* He'd kissed me again, more urgently this time, and we'd sunk into one last, hungry embrace before he had to go.

Vittorio was absorbed in his work; Silvia, by the stove, had dozed off. I might as well have been alone. Love and melancholy, fear and desire – they battered against me like a wave. I couldn't fight any more. I sat still and let them claim me.

24

Vittorio

She used to watch him. He'd got used to feeling her open, curious gaze – had come to welcome it, to soak it up like the warmth of the sun. For weeks, she'd bestowed it on him while he was too self-conscious, too hemmed in and disciplined to respond. Now he's watching her, and she is lost in her own world. Soft, downcast eyes fixed on the table before her; one hand gripping the other as if for comfort, her face flushed and sombre.

Vittorio knows then that his instinct was correct. Marta is in love, and not with him.

He tells himself that it doesn't matter. He tells himself that he cannot even really be her friend. And what would she want with him anyway? A priest, sick in body and broken in spirit; a forty-two-year-old innocent who last kissed a girl when he was sixteen. Even if by some miracle she did want him, even if he could forget his vows, jettison all his discipline and scrub away the indelible mark of his consecration, it would be too late. She's had enough sadness in her life without him blighting it any further. Let her love Mr X. Let Mr X love her, for that matter. It would be only right, and good, and natural if he did.

Once the first surge of pain subsides, there's a certain relief. He can see himself clearly now, as if from the outside. Exhausted and ill, his senses befuddled, grasping for consolation in the well-meaning interest of a kind-hearted young woman. It's embarrassing. Vittorio can only thank God he had enough wit left to realise all this before he made a fool of himself; or more of a fool, he thinks, remembering his confession to Fulvio. But he can't afford to get caught up in that now – not when he has work to do. He gives himself a mental shake and gets on with it.

He does well, too. He gets through the whole morning's work that way. But then Silvia, stacking up the completed forms, says: 'I'll put these back in their safe place, shall I? I expect Mr X will come by for them later.'

Marta blushes. It's more than a blush: she's radiant with pleasure, suffused with hope. And Vittorio knows that her love is returned.

Just so, he tells himself. That's natural, and right, and good.

She's watching him now. Her look is a silent plea: *Tell me he's coming*. He has to clear his throat. 'I dare say he'll pass by. But I can't tell you when, I'm afraid. I haven't managed to speak to him lately.' And he busies himself packing his things away so that he doesn't have to see the disappointment written on her face.

They say their respective goodbyes and he goes out. He's halfway down the stairs when he hears hurried footsteps behind him, and turns. Marta, her cheeks pink and her eyes shining, terribly close to him in the narrow staircase. He can smell something like incense – roses, it must be roses – and his heart is thumping, battering at his ribs like some poor, demented thing in a cage.

'*Father Vittorio*,' she says, and clutches at his sleeve. '*I'm glad you're feeling a lot better. But you'll take care, won't you? Chest infections can be so tricky. You can't afford to have a relapse, and we don't want you to, above all. So promise me you'll try to rest and get as much fresh air as you can. Please?*'

She's so near that he could reach out and touch her face, bring her lips to his. He looks down to ward off temptation and there are her fingers, gripping the fabric of his sleeve. He wants to cover them with his own but he mustn't. He's still staring at them when she lets go, snatching her hand away as if she's been reprimanded.

'*Sorry*,' she says. '*I'm being too familiar. I shouldn't tell you what to do. It's just that...*'

'*It's all right*,' he manages to say. '*You mean to be a friend. Go back upstairs, Marta.*'

She doesn't move. '*Promise me first that you'll take care of yourself. You have to.*'

'*I promise. Please go now. I'll see you...*' His English is failing him. '*When I next am here, I'll see you.*'

'*Good.*' He can hear the smile in her voice. '*I'm glad. Goodbye, Father Vittorio.*'

And she turns and mounts the stairs. Vittorio walks down, through the back office and through the curtain out into the shop. It's only when he sees Bernardo look up from the printing press, oil can in hand, that he realises he didn't wait and listen as he usually would, to make sure that the place was empty: which, thank God, it is. Had there been customers – the wrong sort of customers – he could easily have drawn fatal attention to the operations going on upstairs.

'All right, Father? You finished for today?'

'Yes. Could you…?' He gestures at the door, and Bernardo moves to unlock it. 'Thank you. Goodbye.' And he steps out into the warm sunlit air. The city lies before him, devastated, a rubble-strewn mess. He looks away and turns right, following the curve of the street as it winds downhill. He'll go straight back to the Gesù, see if don Francesco has anything for him to do. And if he doesn't, there's always the library.

By the time he reaches via Peschiera, panic is rising, constricting his chest. He turns right and heads for the bar, the one where he saw Fulvio last. He peers in through the plate-glass window, trying to look inconspicuous and knowing he must be failing. But Fulvio isn't there, only three somewhat less ancient men playing cards, and the owner, gloomily drinking coffee (or, more likely, some dreadful coffee substitute) behind the counter.

He should turn back, but his feet carry him on, along via Peschiera, onto via Assarotti and to the left. He walks past the German headquarters with its guards and its leering windows and its foul red-and-black banners, his eyes fixed on piazza Corvetto and the rump of Victor Emmanuel's horse. He feels urgently now that he must talk to someone; that he must talk to Fulvio. But he walks a full circuit of the piazza and can't see him on any of the benches. Vittorio doesn't know what to do. His throat is aching and there's a terrible knot at the apex of his stomach, right under his ribs. He sinks down onto the nearest bench, pulls out his breviary and opens it, shielding his eyes with his hand. And for the first time in days he struggles to breathe.

A touch on his shoulder. He risks a glance to his left and sees a pair of legs in grey slacks, battered brown brogues. It's Fulvio, thank God. 'Hello, Father. Were you hoping to see me?'

Vittorio nods. His vision is blurring with tears; he doesn't trust himself to speak. He fixes his eyes on the page before him and watches the words dance, shifting in and out of focus.

'You're lucky I haven't anything else to do with my days,' Fulvio says, sitting down next to him. 'Well, I shan't ask you any questions now. That's what's fatal, in my experience. Here's what we'll do. You stay like that, with your hand over your eyes just so, and we'll pretend you're hearing my confession. Because people do that, don't they, if it's urgent? Even outside on a bench?'

He nods again.

'Good. I won't confess to you, of course – I'm not about to start all that up now. I'll just talk about any old nonsense until you've had a chance to pull yourself together. And that's before we get to the matter of the duck,' Fulvio says, abruptly loud. 'Lust, gluttony and wrath at the very least. I can't begin to tell you the things that duck and I got up to. It would set your… all right, she's gone. Sorry, Father Vittorio, some nosy old bird wanted to sit right next to us. She's taken herself off now, face like a slapped arse – excuse my language. I had an auntie like that on my mother's side; well, an auntie by marriage. Awful woman. Every time she came to the house she used to insult my mother. "Oh, my dear Agnese, what an original hairstyle. I would never *dare* show off my ears like that." Stupid cow. Now her husband, my uncle, he was the gentlest soul you could wish to meet – like my mother, for that matter. I remember the time…'

And he goes on like that, trotting out old stories and rehearsing family grudges until Vittorio's throat stops hurting, the knot in his stomach loosens, his vision clears and he can sit up again, and breathe. 'Thank you,' he says. 'You saved me.'

Fulvio snorts. 'Don't go all pious on me, Father. I only did what any man would do. The question is…' He lowers his voice. 'The question is, are you ready to talk about it now? Can you?'

'I think I can,' Vittorio says. 'I think I'd better.'

25

Anna

Massimo came to the house that same evening. I'd been longing for him to appear. But once he and I were actually alone in the kitchen, I found myself looking down and away, trying not to meet his eye. I felt suddenly vulnerable, as exposed as if I were again half-naked in his arms. And above all I was afraid: afraid that he'd regret what we'd done, that our working relationship would have to end. That I'd fallen, finally and completely, in love with him when he hadn't fallen in love with me.

He pulled up a chair next to me and handed me a little rectangular parcel. 'Something for you. Not Conan Doyle, I'm afraid, but the best I could lay my hands on.'

Inside was a 1921 Italian paperback of Leblanc's *Arsène Lupin, Gentleman Burglar*. Massimo couldn't have known this, of course, but I adored the Arsène Lupin stories and had lost my own little collection when I'd lost my home. I looked at him now and he looked back at me with such pleasure, such evident affection that I couldn't be afraid any more.

'It's wonderful,' I said. 'You can't imagine. Thank you.' I leaned over and kissed him, and he kissed me warmly back.

'Come on,' he said, and squeezed my hand. 'The list is in there somewhere. Let's get to work.'

Commendatore, I wonder if you could ever understand what I felt in that moment. In the five years since Stefano died, I hadn't had anything that was truly mine. I didn't have a job, or a family, or a lover, or any task ahead of me other than surviving: a task that was merely stressful and dull at first, but that became all-consuming when the Germans arrived. Even that little flat in Carignano wasn't mine, any more than my room at Bernardo and Silvia's was. But now I had two things that gave my life clarity and purpose. One was my work for the clandestine organisation I now know to call DELASEM. And the other was Massimo Teglio.

You'll tell me, of course, that you also had a purpose in life. I was sick of hearing it by the end: the founding myth of Giovanni Battista Marinaio, the self-made man. How you'd built your business from nothing, forged a glorious family dynasty (or so you claimed), set a glowing example for generations to come. I became very good at pretending to listen when I worked for you.

I should have listened, really listened, because that same, self-aggrandising drivel you spouted over and over again wasn't mere bluster. It was your creed. And so when you assured me in November 1938 that you would certainly keep me in my job – because the Racial Laws, as they stood, didn't oblige the head of a private shipbuilding company to fire his Jewish employees – I shouldn't have believed you even to the tentative extent that I did. I should have gone home that evening and told Stefano: *Look, I've done my best, but my employment at Marinaio e Figli is over. Let's cash in our savings, beg or borrow whatever else we need, and ask my parents now, right now, to help us get an American visa. If you're so determined to finish your degree first, you can stay here and do that alone. I'm going to my family, to a country where I won't be punished simply for having a Jewish father. I'll see you there.*

But I let myself be persuaded. By you, to some extent, Commendatore. Of course I didn't believe that you really valued me as you claimed you did. I certainly didn't believe your effusive nonsense about finding a way to keep me even if the law should change for the worse tomorrow. But I knew how much you relied on me in your day-to-day business, and I thought you might have just enough sense to value that; not to dismiss me until you were actually required to do so.

It was Stefano, though, who finally convinced me to keep up the compromise. *We're so close to our goal*, he said, *surely you can bear to suffer for a little while more? Just a little longer and we'll have enough set aside to start our new life in America. A little longer and I shall have finished my studies, and then I can find work anywhere in the world. And my parents will be so proud*, he said, *when I land a brilliant job at New York Ship or the Brooklyn Navy Yard or Caddell. A job for life, a job to sustain both of us and our future children. Just think what a wonderful difference a few more weeks, a few more months can make.*

It wasn't the first time he'd made that speech. He'd given it in July, when the Manifesto of Race was published; in

September, when Jews were excluded from the schools and universities; and on various other occasions, too, whenever I grew nervous about what might come next. With every repetition it lost some of its power, but I still loved and trusted him enough to go along with it. It seems incredible, but I loved him even more than I hated you. So on this occasion, too, I agreed to stay a little longer, although I really didn't want to do any such thing. But those few more weeks, those few more months I promised to endure… they never materialised. It was a matter of days before you called me into your office and asked me to sit down.

You didn't even have the grace to look embarrassed. 'I've been thinking about our conversation,' you said, fixing me with a fishy eye as if I were the one in the wrong. 'About continuing your employment. And it's simply impossible. It can't be done.'

For a moment, I thought that I had lost my wits. I remembered asking you quite factually whether I would be let go, and I remembered you assuring me – puffing yourself up with the magnanimity of it all – that I would be kept on. And here you were, speaking to me as if I had somehow petitioned you to stay, and you had been weighing it up all that time.

'What do you mean?' I asked.

'I cannot keep you here,' you explained, shaking your head at my stupidity. 'It's true that I could, in legal terms, since this is a private enterprise. But the fact is that my clients are important people. Respectable people. Some of them are very prominent in the Party. I cannot expect them to trust me if my own secretary, the person who handles all their most sensitive information, is a Jew.'

I couldn't speak at first. I was used to bearing your insults, your changing moods and your endless caprices, but to hear that said – by you, by anyone – was viscerally shocking.

'But there's never been any such issue before,' I said at last; and I knew exactly what you would say in reply, but something compelled me to make you say it. 'It was all fine last week.'

'Last week,' you said with exaggerated patience, 'you weren't a Jew. Not in the eyes of the law.'

I fell silent; you took my silence as agreement. 'I knew you'd understand,' you said. 'I have to protect my business, you see. These are difficult times, and I must think of my higher duty.'

My higher duty. I could have laughed; I almost did. 'May I go now?' I asked, and you waved a gracious hand and told me that I may. I went to my desk, stuffed my latest paperback into my handbag, took my coat and walked out.

Outside it was grey and cold and the rain was horizontal. I was angry at you, of course, but in a strange way I was also relieved. It was over. I couldn't be made to keep going any more, because you had dismissed me – the decision was out of my hands. Once Stefano got home, I'd sit down with him and we'd work out what to do next. It wouldn't be easy, but we loved each other. I was sure we'd find our way.

I didn't know I was about to lose everything.

When the evening's work was finished, Massimo reached for my hand. 'Well,' he said, 'where shall we go? I should very much like to squire you around town, show you off to everyone. But where to start? That's the question.'

'Oh.' For the first time, I couldn't think of a single idea. All I could think about was his skin against mine, his thumb tracing gentle patterns in the hollow of my palm.

'Spianata Castelletto?' he prompted. 'Piazza San Lorenzo? Botanical gardens? Mind you, they'd be closed by now. I could take you out for dinner, but if I allow myself to imagine that then I'll start thinking about all the things I want to eat, and I'm afraid that would break my heart.'

'I don't want to break your heart,' I said, and he lifted my hand and pressed it to his lips.

'I know, my darling. Don't worry – I trust you with it.'

I couldn't stand it any more. I got up, went to the door and closed it, holding the handle down so the lock wouldn't click and give us away. When I turned around, Massimo was already there. He took my face in his hands and kissed me until I was weak-legged with desire, clinging to his lapels, my head swimming.

'I'd like to kiss you more often,' he murmured at last.

I leaned against him and he wrapped me up in his arms. 'It will all be over at some point,' I said. 'It has to be.'

He didn't respond, just held me tighter. We stayed like that, prolonging our embrace moment by moment until the pressure of time – the looming curfew – became too much to bear and we reluctantly broke apart. I opened the door while he went to the table and began organising the cards ready for packing.

'For next time,' he said, 'you can think about where you'd like us to go together.'

'Oh, I know already,' I said. 'I'd like you to take me dancing.'

26

I could scarcely bear to go to bed that evening. It had become terrible to do so: I would lie there and wonder whether Massimo was managing to sleep and if so, where, and whether he was safe there. When I dozed off, I dreamed of him even more vividly than before. It felt as if I were really lying in his arms with my head on his warm, bare shoulder and my leg flung over his. I was always bitterly disappointed when I woke up and found that he wasn't there after all, and I was in the same small room with the same plain, single, iron-framed bed and the same white walls, so white they were faintly luminous; Bernardo snoring like a walrus down the corridor, Tiberio snoring more delicately by my ear. I'd bury my face in that rather elderly pillow with the feather ends pricking my skin, and I'd will the time away until dawn came, or the siren sounded, and I had to get up again.

Sometimes – and it seems extraordinary now – I

desperately, childishly longed to open the bathroom window, climb down the rope and run wild circles around the courtyard. I could never have done it in daylight, of course. No matter how trustworthy Silvia and Bernardo's neighbours were, such an act would be nothing but dangerous; and not just for me, but for anyone who could be compromised by knowing I existed. But at night, with the windows covered… well, there would be another set of hazards. I'd be lucky not to break my neck, whether getting down or getting back up again. As for running around with the lights off, that was simply asking for a turned ankle or a fractured arm – and then how much use would I be? Sometimes I had to remind myself of that very sternly indeed.

On that particular night, I almost gave in. I was so very sick of being trapped inside, of staying put while Massimo and Vittorio and the rest of them went about their work, and even Tiberio strolled in and out as he wished. I actually went so far as to throw my clothes back on, pick up my shoes and creep along the corridor to the bathroom. I sat on the edge of the bath for a few minutes, arguing with myself, but the urge didn't go away. Eventually I went to the window and pulled back the net curtain, staring down into the dark courtyard. There wasn't much moonlight; it was like looking into a hole. Perhaps that was even better, I found myself thinking. Perhaps my eyes would adjust and I could risk it after all. Even if only to climb down and stand there for a couple of minutes, breathe the cool air, look up at the night sky and not have to fear it.

I was caught up in these thoughts when something

flickered in the dense shadow below. A tiny, fiery roundel, the burning end of a cigarette. Some other desperate soul clearly had the same idea. Were they merely sleepless, or were they hiding, too? The idea that there might be someone else in this very building, living this same trapped and fearful life just a few metres away, was too much for me. I let the curtain fall and went back to my room, where I crawled into bed and wept silent, desolate tears.

Massimo thought it very funny when I told him about my midnight urge to escape. Not surprisingly, because I'd spent most of that afternoon rehearsing the story in my head, finding just the right way to tell it for his amusement. In my heavily edited rendition it was a one-off impulse, the kind of mad, stupid desire that comes over you when you can't get to sleep and the world seems knocked out of orbit. *I might almost have gone through with it, if only to get away from Bernardo's snoring. Imagine if I hadn't seen sense!*

He laughed and put an arm around me, drawing me into his side. We'd been working in the parlour that evening, sitting together on the sofa, while Bernardo did something to the dripping tap in the kitchen and Silvia (and Tiberio) oversaw him. The cards were checked and stamped and we had a little time before he'd have to leave: ten minutes, although that really meant five, to be on the safe side. I slipped my arm around him and rested my head on his shoulder, just as I did in dreams; and I closed my eyes tight and silently begged the clock on the cabinet to stop ticking.

'I don't suppose you want to go on an excursion with

me tonight,' he said, stroking my hair. 'You've had enough excitement as it is.'

His heartbeat sounded in my ear, regular, comforting; he was so warm, and there was an endearing softness around his waist. I could easily have relaxed into it, all that banal and beautiful intimacy, if not for the seconds slipping past and the mortal threats outside. 'You're right,' I said. 'There's nowhere at all I'd want to go, even if we could. I'd much prefer to stay here, just like this.'

'So would I, very much. If only—'

'Tell me something about yourself,' I said, quickly, before he could finish his sentence. 'Something safe, I mean to say – something you can afford to tell me.'

'Something I can afford to tell you,' he said. 'What kind of thing?'

'Anything. How did you start flying? Can you talk about that?'

'Oh, yes. I can talk about that quite easily.' He rubbed my arm. 'Now, that was when I was seventeen. I'd first seen an aeroplane take off when I was still small, with my father – I remember it distinctly. It wasn't what you'd call an impressive display, but the pilot got this basic craft up into the air and brought it back down again, and I thought that was wonderful. It was all I wanted to do from that moment on. So as soon I was old enough, I applied to volunteer with the Air Force.'

My eyes snapped open. Suddenly I didn't feel quite so sleepy and comfortable any more. 'You volunteered for the Air Force? At seventeen? But that must have been in…'

'Nineteen-seventeen, that's right. What, are you shocked?' he asked as I looked up at him. 'I'm surprised your brother didn't tell you all this years ago. I'm certain it was one of the fifty thousand questions he asked me when we met at the Aero Club.'

'He probably did,' I said, 'but I expect I'd stopped listening.'

'Oh, well, that's nice to know. Anyhow, it was all very bad timing. It took a long time to get my licence, and by the time I did, the war was over and there was nothing for me to do. My mother was relieved, if nothing else.'

So am I, I thought, but I didn't say it.

'I wasn't about to stop flying, though,' Massimo went on. 'I got my civil aviation licence, and I learned to fly seaplanes. I had twenty years of joy that way, before everything went to hell.'

I wrapped my arms around him and kissed his cheek. 'I'm sorry,' I said.

'What for?'

For making you relive it. For everything that's happened. 'All of it,' I said. 'I'm just sorry.'

'Well, you oughtn't to be,' he said. 'Damn little you can do about it. Nice of you, though,' he added, and returned my kiss.

I didn't want to, but I glanced at the clock and saw that our time was nearly up. Along the corridor, Silvia and Bernardo were squabbling about something or other, his quiet bass mingling with her aggrieved alto.

Massimo sighed. 'That's my cue to leave. And now I'm sorry.'

'I wish you could stay longer,' I said. 'If I'm quite honest, I wish you could stay all night.'

'Do you? I don't.' Before I could react, he drew me closer

and went on in a soft, low voice: 'Because if I could, if it were safe, then I'd ask you to come home with me instead. And I'd hope desperately for you to say yes.'

I was beside myself with longing. I thought I might never sleep again. 'I would,' I said. 'I'd definitely say yes.'

'One day, then,' he said; and I shan't ever forget it, because Massimo never usually said things like that. He was too pragmatic, too sensible, too much like himself to talk about a future that may or may not come.

I smiled at him and he smiled back at me: that beautiful eye-crinkling smile that I loved. 'One day,' I said.

27

Massimo and I didn't waste any more time with imaginary walks after that. We did our work, processing as many false documents as we could in tense but companionable silence; and in the leftover minutes we sat close together and talked. Never about anything very sensitive – the door, after all, was almost always open – but about the kind of minor, inconsequential things that assume colossal importance when you're in love. I salted everything he told me away in my memory, along with every touch and every kiss. I knew it all by heart. I still do.

He loved music, and liked to sing in the bath. He'd failed to finish his degree ('with only one exam left to take,' he said with a grin, 'just to make a truly awful job of it'). He was used to having a moustache, and felt odd without it. Left to his own devices, he'd sleep until noon. These were a few of the more innocuous things he told me; I've kept the rest for myself.

But sometimes we strayed into painful topics, as you

might brush against an open wound. In late May, on the eve of Shavuot – I was quite oblivious to the Jewish holidays, which my father never observed, and would never have known had Massimo not mentioned it – he happened to tell me that his own family was not very religious. He himself had only ever attended prayer services when they were a man short of the ten required for a minyan; someone or other would run across from the synagogue to ask him to join in. 'If I was at home,' he said, 'I'd usually go. It's not that I cared much for the ritual, but I liked the people involved.'

When he told me about that, I felt sick. All the distressing images, the fragmented bits of information I'd managed to gather about the raid on the synagogue flooded in at once. 'Then you live nearby,' I said.

Massimo hesitated. 'I used to, yes. Right next door, in fact.'

'Were you there when… when the Germans…'

'No,' he said firmly. 'No, they came looking for me, but I wasn't at home. I was lucky. I've moved elsewhere now, further away.'

'But you know what happened?' I was desperate to find out more, to gain some coherent picture of the event that had haunted me over the last months.

He was watching me, just like the first time we met. 'I've pieced it together,' he said after a moment. 'More or less.'

'Tell me,' I said. 'If you can bear it. Please.'

And he put his arms around me, pulled me close and began to talk in a gentle, matter-of-fact voice. I listened, and terrible images filled my mind: some familiar, some new. The caretaker's children held at gunpoint; the caretaker, Bino Polacco, forced to telephone every member of the synagogue and ask them to come to a meeting the next morning. The Germans lying in wait for those who trusted and came; Rabbi Pacifici, dragged to the temple and beaten until he was bloody. The rabbi and his wife, Wanda Abenaim, had been among those arrested, imprisoned and deported: more than 250, by Massimo's estimate. I now know the exact number: 261, of whom just twenty returned.

'That's all there is,' Massimo said at last. 'I can't tell you any more. I don't know any more. I don't...'

His voice trembled and failed. I was helpless, numb with anger and despair. All I could do was hold him, rubbing his back as his shoulders shook and his tears trickled into the collar of my blouse. 'Sorry,' he said after a while, into the crook of my neck. I shook my head and held him tighter.

The curfew broke us apart, as it always did. Massimo let go of me, dried his eyes, blew his nose, cleared his throat. He rose, a little unsteadily, and picked up his hat and coat while I fussed around gathering the cards for packing. Then he gave me a kiss and went out, his head bowed. We never mentioned religion again.

I didn't hear the full story of the raid until after the war, and not from Massimo, but from a priest friend of his who was involved in DELASEM. Don Francesco, a sweet man in round glasses and cassock who reminded me painfully, at first glance, of Vittorio. Massimo, he said, had spent the night before the so-called 'meeting' hiding from the Germans. The SS had come to arrest him – they had found his name in the synagogue registers – and he had narrowly got away from them, running upstairs and out through the door that led to the uppermost terrace of his building. He listened to the cars and trucks moving in the dark and he knew that the raid was imminent. 'Because he had no doubt it was coming,' don Francesco said. 'He was sure it would happen from the moment they raided the ghetto of Rome.'

As soon as morning came, Massimo walked downstairs and out into the street as if he had nothing to fear. He went from bar to bar and telephoned everyone he could think of, telling them to stay away from the temple. He must have saved some lives that day; as did his Catholic neighbour, a woman called Romana Rossi Serrotti, who ran out on her balcony and warned the approaching Jews to turn back and flee. For that simple kindness she was arrested and held in Marassi prison. But neither she nor Massimo nor anyone could save Rabbi Pacifici, who was in hiding in a place allocated to him by the archbishop's office. He, too, had received an invitation from Bino Polacco: this time to meet in secret at the Galleria Mazzini, where the Germans were waiting for him. Don Francesco had tears in his eyes as he spoke of the rabbi, whom he'd admired.

When I first heard all this, I was taken aback. Massimo hadn't escaped the SS by mere luck: he'd acted quickly, and he'd risked his life all over again in the hope of saving others. Of the many secrets he'd kept from me, that one made the least sense. If you had been so courageous in a situation like that – if you had managed to warn even a few people – then why would you hide it? What was there to lose?

But then I found myself lying awake, imagining him shivering on the terrace in the cold November night while the Germans laid a trap just below, and I realised that I had been very stupid. Of course, Massimo hadn't just wanted to keep me physically safe. He'd wanted to protect my heart, too, and that informed every choice he made during our time together. I'm still discovering the things he did, both for me and for others. I may never arrive at the end of them.

28

Vittorio

His love doesn't hurt; well, not like it did. It's become a quiet, everyday pain, nagging at him now and then, like a bad hip or a questionable knee. He can live with it.

Talking to Fulvio helped, although he ought never to have done it. If he's learned one thing from hearing confessions – apart from the boundless human capacity for the most banal kind of sin – it's how easy it is to assemble a coherent picture from details dropped thoughtlessly here and there. But the need was too powerful to resist, and so he'd kept it vague, talking about Marta and Mr X as if they were characters in a cheap play: two-dimensional, clichéd shadow people against a painted backdrop. Even so, he feels uneasy.

'So this chap she's taken up with,' Fulvio had asked, 'what's he like? One of those smooth types, I imagine him.'

Vittorio thought of Mr X, his silk ties and his well-cut jackets. 'He's certainly elegant,' he said.

'Oho!' Fulvio snorted. 'I know the sort. But don't you

worry, Father – a clever girl like your Marta won't be taken in for long.' He said it as if Marta really were Vittorio's; as if his love could ever come to anything. It was wrong, of course, but it was shamefully pleasing. 'No, no, no,' Fulvio went on, becoming indignant, and then remembered himself and lowered his voice. 'She'll get tired of him – you can be certain of that. What did you say he was again? Something in trade?'

'I believe so,' Vittorio said, although he had no idea what Mr X had done before DELASEM. Trade had seemed a safe enough choice – it could cover anything from munitions to tinned fish.

'Well, that just won't do for the kind of young lady who reads. She'll want someone she can talk to of an evening. And he's sure to be a dreadful bounder. Only a matter of time before she sees him for what he is.'

Vittorio's conscience stung him at that point. 'I don't think he is a bounder,' he said. 'He seems quite honourable, really. He does good things for the poor,' he added, 'and he brings her books.'

'He brings her books? As presents, you mean?'

'Yes.'

Fulvio blew out his cheeks, shook his head. 'I'm sorry, Father. You're done for.'

That *had* hurt at the time; Vittorio had needed to take refuge in his breviary. But in the intervening days, Fulvio's words have stuck in his mind. He's found himself repeating them silently, almost like mental prayer. *I'm sorry, Father. You're done for*. It's strangely soothing; above all, it's true. The more he repeats it, the more it sinks in – and now he isn't sad or angry or envious any more. He's mostly worn out, with a dragging tiredness that grows stronger and stronger until one morning he's too feeble even to shave. He picks up his razor and manages a couple of uneven strokes before he has to put it down again, his arm trembling as if he's just lifted a tremendous weight.

Vittorio can't understand it. He's been sleeping heavily, falling unconscious the moment he gets into bed and waking with difficulty at the morning bell. He ought to be rested, but he isn't at all. He sits down on the bed – just for a moment, just until he can get his strength back a little – and feels the exhaustion pull at him again. In the back of his mind, a small, clear voice is warning him that all isn't well; that this could be the coming of the end, the start of his body's final decline. But there's no time for the warning to register. He's already sinking onto his side, eyes closing, and his head doesn't even touch the thin feather pillow before sleep swallows him whole.

He wakes to the sound of a bell: not the community bell that regulates his day, but the big bell, the one in the tower. As he lies there – still, somehow, exhausted – he counts the chimes all the way to eleven. *Eleven.* He's missed Mass, and he should have reported to don Francesco three hours ago. Adrenaline surges through him and he pushes himself up and off the bed; resisting the urge to lie straight down again, he clumsily washes and dresses, and stumbles out and down the stairs. He isn't even sure where he's going. He usually meets don Francesco in the parlour, but he's hardly going to be there now; he's probably out doing his own work, or else with Cardinal Boetto, or Mr X, or God knows who else. But he can't think of anything better. And so he continues in the direction of the parlour and prays that don Francesco is in there after all, or near there, or somewhere in his path. He has to focus so hard on the simple business of walking, of placing one foot in front of the other, that he nearly cannons into someone coming the other way.

'Steady on!' the other man exclaims. He's wearing sharply creased trousers and distinctly secular shoes, chestnut-shiny wingtips. Mr X. Vittorio can't look up – he's paralysed by guilt and embarrassment and a hot, dark jealousy.

'Father Vittorio,' Mr X goes on, sounding rather friendlier now. 'I'm sorry, I didn't recognise you for a moment. Are you quite all right? Don Francesco was worried about you. Has something happened? Are you ill?'

The exhaustion is setting in again. He resents Mr X for being here, for making him talk when talking requires effort. 'I'm all right, thank you,' he says. 'I'm very sorry. I overslept.'

'That doesn't sound like you. Look, have you time for a chat? Let's go in here, shall we?' There's no need for Vittorio to answer, because he doesn't have a choice: Mr X has an iron grip on his arm and is shepherding him towards the open parlour door. 'Have a seat,' he says, and Vittorio sits down at the table. He has a fierce urge to rest his head on his arms and sleep, sleep, sleep. He hears the door closing as if it's very far away, and then Mr X sits down opposite, takes out a cigarette case and offers it to him.

'I presume we can smoke, since there's an ashtray here. Go on, Father.'

Vittorio nods his thanks and picks a cigarette from the

case. It's a rather cheap-looking thing in plain metal, as is the lighter he's offered next. Vittorio is surprised for a moment: he'd expected something else, something heavy and monogrammed. But that's stupid of him, of course. Mr X would hardly go around carrying a cigarette lighter with his real initials on it.

They sit in silence for a moment. Vittorio takes a deep drag on his cigarette and waits for the nicotine to take effect, but it doesn't, not today. All he feels is a muted whisper of pleasure, not nearly enough to justify the effort involved in smoking the thing. He stubs it out in the metal ashtray and sits back, trying surreptitiously to brace himself against the edge of the table. Mr X is watching him; Vittorio can't look him in the eye, so he looks at one of his eyebrows instead. (They do rather command attention.)

'Your cough really has gone,' Mr X says, and the eyebrow twitches. 'It's stayed away, too.'

Vittorio nods and brings out his lie: 'Yes. I had a chest infection, but it's cured now. It's extraordinary how something like that can drain you.'

'Quite so. But you're still not well, are you? Forgive me, Father Vittorio, but you look dreadful. If you're not feeling up to—'

'I'm perfectly all right.' He knows he's answered too fast, that he sounds defensive, and he curses himself for it. 'It's just today. There must be something going around, some virus or other… I shall be fine again soon.'

Mr X doesn't answer, just continues to watch him. Vittorio knows this tactic – he's employed it himself in the confessional a thousand times. The horrible thing is, it works. He has to fight not to open his mouth and fill the silence, adding on details and justifications that will only undermine his story. But he does manage it, and eventually Mr X says: 'Well, then you must go back to bed for today, at least. I shall let don Francesco know that you are temporarily laid low, and not to worry.'

Back to bed. It's all he wants in the world. 'Thank you.'

'You can report to him here at your usual time, tomorrow morning.' Mr X gets to his feet. 'If he can't be there, I shall. All right?'

'All right,' Vittorio says as lightly as he can. But he knows he won't be well tomorrow morning, either, or the day after, or the day after that.

'Rest well,' Mr X says. 'Good day, Father Vittorio.' He goes out and Vittorio slumps forward with his head in his hands, trying to summon the energy to stand up. If he doesn't move now, he'll fall asleep right here. He plants his hands on the table and levers himself to his feet, and then sets off, step by dragging step, along the corridor and up the stairs to his room.

He doesn't pull back the covers. He doesn't even take off his cassock. He simply lies down as he is, on top of the bedclothes with his shoes still on, and goes to sleep. His last waking thought is that, no matter what it costs him, tomorrow morning he must do all he can to stay vertical.

29

The world outside is full of Germans. It's not that Vittorio didn't see them before. He was always aware of them, always on the lookout for a field-grey object in the margins of his vision. But he couldn't afford to stop and look at them, either. If he'd allowed himself to take in the sheer scale of their presence – if he'd let their brutal display affect him – then he'd never have been able to go outside at all, much less do his work.

But whatever filter was protecting him has gone, washed away by exhaustion. Now he's half-walking, half-stumbling across piazza De Ferrari, that day's list tucked into his inner breast pocket, and Germans are all he can see. Patrolling in groups and loitering by cars, standing vigilant on corners, conversing in knots. A few of them look as he passes by. No doubt they always do, but today he notices and it throws him; he trips over his own feet and has to steady himself against a lamppost. The Germans laugh, thinking he's drunk. *Schaut mal, der ist ja besoffen, der Priester!*

Silvia and Bernardo's seems an unimaginable distance away; it might as well be on the moon, but he's promised that he is up to going and so he must go. He strained every sinew keeping himself upright and awake through that morning's meeting, assuring don Francesco – and he's both guilty and relieved that it was good, gentle don Francesco he had to lie to – that he was still a little tired, but already much better, thank you. And he convinced him. For a moment, he even managed to convince himself, so much did he want it to be true.

It isn't true, though, and his path is lined with temptations. If he sits down, he knows he won't get up and go on. The chairs set out in front of the bars of the Galleria Mazzini call to him. Reaching piazza Corvetto, he forges on past the benches, refusing to look left or right in case Fulvio happens to be there; his sympathy would be altogether fatal. As he begins to climb via Assarotti, his muscles sing with pain and his nerves are taut. The German headquarters loom up on his right and he wishes he'd taken the longer way, the back-streets route he took with Marta, because today it's like walking past the mouth of Hell.

After that it's the endless rise, rise, rise of the street and the sun beating down on him, so that by the time the Waldensian temple comes into sight he's so weak that he fears he might faint. He turns into via Curtatone and allows himself to rest for just a second, propped against the wall of the temple, in the hope of recuperating a little strength. But it's no good, and he arrives at the Tipografia Guichard sweaty and palpitating.

Bernardo greets him with wide eyes and a shake of the head. 'You'll sit down, Father,' he says – it's very much a command – and he takes Vittorio by the shoulder and steers him into the back office, where he pulls out the big chair at the desk and all but pushes him into it. Vittorio sinks into the battered old leather chair with its high back and soft, hollowed-out seat. It's an unbearably sweet feeling.

'What's happened, Father? Aren't you well? I'll 'phone Dr Rostan,' Bernardo says. 'Ask him to come as soon as he can.'

'No,' Vittorio blurts out, panicking. 'No, please don't. I'm fine. I'm just a little tired, that's all.'

Bernardo snorts. 'You're more than a little tired. Anyone can see that. If you'd just let me—'

'No.' Vittorio tries to look Bernardo in the eye, but he's so exhausted that his vision keeps blurring and refocusing; he's blinking up at him like a drunk or a mystic. 'Please don't call him. There's really no need. Please.' He knows he sounds desperate. He can't have Dr Rostan see him like this; he can't stand to hear what the doctor might have to say. 'I'm just tired, truly I am. I had some kind of virus. You'd only be wasting his time.'

Bernardo looks at him rather like Mr X did before: assessing, sceptical. 'If you insist,' he says after a moment. 'But you'll let Silvia have a look at you, at least.'

Oh, thank God. 'Yes. Yes, of course. But could she come to me here?' Vittorio asks. 'I don't want to worry Marta.'

Bernardo nods. 'Probably wise,' he says gruffly. 'Stay where you are and I'll fetch Silvia.'

'Thank you,' Vittorio says. He lets his head nod for just

a moment, barely long enough to blink, and when he looks up again Silvia is already there.

'Tired, are we?' She's studying his face; her mouth is a tight line. Vittorio feels as vulnerable as if he's stripped off for the doctor.

'Yes,' he says.

'What kind of tiredness? Are you sleeping? Not sleeping?'

'I'm sleeping.' Even saying the word makes him crave sleep. 'I sleep all the time. It's the only thing I want to do.'

'And do you wake up feeling rested, or do you just go on being tired?'

'Yes,' Vittorio says. 'I mean to say, I keep being tired. I don't feel like I slept at all.'

'Heart skipping a beat? Any mouth ulcers? Sore tongue?'

'Heartbeat, yes.' He moves his tongue around his dry mouth. His lower lip sticks unpleasantly to his bottom teeth; probing it, he finds a small raw patch. Another sensation he'd managed to blot out. 'Ulcer, yes. Ow.'

'Right. Now, would you pull down your lower eyelid for me? Like this,' she says, and demonstrates, dragging her eyelid down with her index finger to expose pink shiny flesh.

Vittorio does as he's told, and Silvia makes a face. 'Yes, I thought so,' she says. 'Looks like anaemia to me.'

'Anaemia?' It sounds so innocuous, nothing like this bone-deep, sucking exhaustion.

'Not enough iron in your blood,' Silvia explains. 'It's quite common – well, for some people. I expect you haven't had it before. Men don't, generally,' she adds. 'For obvious reasons.'

'I see,' Vittorio says, although he doesn't.

'But if you've been sick with this infection of yours, and fasting, and then when you *do* get to eat it's hardly nutritious stuff, the Lord knows... well, it's not surprising if you're running a deficit. You probably just need a tonic.'

'A tonic,' he repeats. He can't remember when he last had to take a tonic, not as an adult. But he can taste, well over thirty years on, the sticky, sickly honey-sweet stuff his nurse used to make him drink – for his lungs, supposedly. All it ever did was coat his tongue with sugar and make him feel slightly sick. 'Would that really help?'

'Of course it would,' she says. 'A couple of spoonfuls of iron tonic a day, and you'll be right as rain. It's a miracle-worker, that stuff. I have a spare bottle, if you'd like.'

'Please,' he says. It's all he can say.

'I'll fetch it,' Silvia says, and then the shop doorbell rings and Bernardo, on the other side of the curtain, clears his throat and says: 'Customers. New ones.'

'On second thoughts, let's go upstairs. Come on, Father.' Silvia sets off and Vittorio follows, but he thinks longingly of that forgiving leather chair.

'Marta knows you're here, of course,' she says quietly over her shoulder as they climb the stairs. 'She heard the doorbell. But don't you worry. Marta, dear?' she calls out, and now Marta herself appears on the landing. She has on a dress, a blue cotton dress with yellow flowers, and her hair is tucked behind her ears. Vittorio's throat is tight and he has to clutch the handrail; the iron is cold against his damp skin.

'Yes?' she says, and smiles down at him. 'Hello, Father Vittorio.'

'Our friend here hasn't had a good night,' Silvia says

briskly. 'He's going to have a little sit-down before you start work. This way, Father.' She takes his arm – everybody, he thinks resentfully, feels quite free to manhandle him these days – and guides him along the corridor towards the parlour.

'What shall I do?' Marta's voice sounds behind him. He can't look around. 'Can I help at all?'

'You brew some tea and make a start on the cards, if you like. He'll be with you shortly. Have you got the list, Father?' she asks, and Vittorio reaches into his breast pocket and hands it to her. It's crumpled and slightly damp. 'There you go, dear. Now come with me,' Silvia continues, lowering her voice as Marta's footsteps retreat into the kitchen. 'Sit down and I'll fetch the tonic. You can have a dose now and a little rest, I think, before you try to do anything. You're practically cross-eyed.'

Vittorio lowers himself onto the sofa. It's not especially comfortable, but even sitting down is a profound relief. By the time Silvia returns with the bottle of tonic, a folded blanket tucked under her arm, his eyes are already closing.

'Drink,' she commands, and brings a spoon to his lips as if he were a child. He's beyond dignity now, beyond discipline, beyond even staying upright. He meekly swallows the green herbal liquid – it's urgently refreshing, as necessary as water on a hot day – and lets himself sink again, stretching out on the hard, uneven couch. The blanket settles over him in a waft of air and wool fibre and then it's dark.

30

Anna

By the time Vittorio finally appeared in the kitchen, Silvia had given up on him and gone to help Bernardo in the shop. I had filled out all the cards, drunk all the tea, and was amusing myself by practising the mayor's signature on the back of the list while Tiberio purred in my lap.

'Good morning,' Vittorio said, and blinked at me. He looked tired, but definitely a little better than before. 'It is still morning, isn't it?'

'Just about,' I said.

'Oh, well.' He rubbed at his eyes. 'Is Silvia downstairs? Do you want me to fetch her?'

'There's no need,' I said. 'Not on my account. Unless you would prefer…?'

'No, no. I think we're quite all right as we are. I'm just sorry I can't speak English with you. My mind, today…' He shook his head and sat down in his usual chair. 'It's too much effort. I have anaemia, Silvia says. She gave me a tonic and I must say, it's helping somewhat, but I'm still wiped out. Let me see what you've done,' he went on, reaching for the cards. 'Oh, you've filled in the details already. You're very efficient. Pass me the list, would you?'

'Here you are.' I turned the list over and passed it to him, but he'd already spotted the signatures on the reverse.

'These aren't bad,' he said, inspecting them. 'You have a good eye, in fact. Soon you won't need me at all.'

It was a joking remark, of course, but there was something in the way he said it – some small, sad note that made me want to reach out and touch his arm, offer him some kind of comfort. I knew I mustn't, so I stroked Tiberio's ears instead; he raised his head and pressed his face into my hand, his nose a cold whisper against my palm.

'All right,' Vittorio said. He took a card from the pile and lined the list up next to it. 'I shall deal with these now, but perhaps you and... you and Mr X might double-check them afterwards. Just to be sure.'

'Maybe you shouldn't work today,' I said. 'Maybe you should go home and sleep until you're well again.'

'No. No, there's no need for any delay. I'm really feeling much better already. And besides,' he added, with the hint of a wry smile, 'I must think of my higher duty.'

It was an innocent phrase in itself. Anyone might have said it; but only one person had ever said it to me. Surely there was no way that Vittorio – my friend, my comrade, my rescuer – had anything to do with *him*. It was simply impossible. That's what I told myself, but I still felt sick.

'That's quite a declaration,' I said.

Vittorio picked up his pen. He was already focused on the list in front of him. 'Oh, it's just something my father used to say.'

'Your father,' I echoed.

'Yes. I can't remember if I mentioned him to you before. He's... well, shall we say that he's a character? I think that would be the most charitable way to put it.'

'What does he do?' Even as I asked the question, I knew that I oughtn't. It would have been better to drop the subject and pretend it never came up; to content myself with knowing Vittorio as he was, and not to worry about who his relatives might be. But some perverse impulse drove me on.

Vittorio looked up from his work. He set down his pen, just as if this were a normal, everyday conversation – which it wasn't, not for us. 'He's a shipbuilder,' he said. 'He has a yard here in Genoa, or he did, anyway. It's probably been blown to pieces by now. He and I haven't spoken in a long time – oh, twenty-five years.'

'That must be strange,' I said. I was feeling rather faint, and I couldn't decide whether I was horrified or fascinated that Vittorio had chosen today, of all days, to be so forthcoming. 'Living in the same city and not being in touch. You really don't talk to him? You don't see one another at all?'

'No. This is hard to explain to... well, to someone like you.' That wry smile again. 'Please don't take that the wrong way. But you love your mother and father, don't you? And you know that they love you, even if they can't help you right now.'

'Of course I do.'

'Well, there's no "of course" about it for me,' Vittorio said matter-of-factly. 'When I joined the Society of Jesus, I had to leave my family behind. I know many Jesuits, good and dedicated Jesuits, for whom that was a terrible struggle.

They understood what was required of them, and they did it, but it was painful and they grieved. It wasn't painful for me. In fact, it was very easy, because my father was an unpleasant man – a nasty, bullying, angry man – and I'd had enough of him. When I told him that I wanted to be a Jesuit like my teachers at school, he took it as a sort of criticism, and I suppose he was right. I liked them better than I liked him. Anyway, he threatened to cut me off, so I let him. It was that easy.'

'And your mother? Did she cut you off, too?'

'My mother…' He sighed. 'When I was a novice, family members were allowed to visit twice a year. She came once, and then never again. Perhaps he stopped her, or perhaps she decided that on her own. I used to wonder, but I don't any more. What's the point?'

'I'm sorry,' I said.

'It's quite all right. It was all a very long time ago. But it's funny, you know: I can still hear my father sometimes. Always at the oddest moments, like just now.' He made a face – the commendatore's face – and he said in the commendatore's voice: '*Look, son, it doesn't matter what you've got to say about it. I must think of my higher duty.*'

And, oh, I could see it now. Age him thirty years and bulk him out; give him a moustache, whiten the hair and strip away the cassock, clothe him in English tweed with a fat-knotted necktie and a watch on a thin gold chain and a mustard-yellow waistcoat straining at the buttons. It was him. *He* was him.

My horror must have shown on my face, because Vittorio frowned. 'What's the matter?' he asked, and I quickly looked away. Tiberio, sensing my nerves, jumped down from my lap with a thud and stalked off.

'Nothing,' I said. 'Nothing at all.'

'No, something is wrong – I can tell. Are you shocked? I oughtn't have told you all those things about my parents.' He shook his head. 'Self-indulgent of me.'

'It's all right. I asked to you to tell me.'

'Still. It's unpleasant, and you have enough unpleasantness to be going on with. I should have thought before I opened my mouth. I'm sorry, Marta.'

I couldn't bear his solicitousness. It made everything worse. 'I'm sorry for you, that you suffered like that,' I said. 'I'll make some tea.' I stood and tried to pick up my cup and saucer, but that was a mistake. My hands shook violently and the china rattled and threatened to fall. I had to set it all down again; and sit down, too, before I stumbled.

Vittorio was looking at me and there was something terrible in his expression, the same cold horror I'd felt just a moment before. 'Hang on,' he said in a pale, quiet voice. 'You know my father. Don't you? You know my father and he said something, did something... I think you'd better tell me.'

Commendatore, I tried so hard to spare him – not for your sake, but for his. I began by telling him the blandest, the most stripped-down and flattened-out version of events I could possibly concoct. I had worked as your secretary for four years, and then, when the Racial Laws came in, you had dismissed me. I'd been upset at the time, yes, but when I thought about it – I said, swallowing down my nausea

– when I actually thought about it, you had only done what countless other men in your position had done. You had acted to protect your livelihood. Really, my upset was with Mussolini, not with you.

But Vittorio was my friend, and he was your son. He wasn't fooled for a moment. 'But that's not it,' he said. 'You're not being honest with me, Marta. You're trying to spare my feelings, but I don't need you to do that, and I don't want it, either. You must tell me the absolute truth. You won't hurt me and you certainly won't shock me. Nothing he does could shock me.'

So I told him what you'd promised me, and how you'd gone back on it. I told him what you'd said about your important Fascist clients. I recited the line about your 'higher duty,' and saw a look of disgust cross his face.

'I hated working for your father,' I said. 'I hated him – I'm sorry, I did. That's the truth. He was a bully and a boor, and whenever something reminds me of him, I become terribly angry at how he treated me. That's why I got upset just now. So I was happy when he let me go – I walked out and I didn't go back. It was all over and I never, ever saw him again.'

I thought that might satisfy Vittorio, but it didn't. He leaned forward. 'And then what happened?' he asked.

31

VITTORIO

He didn't know what he'd expected to hear, but it wasn't this. He's hurt and shocked and angry, just as he promised not to be, and he mustn't show it. All he can do is sit with her and listen, and act like the man he desperately wants to be. The man he wants to be for her.

'My husband... he didn't react very well when your father let me go,' Marta is saying now. Her shoulders collapse. 'I loved Stefano very much and he loved me, but...'

'Go on,' Vittorio prompts. He already dislikes this Stefano.

'He didn't *understand*,' she bursts out. 'Not really, not properly. He knew I hated it there, and he knew that I was afraid. He knew how much I missed my family and he knew – I thought he knew – what a big compromise I had made for him. Every single day I went to work for your father was a sacrifice by the end, even the days when he was perfectly pleasant and didn't do or say anything nasty at all. Because I never knew when he would, you see, and I was always bracing myself. Every day I was a little more...'

'You were brutalised,' Vittorio says, thinking of the father he grew up with: the capricious autocrat, the dark shadow in the home.

'Yes, that's just it. I was brutalised. Some days I had to come home and go straight to bed. And Stefano would take care of me – he'd do everything to make me feel better, but then he'd say: "Hang on just a little bit longer, darling. We're so close to our goal." And that's the thing – we *were* close. He had just one exam left to take. We almost had what we needed to go to America, like he promised we would, and be with my parents and my brother, and…'

Her cheeks are wet. She scrubs at them with the back of her hand. 'I'd done everything,' she goes on. 'I'd done everything I could, and there wasn't anything more to do. There just wasn't. He'd told me over and over again how happy his own parents would be when he got this fantastic job over there, the one he was sure his degree would get him. We'd done everything by ourselves up to that point and we hadn't asked for help from them at all. I thought we could ask now. That's the thing about growing up in a nice, happy family,' she says with the ghost of a smile. 'You rather think all parents are like yours. Mine would have insisted on helping, would have sent whatever they could scrape together, but I knew they were only just surviving. My brother was picking up menial jobs where he could and studying in the evenings. My mother was teaching English to immigrant families. My father had a job at the City College, and he loved it – but his health was getting worse, and so were his doctors' bills. No, I couldn't ask them.'

'But Stefano's parents would help?' he asks, and she sighs.

'No. Stefano refused even to ask. He said that going to

them for help would be a failure. They'd see it that way, and so would he. He wanted to keep on managing all by himself.'

'But he wasn't managing all by himself,' Vittorio says, indignant. 'He was managing because of you.'

'That's what I told him,' she says. 'I screamed it at him, in fact. I hate raising my voice, but I did then, because I was at the end of my tether. The worst part is that he didn't even shout back. He looked at me as if I were quite stupid, and said something he'd never, ever said to me before.' She takes a breath. 'He was the one with the career, he said. He was the one with the name, the connections, the prospects. It was because of him, he said, that me and my parents wouldn't end up rotting in filth, crammed together in some New York slum. He didn't say I should be grateful that he'd taken me on, that I was worth less than he was. He didn't have to say it.'

Vittorio wants to go to her, gather her up in his arms. He wants to kiss away her tears. He wants to tell her that she is worth more than anything or anyone in the world, certainly to him.

He holds out his hand, palm up, and she takes it.

'He was right in one way, though,' she says. 'I was stupid. I should never have stayed with him in the first place, and I shouldn't have kept on staying. You know, my mother – she would never have stopped me – but she said to me a few times before she and my father left: *You know you can still come with us.*' She speaks the words in English and there's a cadence to her voice, a genteel Scottish lilt. '*If you want to stay, then of course you must stay. But you can change your mind – you know that, don't you? There's no shame if you do*. Do you know what that was? That was a lifeline. My mother offered me a lifeline and I didn't take it.'

'But you couldn't have known what was coming,' Vittorio says. 'Could you? That must have been years before the Racial Laws.'

She nods. 'That was in thirty-four.'

'Well, then. And you couldn't have known about my father, either. I'm sure he was very charming at first. Perfectly easy to deal with until the moment when… well, when he wasn't any more. I've seen him do that many times: to servants, to employees, to my own mother.' He's warming to his theme now. He squeezes her hand and she gives him a faint smile. 'How could you possibly have known what he was until you were already in his grasp? How could you know what the government would do? Marta, you can't blame yourself for a decision you took when you were very young and in love, and you can't blame yourself for trying to make the best of that decision. You mustn't. There was so much you didn't know until it was too late.'

'But I might have known what Stefano was like.' Her voice is quiet, steady. 'I married a man I barely knew and I thought that just because he was in love with me, he would also be my friend. I thought that he'd understand me, value me, just like my mother valued my father. I believed that was the very basis of love. And that, Father Vittorio, was a dreadfully stupid mistake.'

He keeps hold of her hand while the story unfolds. Stefano would not go and talk to his parents, and Marta's attempts to plead with him only hardened his resolve. He was determined to talk to the commendatore instead. ('How I hate that title,' she says. 'A knighthood for services to Fascist industry. But it was so perfectly him. He used it with everyone.') He was sure that he could make him see sense and give Marta her job back. The fact that she didn't want it back was, of course, neither here nor there.

Marta had known – just as Vittorio knows – that this was a bad idea. But nothing she said could persuade him not to do it.

'He was simply convinced of being in the right. And he believed that your father would listen to him, because they were both men, and from the same class – well, no, his family was older and better than yours. Sorry, Father Vittorio. I tried to tell him that the commendatore would never, ever tolerate someone questioning his judgement. Especially a younger man, and *especially* one from an old-established family. You know how he is.'

Vittorio nods. 'All too well.'

'And you can probably imagine how it went.'

His stomach twists. 'I think I can.'

'Stefano came back from that meeting quite changed,' she says with a small, bitter laugh. 'He was shell-shocked. He kept saying: "I had no idea how vile that man is. Sweetheart, can you ever forgive me?" And I rather had to, in the moment – though I didn't forget that I'd told him plenty of times exactly what your father was like, and he hadn't listened. Anyway, now he was convinced that we must go and speak to his parents. I believe he even thought it was his idea. He was nervous, of course. Captain Pastorino, his father, was rather a forbidding man. But we sat together and rehearsed all the reasons why they should help him. None of them involved me or my family; that was simple common sense. It was all about him making a brilliant career abroad, just like the captain had as a young man. Bringing glory to the family name in a new field, that sort of thing. They were perfectly sound reasons and, in any other circumstances, I'm sure they would have worked. But it was already too late.'

Her hand is chilly in his, fragile and still like a dead bird. He doesn't know what she's going to tell him, but he knows it's something terrible and he knows, with a dreadful certainty, who is behind it.

'What did he do?' he asks. 'What did my father do? Tell me, Marta, please. Don't hold back. You must tell me everything.'

32

ANNA

What you did, Commendatore, was almost an act of genius. Having subjected Stefano to the full blast of your fury, you clearly realised that you couldn't afford to do that again. You can vent your anger that way, but you can't really hurt a man's reputation unless you contrive to appear like the reasonable party to the rest of the world. And you wanted to hurt Stefano, like you wanted to hurt anyone who put you in the wrong.

So you did something very strategic. You 'phoned up Captain Pastorino, whom you knew socially and had very nearly managed to charm, and you explained in restrained and sorrowful tones that his son had come to you to plead for his wife's job. You admired his husbandly loyalty, but – and it pained you to admit this – there could be simply no question of your employing me ever again. You didn't want to go into details. It was all too sordid, but since he insisted on knowing... well, a couple of things had gone missing just recently. Blueprints, specifications. The kind of thing that would reap a nice sum of money from a rival shipyard, in Genoa or abroad. The kind of thing, come to think of it, that just might interest a foreign government.

Of course, you hadn't wanted to involve the police: this was such a delicate matter, and you were mindful of my in-laws' reputation. But if there was even the slightest possibility that I might have taken these things, to which I had easy and unmonitored access, then you couldn't afford to take any chances by keeping me on. The Racial Laws had provided a useful occasion to dismiss me without anyone being forced to lose face, and so that is what you had done. You felt rather sorry for me, you said, heaping on the insinuations: the poor little Jewish girl with her disgraced father and her disreputable half-foreign family, all of them overseas – in a major shipbuilding city, as it happened – and no doubt struggling to live. But above all you felt sorry for the Pastorino family, and especially for Stefano, who was so trusting.

You couldn't have picked a better audience for your lies. Captain Pastorino was extremely conscious of his family's reputation, which rested so very much on his own: a reputation built on honesty, social respectability, and a strict adherence to the code of the gentleman seafarer. He'd been too honourable to kick up a public fuss when Stefano had chosen to marry me, though I'll never know what he might have said about it in private. Perhaps if he'd been at all fond of me, as I naively thought he was, then he would have rejected your insinuations or at least questioned them. But it seems he was all too ready to believe the worst.

I didn't make poor Vittorio suffer by describing the scenes that followed your telephone call. I said only that your strategy had worked. Stefano tried to defend me to his parents, but it came to nothing; the angrier he became and the more he defied his father, the worse the atmosphere grew, until I begged him to stop and let it blow over. But he didn't listen to me then, either. Soon, my very existence as a member of the family had become a bone of contention; perhaps it always was. Stefano pleaded, his mother wavered, but Captain Pastorino stood firm: something had to be done about me. It almost didn't matter whether I'd been filching trade secrets, although he clearly believed that I had. I was a liability by my very existence.

'Making Stefano divorce me was out of the question,' I said. 'Abandonment, too. They were a good Catholic family. Stefano did ask whether they might not just send me to my parents in America – I'll always love him for suggesting that. For a moment I thought they might actually agree, but no. That would only be a public admission that something was wrong. They couldn't send me away.' I had to take a breath as the memories threatened to overwhelm me. 'But they could send him, at least for a while.'

'Oh,' Vittorio said, and now he took my hand in both of his.

'There was a merchant ship leaving for Buenos Aires in a few weeks' time. Stefano would go with it, follow in his father's footsteps like his older brothers. The ship was the *Antonio Montaldo*,' I said, and I hoped that he would recognise the name, because I couldn't bring myself to tell the story.

Vittorio sucked in a sharp breath. He knew. Every Genoese knew, of course. The *Montaldo* had never made it home. It had been sunk by night as it lay at anchor off the Spanish coast, torpedoed by an aircraft from the Condor Legion, Franco's German-manned military corps, on suspicion of carrying supplies to the Republicans. A handful of crew had made it to shore, but the others…

'I'm sorry, Marta,' he said. 'I'm so very sorry.'

'And that was it.' Even five years on, I could still relive the pain of the events. The news reports, the waiting and then, eventually, the telegram. Sitting on the floor of our little flat, my universe collapsing around me. 'I was on my own,' I managed to say.

'Didn't Stefano's family look after you? They really should have,' he said severely, 'if they claimed to be good Catholics. They had a duty to you.'

'No. They kept their distance, and I left them to it. After everything that had been said, I couldn't pretend that we were just like any other family in mourning. But once… once, I asked his father for help.' My cheeks were burning at the memory of it. 'I'd been looking for a job for months, since your father dismissed me. But nobody would have me, not even in the sectors where I was allowed to work. I could pick up a bit of typing here and there, but it wasn't enough – I was desperate. All I wanted was to get to my family, and I knew that would take months to arrange. I thought that perhaps, now Stefano was gone, Captain Pastorino might be willing to help if it meant that he could be rid of me. I begged him for work, references, anything that would get me through until I could go to America. I begged him to use his connections to get me a visa faster. It was humiliating,' I said. 'It was the most abasing thing I've ever done.'

'And he wouldn't help, I suppose,' Vittorio said.

'No, he wouldn't, or not with that. He said he'd make sure I got some small amount of money from a seafarers' charity he helped to administer. The way he said it, he made it sound like I'd actually asked for money. And I hadn't. I'd have preferred any other kind of help, but he wasn't prepared do anything that might tie his reputation up with mine. I would have to manage my affairs alone.' He'd said rather more – about my character, my claims on the family, my relationship with his son, the very fact of my daring to come to him – but I didn't want to inflict that on Vittorio, either. 'And so I did manage alone, until you found me,' I said. 'That's it. That's all there is.'

Vittorio sat back, his hands slipping away from mine. He looked dreadful, exhausted and hollow-eyed. I knew even then that I'd done something terribly wrong. I should have kept it all to myself. I should have invented some plausible lie, or simply refused to talk at all. I should have told Massimo, if I had to tell someone. There were so many other, better, kinder options.

'I'm sorry,' I said now, and he shook his head.

'Why should you be sorry, Marta? None of this was your fault. It was my father who…' He trailed off and looked at the pile of cards next to him. 'You know, I think you and Mr X should deal with these. If that's all right.'

'Of course it is. Father Vittorio—'

'I need to go.' He pushed back his chair and stood up, passing a hand over his face. 'I'm sorry. And I'm very sorry indeed for what my father did to you. If you'd prefer not to work with me any more…'

'No, I want to work with you,' I said, indignation propelling me to my feet. 'You're a good man and you are my friend. How could I possibly blame you for your father's actions? Or Stefano's, or *his* father's? Please come back and keep coming, so long as you want to – once you're well again, I mean to say. I shall always be happy to see you. Truly I shall.'

Vittorio nodded. 'All right,' he said. 'All right. Once I'm well. Thank you.'

When he'd gone, I went to my room, shut the door and sat on my bed. I hadn't given Stefano more than a passing thought in the last months, I realised. Or even the commendatore. All those remembered arguments and scenes and betrayals – so fresh and so painful, for so long – had been eclipsed the moment the Germans arrived in Genoa, driven out of my head by the sheer urgency of survival. And now I had brought them back to life. I'd given them a new and horrible currency, all because poor Vittorio had happened to say something that reminded me of his father.

He had paused in the doorway as he left the kitchen. 'You won't tell anyone what we discussed, will you? Not because I'm ashamed, or feel bad,' he added, looking away. 'It simply isn't relevant. If you really are happy to work together…'

'Of course I am.'

'Then it doesn't matter, not one bit.' He summoned a smile. 'Goodbye for now, Marta. I shall see you soon.'

'Good,' I said, and gave him my best and brightest smile in return. 'I'm glad. See you soon, Father Vittorio.' But I couldn't forget the look on his face just a few minutes before: that stark, hollow-eyed shock. Whether I'd meant to or not, I'd caused him tremendous pain. I vowed to find a way to make it up to him, just as soon as we got to see one another again; I only hoped he would let me.

33

VITTORIO

He's been wide awake all through the conversation with Marta, galvanised by indignation and anger and love. But now the adrenaline is subsiding. As he walks down via Assarotti, clutching the tonic bottle in its paper bag, all he can think about is getting back into bed. And he will, he promises himself. He'll get into bed and stay there for as long as he needs to, until the miracle tonic has had its effect. Just as soon as he's found don Francesco – or Cardinal Boetto, or Mr X if he must – and made his excuses. He'll sleep and he'll forget all about his father. He'll forget about Marta's hand resting in his.

He's halfway around piazza Corvetto when he hears Fulvio calling him. 'Father? Father Vittorio, over here.'

The old man is sitting on a bench in the shade, looking eagerly up at him. Vittorio hesitates, torn between affection, duty, and a sudden, vicious resentment. *Another one who needs me. Can't I ever be left alone?* And then he feels instantly guilty, because he's the one who's needed Fulvio lately, and Fulvio has been very kind about it.

'Hello,' he says, and does his best to smile. 'I'm sorry I can't stop – I have to get back.'

'That's all right, Father, quite all right. I just wanted to see how you are. What's that?' He nods at the bottle in Vittorio's hand. 'Taken up drinking? You want a nice flask, like mine. Lot more subtle.'

Now Vittorio really does smile. He sits down next to Fulvio and hopes he'll be able to get up again. 'It's just a tonic. I've been a bit run down.'

'I'm not surprised. But how are you doing otherwise, if I may ask?' He leans towards Vittorio, lowers his voice like a conspirator. 'I don't suppose she's seen sense, your Marta? I know, I know,' he says with a wry grimace. 'You're far too decent to steal her away for yourself. But part of me wishes you would. Call me an old romantic, but you're a good soul and you deserve something in this world.'

'Thank you,' Vittorio says. 'I'm afraid she hasn't, uh... seen sense, and I shan't try to steal her away, but I do feel better after our talk. You really helped me,' he adds, and Fulvio beams at him.

'Well, then, I'm pleased. I like to be useful.'

'I must get going,' Vittorio says, although he doesn't want to at all. He wants to sit and rest on this bench, basking in friendship and warm noonday air. 'Thank you again.' He puts his hand out to Fulvio, and the old man takes it and shakes it warmly.

'Take care of yourself, Father. See you next time.'

'Take care.' Vittorio forces himself to stand. His limbs

are heavy and the tiredness is claiming him, relentless and dragging. 'Goodbye, Fulvio.'

By the time he gets back to the Gesù, it's all he can do to keep standing. He looks for don Francesco everywhere: in each of the parlours, in the library, the refectory, even the bathrooms. When he reaches the small chapel at the heart of the community house, he's swaying on his feet.

And there he is, don Francesco: kneeling in the front pew before the tabernacle, his head bowed and his shoulders hunched. Vittorio ought to leave quietly and pretend he's seen nothing. But something drives him forward: need or compassion, he doesn't know. He blesses himself with holy water from the stoup, genuflects to the Presence – he wavers and almost unbalances, saving himself just in time – and goes to sit next to don Francesco just as old Father Hugh sat next to him, all those years ago.

At first, he thinks the other man is too deep in prayer even to notice. But then don Francesco raises his head, crosses himself, and sits back in the pew. His face is streaked with tears; he doesn't even try to hide them, only takes out a handkerchief and polishes the salt from his glasses. He looks very young all of a sudden. And he is young, isn't he? He can't be more than thirty.

'Father Vittorio,' he says. 'How are things going today? Are you holding up?'

And he smiles his meek, friendly smile. But he's so evidently distressed and exhausted that Vittorio wants to lie, like he has so many times already. Say that he's quite all right, that he's ready and willing for any new task. He can't, though, not this time. This time, he has to admit defeat.

'Not really,' he admits. 'I rather overestimated myself this morning. I'm afraid I might need to rest for a couple of days.'

Don Francesco is all concern. 'But of course you must rest. You must do whatever you need. As a matter of fact,' he says, 'it wouldn't hurt for you to lie low. I'm afraid the Germans might be starting to pay attention to our movements. Ever since Passo del Turchino, I've been uneasy.'

Vittorio turns cold. He remembers don Francesco going to Nazi headquarters two or three weeks ago, asking to recover the bodies of the fifty-nine prisoners dragged out and shot in retaliation for a partisan bomb that had killed five Germans. Ten dead Italians for one dead German, that was the rule. The Germans had actually arrested don Francesco and held him for a little while in Marassi prison, suspecting him of being an opponent of the Reich – which he was, of course – but he'd given them nothing, and had eventually been released. The bodies had stayed where they were, heaped in a mass grave at Passo del Turchino, high in the Ligurian hills. And now don Francesco was afraid.

'I'm sorry,' he says.

'Oh, well, I'm not concerned for myself,' don Francesco says, and wipes his eyes. 'These are the risks one takes. But if they do happen to be watching – if they're watching here, specifically, or looking out for priests in general – then it's a good time to be cautious. You're safe so long as you're on Church property, so stay on it for now. Rest until you feel strong enough to work again, and then we shall see how things stand.'

'I will. Thank you.' He doesn't know quite how to ask, but he has to try. 'Don Francesco, are you… will you be all right?'

'Quite all right, yes. As much as anyone could be. It's just that, sometimes…' Don Francesco sighs. 'What was that phrase of Mr Churchill's again? "Blood, sweat, toil, and tears"? Sometimes, Father Vittorio, I wonder how much of those I have left in me.'

34

Anna

By the time Massimo arrived that evening, I still hadn't managed to calm my nerves. I couldn't stop thinking about Vittorio's stricken expression. What good had it done to unburden myself? What could it possibly change, other than hurting him and altering our friendship forever? I felt wretched, and I wished I could throw myself into Massimo's arms and tell him everything. But I'd promised Vittorio I wouldn't say anything about what we'd discussed. If I could do nothing else for him, I could do that.

Massimo noticed, of course. He drew his chair up to mine and took my hands in his. 'Anna, what's wrong? Is something worrying you?'

'It's nothing,' I said. 'Well, it's everything. All the usual things.'

'My poor darling,' he said. 'I know exactly what you mean.'

I looked up into his kind, clever face and wondered just what he'd heard about me when he checked me out all those weeks ago. Of course he'd found out who I was: what I'd married into, all the compromises I'd made. But did he know what I was accused of and know – or guess – that I was innocent? Or did he know only that I'd been dismissed on account of the Racial Laws, and by a man he found thoroughly obnoxious? I suddenly felt that I had to find out. I was trying to formulate some way to approach the question when I realised that he was talking.

'…you'll need your real identity papers, of course. I know you lost them in the bombardment. But don't worry, we can make you a new set. I've brought the blank form with me, and my man at the questura will—'

'My real papers?' I asked. 'What do I need those for?'

'At the Swiss border. That's the agreement: if you can show your legal identity papers with your status as a Jew, you'll be accepted as a refugee. And that's a guaranteed acceptance, thanks to my contacts in the Red Cross. They won't find some spurious reason to turn you away, like they do to so many others. Of course, the price for all this assurance is that you have to travel while carrying both documents, and that's a risk in itself. But the lady who'll be escorting you is completely trustworthy, and she's done this many times before. That at least should be…' His brow furrowed. 'You're not following me, are you?'

'I'm not,' I said, though my mind and heart were racing. *Switzerland*. It rose up before me like a vision, rich and free and peaceful. 'It's a lot to take in – I'm sorry. Please can you tell me again from the beginning?'

'Of course,' he said, and he started to explain. Since taking over DELASEM, he'd established a safe escape route between Genoa and Switzerland. A lawyer friend of his had a sympathetic client, a rich lady whose Swiss estate spanned the Italian border. This lady and her maid would come down to Genoa on separate trains, and each would take three or perhaps four people back with her. Then the new arrivals would apply for refuge through Massimo's contacts, who had been warned of their coming. It was a slow and cautious way of working, and it meant only a handful of people could be moved at one time. But it was better and infinitely safer than taking your chances at the border; or entrusting yourself to some unknown guide, who might extort a large fee only to sell you out, or kill you, or simply abandon you along the way.

'There's huge demand,' Massimo said. 'You can imagine. We have entire families who need to escape, people coming to Genoa from all over to get on one of these trains. But sometimes…' He was holding my hands tight. 'Sometimes, rarely, it happens that a place frees up – that I can fit in an extra person, someone who's alone. I've been waiting to find a place for you, and now I finally have. All being well, you can leave next week.'

'Next week,' I echoed. 'How long have you been…'

'For weeks now, since I first heard about you. I'm very sorry I didn't tell you before. It would have been cruel to give you hope unless I was certain that I could make it come about. And I wasn't at all sure that I could. I could only prepare to seize the chance if it should arise.'

'That's why you asked about my papers,' I said. 'Back when we first met.'

Massimo nodded. 'I know this must be strange for you – it's strange for me, too. I didn't know you, or what you would mean to me. I just saw a young woman who was surviving alone. If we'd never got to know one another, if I'd never come to feel about you as I do, then I'd still have kept on looking for that spare place and I'd still have offered it to you the instant it came up. I always wanted you to be safe. I hope you know that.'

'But I am safe,' I said. Switzerland had already lost its shine. I didn't want to leave Massimo, to stop the work we'd been doing and abandon the people I could help. In that moment, all I wanted was to stay in Genoa with him. I had my work and I had my love, and in everything else I could take my chances. 'I'm safe here. You said it yourself, the Waldensians—'

'No, my darling, you're not safe, not completely. Perhaps you feel safe, and that isn't the same at all. In fact, it can be very dangerous.'

'But—'

'Please,' he said, with an intensity that startled me. 'Please, Anna, I'm giving you a way out. You must take it. I can't lose someone dear to me, not again, not so soon. Don't put me through it.'

This time, I was the one listening as the story spilled out. 'Did you ever wonder why I stayed in Genoa?' Massimo asked, studying my face. 'Didn't that strike you as strange?'

'Of course I did,' I said. 'It was the first thing I wondered when I saw you.'

'But you didn't ask me.'

'No. I tried to put it out of my mind.' I'd tried, but I hadn't always succeeded. In those first weeks, when I'd loved him without wanting to, I'd sometimes lain awake tormenting myself with the idea that he'd stayed on account of someone else.

'And you were quite right,' he said. 'Need to know, and so on. But I think perhaps I ought to tell you now.' He took a deep breath. 'When the synagogue was raided,' he began, 'I was alone. My wife had died the year before. I'd sent our daughter—'

'You have a daughter?'

'Yes. She went to my in-laws in Rapallo at first – they're Catholic, and so is she, technically – she's elsewhere now, but she's being kept safe. It's all right,' he cut across me before I could respond. 'I live with it. I have to.'

'I understand,' I said, but my head was spinning. Massimo, *my* Massimo, was not just a grieving husband but a father, with a daughter he missed and who must miss him. I couldn't imagine his pain. I squeezed his fingers and he squeezed mine back.

'The rest of my family had left town,' he went on. 'My mother and father, my sisters and brothers with their own families. They were scattered around in various places. I know this is a lot to take in all at once, when I've been so tight-lipped up to now.' He grimaced. 'It's not that I don't trust you. In any other circumstances…'

'I know. It's good practice. The less you tell me—'

'Exactly so. Well, my family were more or less safe up to that point. But now the Germans had their names from the synagogue records, I knew it would be easier to hunt them down – and they would be hunted, there was no question of that. I found a way to write to all of them and tell them to run, to take new names and find new places to hide, places where nobody knew them. And they all did, except one: my little sister Margherita. She and her husband Achille and their children were staying at a hotel in Montecatini. The address was in the records,' he went on, growing heated. 'They needed to leave right away. Right away. There wasn't any time to waste.'

'You mean they didn't...' I had to take a breath myself now. 'They didn't leave?'

'Not immediately,' Massimo said. 'They hid with friends nearby for a couple of days, and on the third day... I can scarcely believe it. They *went back*. Just to pack up their things. Achille stayed with their friends – he thought it was men the Germans were after, men they could draft. But the others, Margherita and Lia and Claudio, they were at the hotel when the Fascists came looking.'

'Oh, Massimo.' I was filled with horror: for them, for him.

'When Achille came back in the morning and found them gone, he turned himself in.' His voice was bleak. 'He couldn't have done otherwise. He couldn't have lived with it. The news reached me and I was frantic. I didn't want to leave Genoa until I knew for certain what had happened to Margherita and her family. I knew that there were people at the Curia who were helping Jews – I had friends who had friends there – I went to ask them to help me. I managed to talk to a priest who told me that he could find something out and report back the very next day. I was overcome,' he said. 'I cried out: "But this is a miracle!" And he looked at me, this serious little priest with his funny round spectacles, and he said that the miracle, the real miracle, would be if my loved ones ever came back to me. He knew something, Anna. I swear they all do, him and the archbishop and maybe even Father Vittorio. They know more than we do about what the Germans are up to, though they'll never say it.'

He hung his head, and for a moment we were both silent. 'There was news when I went back,' he said quietly at last. 'Margherita, Achille and the children had been taken to Florence and put on a train heading for the Brenner Pass. My darling, you have to go,' he said, and he looked up now and fixed me with haunted eyes. 'You want to stay and keep working, I know. And I want to keep you – I want you with me day and night, but you must go. You must.'

'But what about you? Won't you come to Switzerland, too?' It was a desperate hope, because I knew him, just as he knew me. But I still had to try. 'I shan't go,' I said. 'I shan't go anywhere unless you go with me, and bring your daughter. I'm quite serious. If you want to save me, then you'll have to save yourself and her as well.'

'My daughter is safe where she is,' Massimo said, 'and that's well away from me. And I have to stay in Genoa. I'm bound up in all this, and I have been since the first day I went to the Curia. Too many people depend on me now. You ought to understand that.'

'No, Massimo, I don't understand. You've told me yourself that you have all these high-up contacts: in the questura, the Red Cross, the church. And some of them value you especially, because you were once valued by a man they admire. You've persuaded them to help others, but you won't ask them to help *you*. And why shouldn't you? You're in far greater danger than any of them.'

'You know that isn't true. The Germans—'

'…will treat anyone as a Jew who helps a Jew. I know that.

And I know they're all taking risks, but we're not talking about ordinary people here, like Silvia and Bernardo. These are powerful men who have their own protectors, institutions, networks they can hide behind. You don't have any of that, so you have to start protecting yourself. It's foolish not to do so, but it's more than that. It's morally and ethically wrong,' I said, with all the conviction I could summon. 'It's unforgivable, and I won't forgive you.'

Massimo shook his head. He was so composed, so sad, that my heart ached because I knew that I had lost. 'Everything you say is perfectly true. If you don't want to forgive me, then I shan't ask you to. But I still don't know what happened to Margherita, or whether I might ever get her back, and I promised myself that I wouldn't leave until I do. Besides, nobody does anything properly unless I'm around to run things – people mean well, but that isn't enough, and you know it. Mistakes end up being made, and those are infinitely costly.' He reached out and touched my face, ran his thumb across my cheek. 'My work will be harder without your help, darling Anna. I trust you as I can trust very few people in this world. But in another way, it will be so much simpler. I know how that sounds,' he said as I closed my eyes and stifled a wave of pain. 'I do know. But it's easier if I have only myself to worry about. And I can keep going if I know that you are safe – that if I survive, and if this ends, then I shall get to see you again one day. Please don't deny me that one assurance.'

It was unarguable, all of it. And I'd turned down a lifeline once before, the one my mother had offered; I knew, deep down, that I mustn't do that again. 'Then I'll go,' I said.

'I don't want to, you're right, but I'll go. Thank you. Thank you for helping me.'

Massimo pulled me into his arms. 'Oh, thank God.' The catch in his voice made my throat hurt. 'I love you. In case you hadn't gathered,' he added with a shaky half-laugh, and pressed his lips to my cheek.

'I love you, too,' I said. And I clung to him, as though he might be torn from me at any moment.

35

Vittorio

Silvia was right about the tonic. After just two days, it's relieved the insatiable exhaustion and finally allowed him to sleep deeply and well, with a satisfaction he hasn't felt in months.

The problem is, that's all he wants to do.

He doesn't meditate, or examine his conscience, or pray the Liturgy of the Hours. He doesn't work in the library. He doesn't wash himself or shave. He can only pick at the meals don Francesco has sent up to him on a tray; he rarely remembers to drink, and even more rarely uses the lavatory. He stays cradled in sleep, waking only *in extremis*: when his bladder irks him, when his joints hurt, when his father looms large in his dreams. Then he wakes with a start and a gasp, and lies there staring into the dark while his pulse races and patterns dance before his eyes. Sometimes the dream lingers like a miasma, and he feels that his father is actually in the room with him, a glowering presence at the end of his bed. Vittorio knows it isn't real – that the brain plays these tricks sometimes. But he still has to say a prayer against evil before he can sleep again.

On the third night, his father is there more and more. On the fourth night, he won't leave. Vittorio prays endless decades of the rosary; he begs St Michael the Archangel to protect him; he turns over and presses his face into the mattress, clamps the pillow over his head, but the vile angry Thing is still there. *Eli, Eli, lama sabachthani? My God, why have you forsaken me?*

When the morning bell rings, he washes, shaves and dresses and goes out into the corridor. The community is silent. The priests are silent, of course: that's the order of things. An hour's private meditation before the day's business can begin, each in his separate room. When was the last time he observed that rule? Vittorio can't remember. He isn't very sure what he's going to do now, for that matter. He knows only that he needs air, and light, and to be away from his room and that sickening presence. He gets into the elevator and goes down to the ground floor, to the door at the back of the church.

Outside, it's quiet. Via San Lorenzo is lined with German cars, but the Germans themselves are scarce. Curfew is barely over and they clearly don't expect trouble, not at this time of day. Only a small group of soldiers, loitering together outside the Palazzo Ducale, cast him an uninterested glance as he begins to walk down the road towards the seafront. Because it's that he needs to see; he knows that now. He knows it's been destroyed, reduced to rubble by bomb after bomb after bomb – from the air, from the sea – and the Marinaio shipyard must surely have been destroyed too. Perhaps if he can *see* that it's gone, his father will stop haunting him and he'll have some peace.

The old port is ahead of him. He can't see the sea yet – there are buildings in the way – but he can smell it. He should really turn left down dark, narrow via Chiabrera, cut a few minutes out of his walk, but he wants to stay out in the open and look at the water. That's something he missed in Rome and London; even in Genoa, he doesn't get enough of it. And so he keeps on walking until he reaches the arched gallery of piazza della Raibetta, and he turns left and follows the ravaged line of the seafront; pausing for a moment when the flat, silvery sea comes into view, letting himself take it in. He walks and walks, following the railway tracks until he reaches the point where Marinaio e Figli should be, but there's nothing. No bombed-out buildings, no broken signage or abandoned hulls. The only sign that this was ever a shipyard is a right-angled slipway that extends, ruined and half-submerged, out into the water.

Vittorio stands and looks at the empty place that once housed his father's pride, and he waits to feel something: relief, perhaps, or compassion, or triumph. But he can't feel anything except a rising nausea. He's aware, standing here in the pale morning sun, that he hasn't eaten or drunk since the previous afternoon. The sickness keeps coming; his head swims, and the ground beneath him starts to tilt and sway like a boat on rough waters.

Someone grabs his arm. 'Easy, son,' a voice says – his

father's voice, the voice of his nightmares. Vittorio stumbles back, but the Thing has hold of him. His free hand goes to the rosary that hangs from his cincture, seizing the crucifix with shaking fingers, pressing the Lord's agonised body into the clammy flesh of his palm.

It's looking at him, the Thing. It's looking him right in the eye. It's older and stouter and pinker and whiter than the Thing that haunts his room, but it's still his father, and its grip feels solid and strong. He tries to pull away and it pulls him back again, its fingers almost crushing his wrist, and he knows that this is something worse than an apparition.

'Calm down, won't you?' the commendatore says, and rolls his bloodshot eyes. 'Christ's sake, you'd think I were the Devil himself.'

'What are you doing here?' Vittorio asks. There's a tremor in his voice that he can't still.

'Same as you, probably. Looking at the wreck of your lost inheritance – and yes, I know you didn't want it; you don't have to tell me again. Will you stop that?' he says irritably as Vittorio squirms in his grasp. 'I'm just trying to keep you upright. I don't know what the Jesuits have been doing to you, but you look half-dead. Come and sit down.'

Still gripping Vittorio's wrist, he guides him to where a pile of shattered stonework and broken girders has been assembled, ready for clearing. He settles Vittorio onto one of the girders and looks around for a place to sit himself, finally perching on a flattish piece of concrete.

'Now, you stay,' he commands, and takes out a flat silver flask from inside his jacket. Silver flask, English tweed. Like Fulvio, but *he* isn't like Fulvio at all. He unscrews the cap and thrusts it under Vittorio's nose; the florid smell of brandy makes his gorge rise.

'No, thank you. I'd rather not—'

'*Drink*,' the commendatore orders, and he lifts the flask to his lips. The alcohol hits the back of his throat and his stomach churns; he bucks forward and vomits up thin green bile, narrowly missing his father's right shoe.

'Damn it to hell,' his father barks, 'what's wrong with you?'

Beneath the weakness and the confusion and the layers of deep-instilled, reflexive fear, something in Vittorio snaps. He takes a cautious sip of the brandy – it stings his throat, but it goes down this time, and stays down, and fills him with a spreading warmth.

'I'm dying,' he says. 'That's what's wrong with me.'

His father is staring at him – Vittorio can feel his eyes boring into the side of his face. He takes another sip of brandy and looks ahead, at the horizon.

'What d'you mean, you're dying?' the commendatore splutters. 'Dying how? Of what?'

'Tuberculosis, probably.' There's a strange delight in being casual, in dropping these words so they hang in the air between them. 'Or it could be cancer, or heart failure. But it's most likely TB. I had it before.'

'I know you had it before. I got you the best doctors, the best treatments. You cost me a bloody fortune and they all assured me that you were better.'

'I'm sure I was, at the time. It can't be cured, though,' Vittorio says. 'It can only go dormant. It did, obviously, and now it's back. I'm surprised your doctors didn't tell you that,' he adds.

He knows his father won't dare explode at him. He's far too conscious of his reputation to unleash his anger in public; and the city is waking up now, cars and trucks filtering past on the road behind them. But he's still surprised when the commendatore shakes his head and says softly: 'That's terrible. Christ, son, you could have told us. Your poor mother.'

Vittorio hangs his head. It's always painful to think of his mother: his sweet, vague mother who never did anything wrong, though as a boy he'd sometimes longed for her to speak up, to intervene when he was the one being terrorised. But then he grew up and left her.

His father puts a hand on his forearm. 'How long have you...' The commendatore clears his throat. 'How long have you got? Have they told you?'

'I don't know. Not long.'

'What does that mean? Months, weeks?'

'Weeks,' Vittorio says, but he knows it might be days.

The commendatore swears under his breath. His hand is heavy, a manacle on Vittorio's arm. 'You'll come home, then. You'll come home and you'll... we'll look after you there. You'll be comfortable,' he says, and his voice trembles so that Vittorio has to look away. 'We'll make sure of it, your mother and I. Your brothers and sister will want to see you, too. You won't deny them that.'

'I don't think—'

'I'm not asking,' his father says, and there's a touch of the old steel. 'I'm not leaving you like this. You're coming home. I've got the car and I'll take you there now.'

Say no, Vittorio urges himself. *Pull yourself together and say no*. But there's something so tempting about the idea:

dying in a soft bed in his family's villa at Albaro, perhaps in his old bedroom with the high ceiling and the trees outside the window. No more lies, no more deception, no more obligations left unfulfilled. And there's a part of him – the part that's still a wounded little boy – that thrills to the tremor in his father's voice. He wants to be loved. He wants to be looked after. He wants, for a dizzying moment, to forget everything.

But there's so much he'd have to forget. Can he really bring himself to pardon this man for every terror he's inflicted, every spirit he's broken, every underhand thing he's done? Can he pardon him for what he did to Marta? He sees her as he first saw her, curled up terrified and alone in the shelter at Galliera, and love drives its thorns into his heart.

'Come on, son.' The commendatore leans towards him. 'Let bygones be bygones, eh? I know it's been difficult between us in the past, but you mustn't worry about that. I'm quite prepared to forgive you.'

Vittorio arrives at the community house weak and winded. The adrenaline that propelled him along – away from the vanished shipyard, away from his father – is running out and he's nauseated again, his heartbeat pulsing unpleasantly in his temples and dark spots floating before his eyes. The elevator doors close behind him and he leans against the wall, trying to collect himself; but soon they open again and there is don Francesco, hurrying along the corridor.

'Father Vittorio! Where on earth have you been? Oh, you look terrible, terrible. Come on,' he says, ushering Vittorio towards the parlour where they usually meet.

'I was watching for you, I must confess. Brother Carlo took your breakfast up this morning and you weren't in your room. I couldn't find you anywhere. Do you need water? Food? Shall I send to the infirmary for—'

'No,' Vittorio says. He swallows, tastes bile. 'No, I'm all right. But I do need to speak to you.'

'Well, if you're sure.' Don Francesco opens the parlour door and waves him through. 'But you must tell me if you want anything. I'm expecting Mr X shortly, just to let you know – hopefully we shall be done before he arrives.'

Vittorio sits at the table. 'I think perhaps... I think he needs to know this, too. But if I could talk to you first, in confidence...'

'Of course you can.' Don Francesco sits down opposite and smiles at him, his hands clasped together. 'You can tell me anything.'

And so Vittorio takes a deep breath and he tells don Francesco the whole story. Well, not the *whole* story. He can't bring himself to tell this earnest young priest that he has fallen in love, abandoned his discipline, lost sight of his vocation. In this more acceptable version, Marta is his dear friend – that, for a Jesuit, is quite bad enough – but the rest is true, at least in outline. It was affection, he says; pure, chaste, foolish affection that drove him to conceal the state of his health for so long. (And his dedication to DELASEM, he almost adds, but something tells him that don Francesco would take that badly; he'd fret about it, and he's visibly distressed already.)

He hadn't known he was dying until it was very late, too late to do anything about it. And then he'd found out that his father had committed that terrible wrong against

Marta and no, he hadn't disclosed it to don Francesco or to Mr X, although he really ought to have done so right away. He knows that. He was so very sick, so far from God. He wasn't in his right mind at all. And then early this morning – he's outright lying now, because don Francesco has taken off his glasses and is sitting with his head in his hands – he'd gone to take some fresh air and to look at the sea, and he'd run across his father taking a walk by the port.

'Go on,' don Francesco says, without looking up. 'Tell me what happened.'

'It went badly,' Vittorio says. 'I'm afraid he said something that… it didn't sit well with me, and there was an argument. I can't remember exactly what I said to him, but I think that perhaps I gave away that I knew Marta and what he had done to her. I can't be sure. But if I did…'

His father's face is before him, congested and angry; his own raw voice rings in his ears. *Was it worth it? Ruining a young woman's life, tearing her from her family, killing her husband and smearing her reputation? And just look, look at all the good it did you. Look at the glorious legacy you're leaving behind.*

'You think he might lash out again,' don Francesco says. He looks up and puts on his glasses. 'Given what he did before. He might try to avenge himself on you or Marta or both – and he knows where to find you, at least. Is that what you're telling me?'

Vittorio nods, miserable. 'Yes.'

'Right.' Don Francesco pushes back his chair and goes

to the window, turning his back to Vittorio. 'This is rather beyond me. I'm afraid we shall need Mr X.'

'I'm sorry—' he begins, but don Francesco cuts him off.

'No, Father Vittorio. Not now.'

They lapse into a tense silence until don Francesco, craning his neck, says at last: 'Ah, here he comes. I'll go down and meet him. I think it's best we speak privately before he sees you.'

'Thank you,' Vittorio says, but it's the wrong thing; don Francesco shakes his head and goes swiftly out. Vittorio is left alone in the little parlour with the loudly ticking clock and the portrait of St Ignatius. And he feels very much alone: isolated and awkward, just like in his novice days when he'd wait in vain for his mother's visit. That wasn't the same parlour, of course; it wasn't the same community house, but it might as well have been. There's a universality to Jesuit parlours.

Time ticks by, and he's beginning to wish he'd given in to don Francesco's entreaties right at the start and allowed himself to be fed or at least given some water. Just as he's wondering whether he can justifiably go along to the refectory and fetch a glass – because his mouth is dry and sour and his head's starting to ache – the door opens and Mr X comes in with don Francesco following close behind, carrying one of the wooden folding chairs that stand in the corridor.

There's no bonhomie this time, no offering of cigarettes. Mr X sits down across from him and fixes him with a steady gaze.

'Tell me everything,' he says. 'I've heard it from don

Francesco, and now I need to hear it from you. From the beginning, please.'

Vittorio glances at don Francesco, who is now seated in the corner, but the other priest won't meet his eye. 'If you would, Father Vittorio,' he says.

'Very well,' Vittorio says, and he begins his story. It's slow going. Mr X is much harder to lie to about his feelings for Marta; he's got that unnerving look about him, the look of a man who *knows* he's being lied to. Perhaps he does know. Perhaps Marta's said something to him, something that's given Vittorio away. Mr X is a man of the world, after all. And God only knows what the two of them confide about when they're alone together, when they... Images flood into his mind – vivid, uncalled-for images – and a wave of heat engulfs him.

'May I have an aspirin?' he asks don Francesco, who glances at Mr X.

'Of course,' Mr X says, and don Francesco hurries out. 'Are you feeling all right? Relatively speaking, of course.'

'I'm fine. Just a headache.'

'Then let's press on, because this is rather urgent. Now, you had reached the part about your father – about finding out what he had done to Marta. I must say, that was news to me.'

'Yes. I asked her not to say anything to you.' The words come out in a rush. 'I must have put her in a terribly difficult position. I should have—'

'The story, Father Vittorio,' Mr X says.

Vittorio bows his head and resumes where he left off. Now he's talking about his father, it's a little easier; indignation carries him along, and he's in full flow when don Francesco comes in with a glass of water and a plate with a slice of bread and margarine.

'Best eat something if you're going to take aspirin,' he says, setting the glass and plate in front of Vittorio along with a small white pill wrapped in a napkin. 'It's hard on the stomach.'

Vittorio crosses himself and picks up the bread with shaking hands. He can't tell if he's hungry or sick, and Mr X is still watching him, but he manages to take a bite and then another. By the time he's eaten the whole slice and drunk the water with the aspirin, his stomach has stopped roiling and the throbbing in his temples is starting to recede.

'Better?' Mr X asks, and he nods. 'Good. Now you can tell me exactly what you said to your father.'

'I can't remember, I'm afraid. I might have—'

Mr X leans forward. 'No, Father Vittorio, I think you do remember. I think you know every word he said to you, and I'm damn sure you know every word you said to him. And I need to hear it. All of it.'

When Vittorio has finished repeating every word, Mr X swears, and then apologises to don Francesco for swearing.

'It's all right,' don Francesco says. He's as white as paper, and he can't look at Vittorio at all. 'Entirely justified.'

Mr X leans back in his chair, drums his fingers on the table. 'Right,' he says. 'We need to sort this out.' Vittorio expected him to be angry, to lose his cool for once and upbraid him, even threaten him. But the coldness that's radiating from him is far, far worse.

'I truly am sorry. I know…' The words are spilling

out, unstoppable, desperate. 'I know you love her. I love her, too,' he says, and don Francesco sucks in a breath. 'Everything I've done, I… I didn't mean to put her in danger. I know I have, but I didn't mean to – you must believe me. Please help her. I don't care about myself, only her. Please.'

Mr X pushes back his chair and stands up. 'Go to the San Martino Hospital,' he says, just as if Vittorio hasn't spoken. 'Straight to the leper ward.'

'The *leper* ward?'

'The Germans don't go in there – too cowardly. You'll be given a bed. I'm sorry, don Francesco, I have to go. Can you get a message to our doctor friend?'

'Of course,' don Francesco says.

'Thank you. Good day.' He strides out, pulling the door firmly shut behind him.

Don Francesco gets up and hurries to the window. 'Forgive me, Father Vittorio, but I must see that he gets away. It's my constant worry.' He's studying the panorama, tapping his fingers on the windowsill. 'He'll go out through the church, of course – looks so much less suspicious. Oh, there he is,' he says at last. 'Just look at that.'

Vittorio doesn't want to look, but he gets up and goes to stand next to don Francesco. And there far below, crossing piazza De Ferrari, is Mr X: not walking, but sauntering past a group of German soldiers. One of them looks at him, and he nods and tips his hat; the German nods back and turns away, scanning for miscreants.

'I don't know how he manages it,' don Francesco says. 'I go out and about, of course, and do what I must do. But *he* makes it look terribly easy, and he's taking such a very great risk compared to me. I feel quite inadequate.'

They watch until Mr X is out of sight, and then don Francesco turns to Vittorio and looks him directly in the eye for the first time since he re-entered the room. 'I dare say he's off to the Guichards'.' His voice, like his face, is soft and expressionless. 'Mr X is very protective of those he loves. And he's very fair to those he doesn't.'

'Yes,' Vittorio says. He's choked with misery, overcome by a mercy he doesn't deserve.

Don Francesco puts a hand on his arm. 'I think you'd better make your confession,' he says.

36

Anna

We were still at breakfast when the doorbell rang three times. Silvia and Bernardo exchanged glances, and then Bernardo put down his napkin, got up and went downstairs. I hovered on the edge of my seat, ready to flee as always, until I heard the familiar sound of Massimo's voice. He was speaking to Bernardo in a low, urgent tone – I couldn't make anything out.

'Were you expecting him?' Silvia asked, and I shook my head. 'Maybe it's time to go, then.'

'Maybe,' I said. 'It's early, though.' Massimo and I had agreed that he wouldn't give me advance notice, but would simply tell me on the day my train for Switzerland was to leave. It made sense, because plans could always change; and I'd thought it would be easier, less painful, to go on living as usual and pretend that nothing was happening. But the reality was agonising. I'd spent several days with my suitcase packed and ready at the end of my bed, with my new, Genoese papers stitched into the lining. Vittorio hadn't come in all that time. Massimo had visited twice, and we'd worked and talked as we always did; but inevitably he'd have to leave, and there was no pretending then. I wasn't sure how many more of those goodbyes I could bear.

Silvia patted my shoulder. 'It might be no bad thing,' she said. 'Sometimes the waiting is… Hang on, here they come. Let's see, shall we?'

When Bernardo appeared in the doorway with Massimo behind him, I knew immediately that something was wrong. 'We have to leave,' Bernardo said. His face was ashen. 'Plan B.'

'Oh,' Silvia said. She was pale, too; she got to her feet, straightened her apron. 'Plan B. Yes, let's…' She trailed off, put her hand to her mouth.

'Come on, love,' Bernardo said, and reached for her. 'Let's go and leave these two to talk.' He led her out and down the corridor, and now Massimo and I were alone. He quickly came towards me, closing the door behind him; he looked as shocked as Bernardo did. I felt sick with nerves and my legs were suddenly weak, too weak to let me stand.

'What's going on?' I asked, though I was almost afraid to know. 'Why did he say that *we* have to leave?'

Massimo sat down next to me and took hold of my hands, just as he'd done when he told me about the escape plan. 'I'm sorry,' he said. 'Something's happened, something I couldn't control. There's been a breach and you're in danger, you and Silvia and Bernardo. I'm afraid you can't afford to wait for the train to Switzerland. I need you to go with them right now, this morning, to Torre Pellice. They've got a house there and contacts, people who'll help to protect you – it's Waldensian country up there, of course. You'll be safer than you are in Genoa. I know it's not what I promised,' he added. 'It's not what I wanted for you, not at all. I wanted to make sure you were really safe. I'm sorry.'

'But what about you? Will you be all right?'

'I have my own Plan B, if I need it. And C, D, E and F, at the very least. Don't worry about me.'

But of course I worried about him. I wanted to beg him to come with us – to come with me, and be relatively safe in Torre Pellice among the Waldensians. I opened my mouth to say as much, but he shook his head and said, with a severity I'd never heard from him before: 'I can't leave my post – not even for you, and you know it. Do as I ask, please.'

I didn't want to, but I knew that I had to accept. 'All right,' I said, and tried to pretend that it really was all right. 'But what about Father Vittorio? He comes here all the time. Is he in danger, too?'

'I've already seen to that. He's been sent to a safe house. And now I'm afraid I have to go.' Massimo's expression was grim. 'I have a hell of a mess to clean up. But I shall be fine, my darling, knowing you're being looked after.' He stood and pulled me up with him, folding me in a tight embrace. 'I love you,' he said quietly, into my ear, as if it were a secret. And he kissed me one last time before turning and walking out, his back straight and his shoulders rigid.

Silvia bustled in just as I was sinking back into my chair. 'Forgive me, dear,' she said, brandishing my 'legal' identity card. 'I went into your suitcase. But I thought we should take this out, and get rid of it, before anyone forgets. Since you're staying in Italy after all…'

'Of course,' I said. I was in a daze.

'It's probably best if you deal with it. Save me knowing anything I don't need to know.'

She was already rummaging in the drawer where the matches were kept. I turned my head away. I couldn't bear to see it destroyed: the card Massimo had made for me, the card that was to assure my future. He'd taken the photograph himself with a Ferrania box camera, the kind we used to have at home. 'No,' I said. 'I can't. You do it, please. I trust you.'

'Very well,' Silvia said. I heard her rip the card into pieces ('I'm doing this without looking,' she said, 'just so you know') and then came the sound of the struck match and the flare of sulphur; there was a smell of paper burning and of something else, something sharp and unpleasantly chemical, before she turned on the tap to wash away the ashes. 'There,' she said. 'I'm sorry I had to do that. But I know you understand.'

'I do,' I said. 'Thank you.'

'And now we'd better get moving,' Silvia went on, her voice softening. 'I know it's terrible to say goodbye to him. I'm sure you're feeling quite dreadful, but just stick it out for a few hours and we shall be home – or what Bernardo calls home – and you can weep as much as your heart requires. All right?'

I looked at her. She was standing and watching me, tilting her head in that way people do when they're being sympathetic, and she was wearing her ordinary cotton skirt and blouse with a light coat and a pair of somewhat battered, comfortable shoes, her favourite big handbag slung over her shoulder. She looked just like she always did; and that was a problem, I realised. That was a very big problem indeed.

'You're not going like that,' I said.

'What do you mean?' Silvia looked down at herself, confused. 'Have I got a stain? Cat hair? What is it?'

'You look like *you*. Not that it's a bad thing in itself,' I added hastily, as her eyes widened. 'But why would you and Bernardo be travelling with some unrelated Sicilian woman? Because that's what I am, according to my papers. What will you say if the Germans stop us? We need some kind of story.' My mind was coming thankfully alive, ticking through the possibilities. 'I think I need to work for you. I could be a cook, or a... a maid. Yes, a maid. Can you dress up, do you think? Look the part of my employer?'

'Oh. Yes, I suppose I can dig something out... I do have some nice things, though I really never wear them. I don't quite feel like myself when I do. But then I suppose that's the point, isn't it? A bit of play-acting.'

'Exactly. If you can bring yourself to be the imperious lady, order me about...'

'...then you can just stay quiet, keep your head down and your mouth shut, and nobody will wonder about it. And it's probably as well you do.' Silvia shook her head. 'I don't think you'd pass for Sicilian, not for a moment. You sound about as Genoese as it's possible to sound. But you'd better change, too,' she said, eyeing my favourite blue-and-yellow dress. 'You've got that white blouse, haven't you, and there's that grey skirt you hate. I should think that would do nicely for a uniform.'

'Yes. Let's both go and change – you tell Bernardo to do his best, too, and I shall meet you downstairs in a couple of minutes.'

'It's a plan,' Silvia said.

When I was alone in my room, the reality of leaving Massimo came rushing in, and I had to pause for a moment and steady myself against the washstand. But I made myself force the feelings down, and concentrated on putting together my 'uniform'. By the time I had got dressed, checked over my suitcase and taken another moment to compose myself, Bernardo and Silvia were waiting for me downstairs in the shop. The sight of them startled me so that I almost laughed.

Silvia was dressed as I'd never seen her before, not even for going to church. She had on an elegant summer suit with an extravagant brooch on the lapel; her hair was pinned up under rather a rakish hat, and she was wearing high-heeled shoes. As for Bernardo, he looked quite different in his three-piece suit with a fine silver pocket watch. Even his moustache looked polished and groomed. Tiberio's basket sat by the door – I wondered if he, too, had been given some kind of adornment, an elegant collar or even a miniature necktie.

'Let's get going,' Bernardo said, taking my suitcase from me and hefting the cat basket in his other hand. 'If we walk smartly, we should be able to catch the next train up to Turin. The less hanging around we have to do, the better.'

'Quite right.' Silvia ushered me through the door and turned to lock up behind us. 'We'll take the steps. That will bring us practically to the back of Brignole station – see?' She pointed to the steep, winding stone stairs that led off down the hill, just across the street, and then to the great, damaged roof of the station a little way off. 'It's much quieter that way. You just stick with me.'

'All right,' I said, and she took my arm and tucked it

through hers. I was pathetically grateful. The last time I'd gone further than the air-raid shelter was when Vittorio had brought me here, the morning after the bombardment. Weeks, months ago now. I felt exposed, standing there with the sun shining down on me; no safe enclosing walls, no place to hide.

'Come on then,' Silvia said. 'Sooner we're off, sooner we're there. Awfully commonplace, I know, but it's true.' From his carrier, Tiberio let out a soft meow, as if to agree.

I nodded and took a breath, the deepest breath I could manage. We crossed the road and began the long, steep climb downwards, among the ruins of Genoa.

Brignole station was full of people. I'd anticipated that, but I hadn't anticipated how it would feel after a period of relative quiet. The crowds surging around me were unbearable, jostling against me, shouting – so it seemed – directly into my ear. No matter how firmly I told myself that this was good, that there was safety in numbers, I had to struggle with the urge to break away and run outside into the open air.

'Stay strong, dear,' Silvia said in an undertone. 'Bernardo will be back with our tickets in just a moment, and then we shall be in a nice, civilised train compartment and all will be well with the world.'

But all wasn't well. There was a soldier bearing down on us, a German. He was fair and red-cheeked with an angry scattering of pimples along his jawline, and I hated him – I hated all German soldiers, but I hated him specifically because I was quite sure that he'd picked us to intimidate, two harmless women standing there in the middle of the concourse with a suitcase and a cat in a basket. He stopped right in front of us, far too close, and held out his hand as if demanding tribute.

'Papers,' he said.

'Well, *really*,' Silvia said, drawing herself up. 'A little courtesy wouldn't go amiss.'

I was afraid for a second that the gamble wouldn't come off; that the German would be provoked by Silvia's show of indignation. But he wasn't provoked, or didn't seem it. He merely rolled his eyes and said: 'Papers. *Bitte*.'

'That's better.' Silvia opened her bag and brought out her identity card. She turned to me and gave me a sharp nudge with her elbow. 'Come on, stupid girl. Show the young man your papers. You simply cannot get the help,' she said to the German, who raised an eyebrow; I couldn't tell whether he understood her, or had merely picked up on her tone. 'Your *i-den-ti-ty-card*,' she said, enunciating the words practically in my face as I rummaged in my own bag. 'Honestly, I despair. I ask the agency for a housemaid, one fit for a respectable home, and this is what they send me. I shall have to send her back, ask for something with a brain in its head. These Sicilian girls are no good. And about time,' she pronounced as I finally located my papers – they seemed to have slipped to the very bottom of my bag – and presented them to the German with shaking hands. 'You're hopeless, that's what you are, Marta. Quite, quite hopeless. I really must apologise for her, young man. She's making your important work very difficult, I'm sure.'

The German glanced briefly at my card and Silvia's and then thrust them back at us. 'Fine,' he said, and he turned on his heel and swept off.

We watched until he was at a safe distance, with his back to us, demanding papers from a young couple with a heap of suitcases and a small child clinging to the woman's skirt; and then Silvia leaned in and said quietly: 'Well, that worked rather splendidly. Your man would be proud of me, I dare say.'

I nodded. I could have hugged her, but I didn't dare, not after the display she'd put on. Bernardo arrived then, thank God, brandishing our tickets; I could have hugged him, too.

'Come on,' he said. 'It's leaving in a few minutes.'

Once we were in our compartment, with Bernardo and Silvia on either side of me and Tiberio's basket settled across my knees, my heart had slowed just a little and I was beginning to feel that it might be all right after all. The only other person there was a white-haired woman in brick-red, beaded draperies, who sat by the opposite window reading a paperback, a large tapestry bag on the seat next to her. As the train pulled out of the station, she opened the bag and took out an apple wrapped in a damask napkin. Looking apologetically at Bernardo and then at Silvia – I, in my drab, schoolgirlish clothes, evidently didn't count – she said in rather a reedy, aristocratic voice: 'You don't mind, do you?'

'Whyever should we mind?' Silvia said, and the woman smiled and thanked her. She took a large bite of the apple and chewed it vigorously, making noises like a horse. Bernardo cleared his throat and buried his nose in the newspaper he'd bought in the station; Silvia, perhaps mindful of her society-lady status – for I knew she had knitting in her bag, and was itching to get on with it – folded her hands in her lap and stared determinedly out of the window.

As for me, I was grateful to the lady in the corner seat. It was amusing to look at her, however surreptitiously, and try to imagine who she was and what she did in life. I decided that she must be something artistic: a painter, a writer, a composer. In fact, on appearances, she would have fit in quite well with my mother's more bohemian friends. My mother loved to surround herself with unconventional characters, even though she herself never shed her Edinburgh respectability. *That's why they're drawn to you, of course*, my father used to say fondly. *You're so very respectable that it's downright eccentric.*

For a little while I entertained myself by wondering what kind of odd things this lady might create in her studio or at her desk, and whether eating apples loudly in enclosed spaces was her only vice, or whether she went in for anything else; like jumping up from table in the middle of dinner to do Swedish exercises, or bringing her own lavatory seat when she stayed at other people's houses. (I wouldn't have thought ill of her for it, not in the slightest. My mother had a very dear friend who used to do both of these things.) But then she closed her book, and I caught a glimpse of the cover: it was a collection of Machiavelli's verse, for which my father had long ago written the introduction. I felt quite tender towards her then, and couldn't bring myself to smile even internally when she reached into her bag and brought out a piece of knitting that looked like a bright-blue, ten-armed octopus. And I was pleased when Silvia really did smile at her, but nicely, and took out her own knitting.

'This *is* cosy,' the lady said happily, and Silvia agreed. I ran my fingers over the wicker surface of Tiberio's basket and wished that I could ask her to lend me her book, even for a moment. I urgently wanted to read my father's words again. But I was a housemaid, I reminded myself: a shy country girl who didn't speak and perhaps didn't read, certainly not Machiavelli.

Outside the window, the thick-wooded hills rose up high and jagged. There must be partisans around here, I thought. I knew from Massimo that they were growing bolder and stronger every day, harassing the Germans from all sides, even coming into the city to do so. I looked and tried to see some sign of life, but the trees were too dense and besides, the partisans were surely too clever to build their encampments within sight of the railway line. I simply had to believe that they were there, and that their efforts would come to something. I had to believe that the war would end; that, one way or another, I would get to see those I'd had to leave behind. And I dreamed, in that moment, of seeing Vittorio – my unexpected friend, who loved old books and English slang and tea with honey. I hoped to make it up to him for the hurt I'd caused; I hoped, above all, to see him well and happy and restored to himself.

I would never see him again.

37

Vittorio

As he packs up his few things, Vittorio briefly wonders what would happen if he didn't go to the leper ward; if he simply got into bed, hid under the covers and stayed there. For a moment he stands with a pair of socks in his hand – they aren't even his socks; they're the property of the Society of Jesus – and considers it, but the moment doesn't last. He has to go; he knows that. Everything he's done in the last few hours has made it impossible to stay. He has ruined everything: risked Marta's life, brought danger upon the entire network, and all because he couldn't control his worst impulses. Who would have thought that twenty-five years of Jesuit discipline would end like this?

He shakes his head and goes on packing: spare shirt, underwear, razor and toiletries, breviary, none of them his; all neatly parcelled up and placed in a leather overnight bag that isn't his, either. But this will all be squared with his superior, just as his departure will be. Cardinal Boetto will take care of it. The situation he has created is far too urgent for anyone to hang around seeking permission.

When he gets out of the elevator, don Francesco is waiting for him by the back door. 'Are you ready?' he asks. 'Do you have everything you need?'

'Yes,' Vittorio says.

'You're sure you wouldn't prefer to change?' Don Francesco eyes him worriedly. 'I can certainly find you some civilian clothes.'

'No.' Vittorio has worn a cassock almost every day for the whole of his adult life. Now he's back in good standing with God and the Church, he can't imagine taking it off. It would be like disavowing who he is. 'No, thank you. I appreciate it, but I shall take my chances.'

'If you really insist,' don Francesco says, 'I suppose I can't stop you.' And then he does something extraordinary. He puts his arms around Vittorio and draws him into a hug.

It's a shock, a terribly welcome shock. Vittorio turns hot – he mustn't cry, he mustn't – a strangled sound erupts from him and don Francesco rubs his back, just as if he were an upset child.

Vittorio can't fight any more. He leans his head on the other man's shoulder and cries: for Marta, for himself, for the unfairness of it all. 'My poor, dear friend,' don Francesco says, cradling him in his arms; and Vittorio feels such a rush of affection for him that he cries even more.

When he's finally hiccuped to a stop, don Francesco gives him a firm pat across the shoulders and releases him. Vittorio quickly turns away and reaches for his handkerchief, mops his face and blows his nose. He's washed out, foolish, grateful.

Don Francesco smiles at him. 'Courage, Father Vittorio,'

he says, and opens the door onto the bright, warm street. Vittorio picks up his bag from where he dropped it and steps out into the world.

The hospital is a long way away, about three and a half kilometres, beyond Brignole station. As sick and slow as he is, it will take him over an hour to walk there. But the idea of standing on a crowded tram – even assuming they're running – and rushing to his destination in a series of stops and starts makes him shudder. This is probably the last morning he'll be free to walk outside in the sunshine; he ought to make use of it. He crosses the road and begins to walk up via di Porta Soprana towards the old city gate that stands at the top of the hill.

But the sun is merciless, the heat already rising. After just a few steps, he's breathing harder; there's sweat rolling down his forehead, dripping into his eyes. He stops to wipe it away, and when his vision clears he sees them blocking his path. Two SS men, and a woman: an interpreter.

'*Sie sind Francesco Repetto*,' says one of the men, the bigger one.

Vittorio doesn't need an interpreter for that, but the woman speaks anyway in a flat, hostile tone: 'You are Francesco Repetto.'

Not 'are you', but 'you are'. Not a question but a statement. He sees himself as they do: a slim dark-haired priest in a black cassock and round glasses, harassed-looking, guilty. They don't know the difference between a standard cassock and a Jesuit one. They don't know that he's at least ten years older than don Francesco, and probably looks twenty. They know only that he fits the description they've been given, and that he's come from the Gesù. How long have they been watching the back door? He thinks of don Francesco's quiet despair in the house chapel a few days ago, his feeling of being hunted. *Ever since Passo del Turchino, I've been uneasy.*

The German snorts. '*Bist du taub?*' he barks. '*Antworte!*'

'Are you deaf,' the interpreter repeats in her nasal monotone, stripping away the question mark. 'Answer me.'

Vittorio knows what he must do. He can make things right, or at least better. He can use his last strength to buy just a little more time: for don Francesco, for Mr X, for DELASEM and all those who depend on it. And then it will all be done, and he won't have to suffer any more.

'Yes,' he says, drawing himself upright as much as he can. 'Yes, I am Francesco Repetto.'

Author's Note

WHAT HAPPENED NEXT

THE ACTION of this story begins in April 1944 and ends around July of the same year. That's no coincidence, because that was a turning point for the two real, historical characters at the heart of the action. In early July, don Francesco Repetto went into hiding after narrowly evading arrest: his role was taken over by don Carlo Salvi who, like him, would subsequently be recognised by Yad Vashem as Righteous among the Nations. Had Father Vittorio's sacrifice really happened, it might only have won him a couple of days.

Massimo Teglio also found himself under severe pressure. Not only don Repetto, but many of his associates and helpers had been arrested or forced to flee. His situation in Genoa was becoming untenable. Thankfully, he had a powerful friend. Achille Malcovati was a wealthy businessman, a highly decorated war hero and a former Fascist who now dedicated himself to helping Jews and partisans. He offered Teglio a safe haven, employing him as a driver so that he could circulate freely. Teglio accepted the offer and went on working from his new base in Milan, where he was not a local celebrity, and where he could operate under the protection of Malcovati's untouchable reputation.

The extraordinary double act of Teglio and Repetto was broken up for now, but the processes they had set into action went on. So did the work of the brave individuals and groups who helped to protect the Jewish population, even as many of their compatriots collaborated with the Nazi-Fascist regime. Historians estimate that at least eighty per cent of Italian Jews survived the war. This is not a reflection of some mythical Italian national trait. Rather, it reflects the sheer persistence and determination of those who committed to the fight, and their ability to exploit a dynamic and often messy situation.

WHAT HAPPENED AFTERWARDS

FRANCESCO REPETTO and Massimo Teglio met *in extremis*, and perhaps in another set of circumstances they wouldn't have met at all. But the gentle-hearted priest and the tough, pragmatic aviator became fast friends for life. Both returned to their native Genoa after the Liberation of 25 April 1945, and each continued to work for the good of his city and community.

Francesco Repetto was at Pietro Boetto's side in January 1946 when the cardinal, long afflicted by heart problems, was struck down by his final sickness; Boetto died in his arms. For the following decades, don (later Monsignor) Repetto was active in a number of roles: as a school and seminary teacher, as chaplain of San Siro Basilica, and as prefect of the Biblioteca

Franzoniana. He was devoted to interfaith work, and his fierce, egalitarian love for the Jewish people was constant and evident long before the Catholic church officially changed its position. Don Repetto died on 14 October 1984.

Massimo Teglio was reunited with his daughter Nicoletta when he returned to Genoa, as well as most of his family. However, his sister Margherita, her husband Achille Vitale, and their children Lia and Claudio, had been deported to Auschwitz and did not return. Over the next years, Teglio raised his daughter and continued to work for the welfare and settlement of Jewish refugees. An agnostic and a fatalist, he showed up to prayer services whenever he was asked. He did not marry again, but in later years found a partner, Francine; he was a much-loved and very entertaining babysitter to the children in his family. He died on 31 January 1990.

A WORD ABOUT NAMES

LIKE MANY languages, Italian has a central feature that English no longer has, or not in common usage: two different forms of 'you'. While today's usage is much more fluid, in North Italy in the 1940s it was very straightforward. If you wanted to express respect, deference, social distance or plain old politeness, you would address your interlocutor as *Lei*. (Or, if you adhered to Mussolini's campaign against *Lei* as a supposed foreign import, you would use *Voi*.) This was the default in the majority of cases. The informal *tu* was reserved for family, lovers, close friends, children or substitute children, people you wished to insult, and God.

Had I written this book in Italian, this built-in mechanism would modulate the various choices I've had to make. Those engaged in clandestine work often used code names or first names with each other as a matter of good practice. This was a particularly urgent concern for Massimo Teglio, whose surname was identifiably Jewish. Even close associates like don Francesco Repetto, who knew perfectly well who he was, made a point of never, ever speaking his surname out loud. They called him *signor Massimo*: another standard Italian usage that doesn't transfer well into English. To others, he was *il signor X*, which works rather better in translation. I smoothed this out by having him be Mr X to (almost) everyone.

Other than Mr X, my characters generally address one another by their first names. For most of them, this is a security measure; though sometimes it also comes from affection, or a commitment to egalitarianism, or simple disregard for convention. Many of the people who appear to be gaily first-naming one another here would be using the formal *Lei* and very possibly also the title *signor(a)*, which would considerably soften the impact.

Finally, two of my protagonists are priests. Francesco Repetto is a secular priest, and his title is *don*, like Guareschi's famous parish priest don Camillo. I believe that's familiar enough to leave intact. Vittorio is a Jesuit, a member of a religious order, so his title is *padre*. For the sake of elegance, I've rendered this as Father. This also fits with my general policy of switching between Italian and English terms of address depending on which sounds better in the moment: since this is a book written in English, with Italian characters who address one another in Italian – specifically, the somewhat Anglified Italian of Genoa – I felt this was a liberty I could afford to take.

A NOTE ON SOURCES

RESEARCHING THIS book was an intensive, demanding and thoroughly absorbing process. I benefited especially from the incisive work of historians including (but not limited to) Michele Sarfatti, Sandro Antonini, Mario E. Macciò, Carlo Brizzolari and Shira Klein; as well as the journalist Alexander Stille, whose *Benevolence and Betrayal* (published in Italian as *Uno su mille*) is an indispensable guidebook to the experience of Italian Jews under Fascism, and includes precious testimony from Massimo Teglio and his siblings Laura and Mario. I also made use of the online resources of the Fondazione Centro di Documentazione Ebraica Contemporanea (CDEC) in Milan, especially the recorded interview with Teglio conducted by Michele Sarfatti, and those of the Centro Internazionale di Studi Primo Levi.

When accounts of a specific event conflict – and they sometimes do – I have always prioritised the version provided by Teglio to Stillc, Sarfatti, Brizzolari and others. Where he or another character tells a story in dialogue, I have taken care to remain faithful to his version while supplying fresh words, rather than reproducing his later interviews verbatim. I have been less faithful with regard to the bombing of the Curia, which Teglio recounted in wonderfully vivid language to Alexander Stille. This is narrated by Father Vittorio, who does not exist and therefore was not there, and his version is heavily shaped by the need for secrecy and his own, already fragile state of mind. (However, I could not resist including a take on Teglio's line about the frescoes.)

I also took advice whenever possible. In Genoa, historian and tour guide Fabrizia Scortecci was an invaluable resource throughout the entire process, sharing her knowledge, helping me find story locations, checking geographical and historical details, chasing down missing information and putting me in contact with other helpful people in the city. Pastor William Jourdan of the Waldensian community in via Assarotti was a fount of useful facts and resources, moral support and theological conversation; I was also privileged to attend services at the temple, and am grateful for the welcome shown to me by the congregation. Letizia Teglio generously shared her memories of her uncle Massimo, both in person and over email; Fernanda Segre advised on the (distinctive and highly secular) Genoese Jewish life of the time and showed me around the beautiful synagogue of which she is secretary. I had extremely useful conversations with Leonardo Vezzani SJ and Cesare Bosatra SJ, two real members of Father Vittorio's community at the Gesù, though I've taken a few liberties in deciding on the layout of the community house and the duration of Cardinal Boetto's stay there. And I owe a debt of gratitude, as always, to my friendly local Genoese dude Nicola Rebagliati; and to his uncle Umberto Rebagliati, who furnished many fascinating details about his memories of wartime Genoa.

Elsewhere, Nicoletta Basilotta of the Kolvenbach Library at the Jesuit Curia in Rome helped me to work out many details of Father Vittorio's discipline and formation. I also received useful input on preconciliar Jesuit life from David Birchall SJ of the London Jesuit Centre and from my good friend Guy Consolmagno SJ of the Specola Vaticana. I have, nonetheless, imagined a personal and spiritual life for Father Vittorio that is uniquely his own, taking liberties where desirable.

Police adviser Graham Bartlett consulted on Massimo's questioning of Anna; naval and aviation expert Matthew Willis was instrumental in the sinking of the fictional *Antonio Montaldo*. Ryszard Hermaszewski and Helena Dixon gave expert advice on Vittorio's extrapulmonary tuberculosis and the medical treatments available to him in Genoa in 1944, while Susannah Rickards kindly read the passages about his anaemia and provided feedback from her own experience; Carol Goodall and April Doyle also furnished helpful insights. Roberto Amato patiently transcribed Teglio's interview with Michele Sarfatti so that I could study the Italian text in detail. Josie von Zitzewitz checked and improved my German dialogue. Fabrizia Scortecci, Nicola Rebagliati, Roni Abramson, April Doyle, Catherine Jones, Emma Darwin, Hilary Ely, Keren David, Michael Carley, Nicole Sochor, Margaret Kirk, Sam Schindler and my father, John, all took a critical look at the manuscript, in part or in full, from various angles of expertise at different points in the process.

Even with all these resources and all of this help, I am bound to have made mistakes, and the fault for those is mine alone. I've also had to imagine details that (to my knowledge) are lost to the historical record, or simply specific to the scenario I have built. Hopefully, my imaginings hold water.

Acknowledgements

THIS WAS a challenging book to write, and I wrote it during a particularly challenging period. Throughout the whole process, I was fortunate to have steadfast moral and practical support from old friends, new contacts, and industry colleagues.

My long-established writing buddies Michael Carley, April Doyle, Catherine Jones and Lisa Glass were just as brilliant and understanding as they always are – which is to say, exceptionally. Equally wonderful were Nicola Rebagliati, Karolina Manka, Jenn Strange, Fabrizia Scortecci, Roni Abramson, Leila Rasheed, Lesley Roberts (and Tina, the emotional support labrador), Sharon Robinson, my dad, John, and all the lovely people at Lo Scorretto in Genoa, my home away from home in the city of my heart.

I am deeply thankful to have worked with Broo Doherty at DHH Literary Agency, without whom this book would not exist in its current form, and her colleague Helen Edwards. Sophia Kaufman (at Harper Paperbacks) and Aubrie Artiano and Laura Palmer (at Head of Zeus) were attentive and sympathetic – and rigorous – editors whose professionalism and collegiality enriched every stage of the process. I'm also deeply grateful to Sophie Dawson at

Head of Zeus for shepherding this book to publication; to Helena Newton for her sensitive and thorough edits; and to Shannon Hewitt (Marketing) and Yasmeen Doogue-Khan (Publicity) for everything they've done to help *Daughter of Genoa* find its readers. And I owe a special thanks to my fabulous agents, Sara Megibow and Helen Masvikeni. Getting to collaborate with all of these people has been a joy, and I truly appreciate their investment of time, work and faith.

My progress on this book was significantly aided by an Authors' Foundation grant from the Society of Authors. Thanks to their generosity, I was able to dedicate precious time and energy to the work I love best.

Finally, I am grateful to Father Luciano, who was exactly the right person to meet while having a book-related anxiety attack in St Peter's Basilica. I hope I have lived up to his encouraging words.

About the Author

KAT DEVEREAUX was born near Edinburgh, and has lived in the United States, Russia, France, Chile, Germany, and Italy, and now lives in the beautiful city of Prague. She is a historian by training and an enthusiast by nature.

Thanks for reading!